Praise for

TOMBOY

"Mix Jo March and Tom Ripley, shake, pour, and take a brisk, bitter swig of Jane Benjamin. You'll be deliriously intoxicated by this bracing sequel to *Copy Boy*."

—GRETCHEN CHERINGTON, author of *Poetic License*

"Riveting as *Mare of Easttown*, binge-worthy as *The Queen's Gambit*, *Tomboy* kept me reading—obsessively—until the very last line."

—DEBRA THOMAS, author of *Luz*

"Chock-full of audacity and adventure—a suspenseful and layered novel from the squalor of Hooverville to the opulence of the Queen Mary."

—ASHLEY E. SWEENEY, author of *Answer Creek*

"Crisp prose, snappy pace, exquisite period details, and a resourceful, resilient, wonderfully flawed protagonist. Fasten your seatbelts. It's going to be a bumpy boat ride."

—MARY CAMARILLO, author of *The Lockhart Women*

"*Tomboy* ascends to a breaking point that will leave you breathless."

—LAURIE BUCHANAN, author of the Sean McPherson novels

"The best kind of seat-of-your-pants protagonist to keep your heart racing as she gets herself into scrapes that threaten her safety but clarify her morality."

—MAREN COOPER, author of *A Better Next*

Praise for

COPY BOY

"Smart, lively, and suspenseful—Raymond Chandler for feminists."
—SHARMA SHIELDS, author of *The Cassandra*

"A stellar debut, mesmerizing as the fog lifting over Nob Hill. Highly recommended."
—SHELDON SIEGEL, *New York Times* best-selling author of the Mike Daley/Rosie Fernandez novels

"*Copy Boy* is a rewarding historical novel with a ferocious, fascinating lead."
—*FOREWORD REVIEWS*

"An expressive and striking story that examines what one does for family and for oneself."
—*KIRKUS REVIEWS*

TOMBOY

TOMBOY

A Jane Benjamin Novel

SHELLEY BLANTON-STROUD

swp

SHE WRITES PRESS

Published 2022
Printed in the United States of America
Print ISBN: 978-1-64742-407-7
E-ISBN: 978-1-64742-408-4
Library of Congress Control Number: 2021924757

For information, address:
She Writes Press
1569 Solano Ave #546
Berkeley, CA 94707

She Writes Press is a division of SparkPoint Studio, LLC.

Book design by Stacey Aaronson

To Andy, for the planting and the weeding

"For whatever we lose (like a you or a me),
it's always ourselves we find in the sea."
—E. E. CUMMINGS

PART ONE

CHAPTER ONE

MONDAY, JUNE 26, 1939

Rivka's Flat, 3528 Clay Street
San Francisco, California

Elsie grabbed my short shaggy mane in her tiny fists and wrenched like I was a horse to rein in and break. Her head slammed into mine, cracking my nose and blinding me with pain. I instinctively bucked, throwing the back of my skull into the wall behind me. My head rebounded and banged into Elsie's again.

The hit that did real damage was the one I caused myself, recoiling from Elsie, my toddler half-sister, my obligation.

Clanging filled my ears and everything turned yellow. I couldn't faint, couldn't let myself drop her, so I slid down the wall to my haunches. She stopped screaming briefly, as if surprised to have communicated something. *She's studying my reaction.* Her forehead shone pink from the collision. Then she reverted to screaming, out of pain or anger or frustration. Or something else I didn't yet understand.

"No more!" yelled our housekeeper Lola, like this was happening to her.

I squatted on the floor, blood flowing out my nose onto my lips and chin. I wiped it with my hand. The back of my head burned.

Lola gripped both my elbows, pulling me up to standing, Elsie still in my arms.

My roommate Rivka rushed in. Her eyes cut over to my nose and she gasped. "Lola, please, don't leave. We need you. We'll raise your pay."

"Money is not the problem," said Lola.

"You cain't do this . . ." My accent slipped out when things fell apart, like whenever a housekeeper quit on us. "We have to go to work."

Lola threw her apron on the floor. "This *here* is the work." She made an angry turn, grabbed her coat off the rack, and charged down the hall and stairwell. The door to Clay Street banged shut behind her.

God, I wanted to follow her. Just to run out that door.

Elsie wasn't done. She arched back, her hands pushing up against my shoulders, trying to bust free of me. "No, no, no!" What was she saying no to? I didn't know what she needed. I never did.

I strained to sing our song, which sometimes worked. "I never let you go, Elsie, never, never, never, Jujee never lets you go." I wrapped my arms tighter around her, rubbing her back. "Never let you go, never, never, never." My head and face changed shape as I lied.

Her screams downshifted to snotty sobs into my collar and her hands moved back into my hair, twining rather than yanking, her little torso heaving with unhappiness and loss.

I looked over Elsie's shoulder at Rivka, who picked up Lola's apron and handed it to me. I used it to wipe my face and pinch my numb nostrils. Everything pounded with noise and emotion.

"Your mother keeps calling," Rivka said, crossing her arms

over her narrow chest. "She wants her back. She has all that space now. It's time to take Elsie home."

"Hang up."

"What?"

"When Momma calls, hang up."

Rivka groaned. She didn't get it. Everything was black and white with her.

Momma did want Elsie back. But the idea made me sick. She had the charisma that could pull you in, tie you there. It took me seventeen years to run, and I failed even then. I brought her with me to San Francisco, rescuing her from the dirt and the fields and her murdering common law husband. I couldn't cut the rope because of Elsie. I couldn't leave Elsie behind.

"This is not about you," Rivka said. In her Czech accent, every word rang brutal. She made it her mission always to critique my flaws and I let her do it because she held the lease, paid the rent, and bought most of the food. Her home, not mine. I tossed in what I could every paycheck. Elsie and I'd been sponging off her for over a year and a half now. That didn't feel great. But I chose it from a slate of worse options.

My pay at the *San Francisco Prospect* hadn't changed since I got there. I'd made fifty cents an hour as a copy boy, fetching coffee and running grafs from cog to cog of the great news machine. Though the pay should have risen to seventy cents when I moved up to cub reporter, my managing editor Mac dropped me back down to fifty because I'd pretended to be a boy to get the job.

Elsie drummed the back of my neck with wet fingers now, her fit run out.

"They'll let me have that column," I said.

"Oh, there's the solution," said Rivka, the cynic.

But I knew it would work. I heard Hedda Hopper earned as much for gossip writing in Los Angeles as Walter Winchell did in New York. Hedda was big time, proof a newspaper would reward a lady columnist for writing about the bad behavior of famous people, and what they wore while doing it. Mac had been hinting such a column might be possible for a while now. Or at least not shooting it down when I hinted.

"I'll bring it up today," I said. "And when he gives it to me, that'll be more money. Elsie and I can rent our own place, and hire somebody good to babysit. Help us for a little longer. Take Elsie today. I'll fix it by tonight." *Maybe*, I thought.

Rivka stomped down the hall to the kitchen. I could hear her rummaging in the ice box as I swayed Elsie back and forth, trying to relax the tension in her body with one hand, pinching my nose with the other.

Rivka came back and handed me an ice pack. I wadded the apron into my pocket and pressed the ice on Elsie's forehead. She cried and pushed it away so I put it on my nose. The cold made me dizzy.

"This is not right for Elsie," Rivka said. "She needs someone, fulltime, devoted to her. She needs her mother."

"I won't do that."

"It's time. Your mother's situation has changed. She has what she needs."

Rivka meant money. Momma had her new husband Jonesie's money now, and his big house. And cash did make everything easier, flattening layers of crisis and challenge that provoked the best in some people, the worst in others, like Momma. Nobody knew that better than me. But I wouldn't give in on this.

"You can practice at home on Mondays," I said. "Just take her today."

Rivka's face bleached, but the way her shoulders drooped, I could tell she wouldn't fight me. She didn't have to be at the symphony today. She wouldn't do any real practicing while taking care of Elsie, not the kind of practice that met her standard, and I did feel contrite about that. But I needed her help.

I peeled my sister off and passed her to Rivka.

"I'll bring home good news. I promise." Again, I thought, *maybe*.

Rivka held the ice pack against Elsie's forehead, making her sputter.

I put on my Oxfords and took my jacket and fedora off their hook.

"You're always negotiating," Rivka said. "No matter what. Everything's a deal you want to make, a promise you'll renege on. We'll settle this tonight."

"Tonight. I promise."

I gripped the rail, escaping downstairs, woozy from the head butting, and opened the door to Clay Street as my bus screeched up. Even the light of a gloomy June sky was too bright, the bus brakes too shrill. I climbed up, paid, took the last empty seat, back in the open-air section, and exhaled from down deep.

The old man sitting next to me stared at my nose with alarm, like he thought there might be a cruel young husband behind the door I'd emerged from. I closed my eyes, raising my face to the mist, and ignored his judgment.

Injury was temporary. I healed fast.

CHAPTER TWO

SEPTEMBER 1930

Rotten Egg Hooverville
Sacramento, California

A swoosh of bug-hunting bats swarmed my head. I squeezed my eyes shut, hugging a cottonwood trunk, rubbing my cheek sore against ridged bark. My breath came in quick sips and hiccups. *This ain't on me.* I heard rustling in the nutgrass below.

"Jump down, Janie."

Momma said it in a plain, reasonable voice, causing me to shiver from scalp to toes. I stared down through cloudy blossoms sloughing off the tree at Momma's upturned face below, drawing me to it, moonlike. Her light-blue eyes twinkled on the outside edges and grew dark approaching the pupil. The closer you examined the dark, the more you saw her angry intelligence and forgot her beauty. I believed Momma could control that effect, growing the light blue to woo you and expanding the central black when she didn't care if you knew the truth.

"You owe me."

Momma always said that.

I jumped out of the tree, landing on the hardpan between the canal and the field, first on my feet and then on my bony bottom. I pushed up, snuffling. My ankle hurt.

"You're a bad girl." Momma said.

"Not, not, NOT my fault." My bottom lip quivered.

"Don't pretend you weren't part of it."

"Mrs. Anderson don't mean nothing to him!"

"You think I care about her?" Momma asked. "Don't act feeble."

Momma headed away from the canal, me following, through the field, toward camp, her faded nightdress glowing in the dark like a lantern. We passed sideways between cotton plants.

"I ain't jealous of that clown," Momma said.

Mrs. Anderson was fake, tin can curls and pancake makeup, while Momma was real, no fuss, shiny black hair waving around high cheeks. Dimpled chin. Petite, womanly shape. What seemed like a soft, lazy behind was really a ball of muscle. I'd seen Momma do a string of cartwheels and handsprings down a potato row for applauding pickers on her twenty-sixth birthday. Mrs. Anderson's attractions were obvious. Momma's were surprising.

I dragged my feet, stirring up dust as I followed her past the cardboard tilt-up kitchen and rusty Model A at our campsite, a slice of gray dirt between the highway and Mr. Russell's' back forty.

I walked through the sheet flap door behind Momma. Daddy lay on the dirt, vomit on his face, feet bare. He'd wet and soiled himself. He looked like a horse I'd seen, killed by a farmer's bullet, long muscles useless because he'd broken his leg. I couldn't imagine how Daddy would have made it home if Mrs. Anderson's husband hadn't driven him, pushing him out of the truck in front of our tent.

She said, "You done this."

"I didn't."

"You were an accomplice."

"But all I—"

"You aided and abetted his playing around, his drinking, his missing work because of it. Ran his love notes to her, ran hers back to him. Don't lie and say you didn't. You were the messenger."

I didn't know what to say, because I *was* the messenger.

"You showed me where your loyalty lies—with your philandering Daddy and that dyed-head hussy."

"That's not true."

"You're either with me or with him."

I didn't want to choose. They were both my parents and I wanted to please them both. But Daddy put me in this situation. And I'd made and remade this choice so often, I figured I could always change my mind later as facts shifted.

"I choose you, Momma."

She snorted, doubtful.

"Let's see about that. You've got a new message to deliver."

She told me what it would be, and I set out to follow her directions, walking through the fields, over the train tracks, down the levy, coming out on the skid row side, where Mrs. Anderson's diner sat, neon lit and smelling like chicken.

When I entered, nobody glanced, though I must have been a filthy sight. I shuffled to the counter and the teenage waitress asked me what I wanted.

"I need to talk to Mrs. Anderson," I said.

The waitress lit up. Must've been a boring shift so far. "Olinda?" she called.

A couple of farmers sitting at the counter, one eating French fries, the other apple pie, perked up, like the movie was starting. They knew Daddy and must have recognized me, too, from all the messages I'd delivered.

Mrs. Anderson came out, red curls bouncing like her bosom.

"Why yes, Miss Hopper. What can I do you for?"

"My momma has a message for you."

Mrs. Anderson had little beads of sweat on her forehead that made her look surprisingly human.

"She says you're a two-bit whore and you better keep your paws off Daddy or she's gonna pull those curls out at the root."

Mrs. Anderson puffed up. Her customers dropped their eyes to their coffee or their biscuits or their fried okra.

"And she says, don't try to figure out how to carry on with this nonsense because you're not up to it. She says your cornbread ain't done in the middle."

The supper audience wheezed and chuckled. Mrs. Anderson deflated to a third of her diner-glamorous self. I made my exit before she could answer and skulked back to our campsite, humiliated to be a low-class Hopper.

When I got back to the tent, Daddy was clean and tucked into his pallet.

"Go on," Momma said.

"I did it."

"Okay then. Not every kid can do what you can. You ain't faint of heart."

That meant something to me. Still does.

She stripped off my filthy overalls and washed me down from a bucket, in and around my ears and my knuckles, all the way round and under my fingernails, the way she did when I was a bitty thing. She brushed my knotted hair and braided it. Then she slipped over my shoulders a thin white nightgown cut from the same bolt as her own.

I lay down on my pallet and she rubbed my back, singing an old tune of Granny's, *"I love you, because you're mine, because you're mine."* And, in spite of my resentment, it did reassure me to know I belonged to someone, even Momma.

CHAPTER THREE

MONDAY, JUNE 26, 1939

The Prospect — Fifth and Mission
San Francisco, California

"Jesus, fistfight in the soup line, Benny?"

Mac slapped the side of my head, sending a wave of pain all the way to my toes.

He treated me like I was a male cub reporter, which I mostly appreciated, if not today. He blew by in a smoky gale, toward the spine, the spiral staircase at the center of the *Prospect* newsroom.

"Mac, wait ..."

I watched him take the stairs two at a time, no touching the handrail, no looking back. Mac was a showoff who didn't respect even powerful, big money men who weren't also boyishly athletic. He thought everything hung on that.

He'd been good enough to me, hiring me with no experience, keeping me on in spite of the godawful messes I'd made, promoting me to cub. Still, he wouldn't let me forget I'd pretended to be a boy, Benny, to snag the job in the beginning, even now that I went by Jane. He didn't like to be a sucker.

Some people nurse their grudges. Some people get away with paying copy boy wages for a reporter's work. But Mac could make me a columnist, so I tolerated this.

Besides, he made a reasonable point. I hadn't looked good in months. I wore the same men's suit, Oxford shoes, and fedora I'd worn since I got here. The switchboard girls said I could make it work, that I could look stylish compared to all the men in suits and girls in dresses. But tending Elsie every night and morning got in the way of the other tactics they advised—slathering on Pond's cold cream, applying lipstick, dangling painted glass earrings—everything that would prove I was Jane, not Benny anymore. For months, I'd dropped the girly Jane stuff because of the toddler Elsie stuff.

I pressed my hair down behind my ears, pinched my cheeks, blinked my blurry eyes, trying to look less like somebody stuck in the drunk tank. I sat on a hard bench with nine other cubs, all guys, around a large metal table in the middle of the newsroom. Even the copy boys had a cushion on their bench. I had to pick splinters out of my pants after a long day riding the pine, waiting for the assignment that would lift me above this pack.

I asked Wally, the cub to my right, "Why's everybody running already? What makes it such a rushed dang day?"

"What happened to you?"

"Nothing, just a stupid . . . walked into a door. I was tired."

"You get klutzier and klutzier." Wally stared up at the ceiling with a worried face, the pointed black tips of his bangs poking into his eyelashes. "Publisher's in house, before he goes out to catch the train for the boat."

There'd been a lot of talk about that, on the front page of every San Francisco paper, under the fold, below reports of Japan spreading its blockade down the China coast and rumors of Lou Gehrig retiring.

A local girl tennis player, Tommie O'Rourke, was playing at Wimbledon, in England. San Francisco wasn't such a cosmopolitan place that the bigwigs would ignore something like that. And the bigger the wig, the more likely they'd be taking a train to New York and sailing to England to be there when Tommie won. That included Edward Zimmer, the *Prospect's* publisher, who was supposedly planning to make it there in time for the women's championship match.

Muckety-mucks weren't the only ones hanging on Tommie's story. She'd grown up in a poor family in the Sunset District, learning her sport on the free courts in Golden Gate Park. One sports reporter claimed that background made her better. He said she'd played on rough surfaces, developed a rough game. Tommie wasn't some thoroughbred who'd injure easy or stop playing if she was hurt. So they portrayed her as The City's scrappy hometown heroine, fighting her way to the top. Locals loved it. The fact she was a bombshell didn't hurt.

I wasn't a city kid like Tommie, but the tomato fields required rough play of pickers like me, and I had scrapped my way out of there, so I mentally put my own face over Tommie's in those articles, though I wasn't exactly a bombshell.

"I don't know what Zimmer can do in just one morning to get everybody so riled up," Wally said. He didn't have my aspirational imagination. Our absentee publisher's visit offered a rare chance to please the alpha male. The whole newsroom would be circling for scraps and I wasn't going to miss my chance.

Head and nose pounding, I raced up the spine to the third floor, where Zimmer stood facing a collection of reporters admiring a new Zenith radio, a beauty, four feet tall, gleaming wood, huge dials. He stroked its shiny side like a spaniel.

Zimmer was good looking himself, about forty, powerfully built, with dark wavy hair, swarthy skin, a jutting jaw, and a thick mustache. Very attractive, except for the fact he likely spent too much time in front of a mirror.

"This lady's full of it, fellas," he said.

Other than me, odd one out, it *was* all fellas standing round. The only other *Prospect* girls were the ones at the switchboard and reception desk and Mac's secretary, Sandy.

"Everybody's 'blah blah blah' about *training*," Zimmer continued. "But that isn't it. You've gotta have *talent*. You can't teach talent. It's in you or it isn't. You can build skills on top of talent, but skills are useless without talent."

I pushed my way into the front of the group to listen to our publisher prophet. But now the nasal voice of a British interviewer blared over the radio instead.

"Miss Carlson, fans the world over admire Tommie's many successes—tennis, singing, clothing design. Is there anything she can't do? Is she just a born natural at everything?"

Miss Carlson cleared her throat. "All that extra dilutes Tommie's success. I tell her, just practice tennis and play tennis. That's all. If you want to be great, devote yourself. Stop derailing your progress with attention seeking—"

"Well, eager listeners," the radio interviewer interrupted, "you've heard from Edith 'Coach' Carlson, with a message for her player, Tommie O'Rourke—quit playing dress-up and get serious. Ha! Looks like there may be a cat fight in the ladies' locker room!"

All the guys around me laughed in a great exhalation, as if relieved to hear Coach take down Tommie, and the radio interviewer take down Coach, setting everything back in its natural order. I wanted to topple the natural order.

Though the world lined up against her, as it did against poor girls everywhere, Tommie had made it to Wimbledon. And now her coach was telling her to stop thinking of all the things she could achieve? *They stay on top by keeping you down.*

Even so, the way that radio interviewer interrupted her,

chuckling about a *cat fight*, that rubbed me wrong too. Against my will, I felt a little something on behalf of Tommie's coach.

"Girls just can't," said Harry, reporter to my left. "They're not wired that way."

"What are you talkin' about, dope?" said Monty, a known devil's advocate. "Tommie can do anything. She caught for Lefty O'Doul, coulda played baseball herself! She'd outmatch you!" Monty pantomimed a right jab.

"Whoop-de-do. That was for O'Doul's fans. Sure, yeah, she's talented. But I'm saying she hasn't got it in her to go all the way. She'll fall in love, have babies. She'll be a flash in the pan. I'm right! Coach is right!" Others chimed in, agreeing, disagreeing.

They may as well have been talking about me. It was almost impossible to try to do something great while changing diapers. And not to let anybody know about it either? If Mac found out I was raising Elsie, he'd fire me and give my job to some guy, even if that guy had a baby himself. It looked to me like a whole lot of guys rose up without talent or practice. They just rode the current.

"Coach does pose an interesting question," Zimmer said. "Is it best to try a lot of things, be so-so at everything? Or is it better to focus, to apply greater discipline? Take Mac . . ." Everybody gawked at our editor, who was about to be made an example. "You've led quite a varied, adventurous life, haven't you, friend? Do you like the way that's adding up? Proud of your accomplishments?"

His insult hushed the crew, who longed to curry favor with the publisher, but liked drinking beer with the managing editor.

Mac had worked at a lot of things—farmer, coal miner, logger, golf pro, banker—before becoming a newsman. I thought maybe he saw something in me because we both had a little dirt under our nails. I liked that about him, too. But the publisher calling him out in front of reporters? Not good. Mac's face went red, and I felt the sting too.

Zimmer started toward the elevator, leaving his comment there. Mac followed, hands jammed in his pockets, shape of his fists visible through fabric. I elbowed myself fourth or fifth in the parade.

Mac said, "So, about the gossip thing . . ."

Here we go. This is it.

As I stepped up to the elevator, Smitty, the geezer elevator operator, closed the doors with a jolt and a smirk.

I rushed to the spine and took the stairs two and three at a time, barely catching the edge of the steps, arriving as the brass elevator doors opened again.

Holding a lever curved into a capital P, Smitty delivered his line, "Second floor, *Prospect* newsrooooom—where facts become story!"

Zimmer boomed, "Smitty, the paper's very voice!"

A pack of cubs gathered, clearly hoping Zimmer would see their faces in the crowd and choose them—*You! Be the baseball guy! You! You're on business. You! The government desk!*

Their faces glowed with unwarranted faith.

Mac called out, "Jane!" Not Benny. "Over here!"

The crowd cracked, making room for my approach.

Some rare moments were like this, opening to just what I wanted, just when I wanted it.

"Mr. Zimmer needs help," Mac said. "I told him you're the one."

"Sir," I said, smiling the way I thought a gossip columnist might, one-sided, smug, smirky, swollen nose and all.

"Hullo beauty," Zimmer said, eyebrows raised. "How's the other girl look?"

"Other girl's a door, sir. Bad morning." I cast my eyes down, then quickly back up, remembering to feign confidence.

"Right, right," he said, like he doubted the door. "I've heard about you."

Thank you, Mac, thank you, thank you.

"Met your mother—Kate, isn't it?—last night at Jones-at-the-Beach. Told me about her daughter, tearing things up at my paper." Zimmer laughed, wiggling his thick brows at Mac.

Coffee milk curdled in my belly.

"Did Jonesie tell you about his horse?" I asked, moving this conversation back on socially safe ground.

"Didn't talk to Jonesie. Just your mother."

He scrutinized my lips, my throat, and my feet. This is what people did when they learned I'd passed for a boy. Momma must have told him.

At seventeen, I fought my father, defending my mother. At least I thought that's what I was doing. I believed I'd killed him and ran away, stole a car and drove to The City. Rivka took me in. To find a job I cut off my hair. I made a few other stops along that route but that's basically how I got on at the *Prospect*. I was born Jane Hopper but became Benjamin Hopper, taking the name of my dead twin brother. When the time was right, I spoke up about who I was and renamed myself Jane Benjamin.

It gave Momma a good story. I was some of her best material. Jonesie had his barroom set pieces. Momma had me, a story she played for laughs. I didn't have to inspect it too closely to see the disrespect.

I breathed through my nose, trying to calm myself.

Mac was telling Zimmer about Jonesie's horse, Bullet, who

Jonesie invited into the roadhouse on special occasions. It was a schtick everybody liked. An eccentric bar owner sold more cocktails. I faked nonchalance while they talked.

Zimmer laughed at Mac's punchline but I didn't hear it.

"So, Jane," Zimmer turned back to me. "I need you to buy a train ticket, leaving today, to New York, and then the *Queen Mary* from New York to Cherbourg, on to Southampton, England. Make sure the days and times line up. Ship's got to arrive in time for the Wimbledon ladies' championship match, July 7. Then a return trip—that date's flexible. Got it? Right now?"

"San Francisco to New York to Cherbourg to Southampton. How about Wimbledon?"

"Sandy bought that."

I waited.

"Right now?" he repeated.

I waited a second or two more, long enough for, "Then we'll talk about this gossip column," but that didn't come.

"Yes sir, on it."

I headed back to the metal table and pulled one of three telephones to my spot. All the cubs had seen him hand me this assignment so nobody fussed about my grabbing one of our shared telephones. In fact, envious sighs were heaved around the table because I was doing this bit for Zimmer, whereas I was aiming not to completely deflate. This was not what I'd aimed for. And I didn't like the way Zimmer had surveyed me and my nose, like damaged goods.

But I was a *bounce back* person. He hadn't offered the gossip column. Yet. He'd given me a task and I'd do it right. The problem was timing. He planned to leave today? I was more overwhelmed than usual, what with the head butting. I sneaked a look around to make sure Mac and Zimmer were no longer nearby.

"Hey," I said to the cubs, Wally, Barry, Quentin and Shawn. "Who's got time?"

"What, Tom Sawyer wants us to whitewash a fence again?"

"Help me do this thing fast and I'll buy first round at Breen's."

Wally nodded eagerly, thirsty already. Barry said, "Two rounds."

I couldn't afford to buy any drinks at all but I'd figure that out tonight.

"You two, find a train from here to New York. Round trip. Today! I'll call about the boat from New York to England."

"Well for starters, no train leaves from San Francisco," Quentin criticized. "You gotta take a ferry to Oakland."

"Or Alameda," said Shawn.

"So, you want a part of this?" I asked.

"Nah, go on," Shawn said.

"I'm in," said Quentin.

I picked up the telephone and said to the switchboard girl, "Meredith, plug in. About to start ringing."

"Yippee. I hate snooze time."

I called Quentin over.

"Connect Quentin with whoever tickets the *Queen Mary*."

"Aren't you coming up in the world?"

"Any day now."

Fifteen minutes later, Wally waved a moleskin over his head.

"Hey, turns out the *Challenger*'s the best deal, with the sleeper cars and all. Changeover in Chicago, and on to New York."

"Bingo!" I grabbed his notebook.

"Only just," Wally said, "it's all sold out."

"Why'd you waste your breath?" I pointed at Barry.

"*City of San Francisco's* it. Takes the Overland Route to Chicago, starting with a ferry from here to Oakland. He'll catch the boat at 3:45 p.m., it drops him straight at the Long Wharf, then he'll catch the train at 4:11. This one's fast. It covers 2200 miles to Chicago in thirty-nine hours, thirteen minutes, over two mountain ranges!" Barry had a train to sell me. "Makes it to Chicago in two nights total."

"And from Chicago to New York?" I asked. "Can he do it in, what . . ." I scratched out the math in Wally's notebook. "Sixty-two hours?"

"Yep." Barry explained the details of the journey's second leg on the *Fifth Avenue Special.* "From the ferry to New York, three nights, 60 hours, 35 minutes." Wally slumped, having lost the contest to find the winning train. I tossed him his moleskin.

Zimmer could arrive in New York in time to board the boat to England.

"Just one problem," Barry said.

"What!" I growled. The clock was ticking.

"He's gotta go coach. Too late for a Pullman—all booked—this is the day of."

"What's the difference between coach and Pullman?"

"Everything."

"Jeez," I said. "Train's as bad as the boat."

"What about the boat?" Wally asked.

Quentin said, "Only third-class tickets left, no cabin class or even tourist class."

"If they're gonna divide everything up by how good it is, they may as well make it easy and call it first, second, and third class," I said.

"That's the point. If you don't know the difference, you're in third."

"Better ask Zimmer what to do," Wally advised.

Hard to picture Zimmer in third class.

I took Quentin's and Barry's notes and hustled over to Mac's office in the corner, where he and Zimmer were talking behind a closed door, voices raised.

I got right up to it, ready to knock, when Mac's girl, Sandy, said, "Halt!"

"What, you're the bouncer?"

"Don't interrupt them. How can I help?"

"It's urgent. Zimmer's ferry leaves soon and I gotta . . ."

"What do you need?"

Everybody wants their little bit of power and, though Sandy presented as just the cute type—bouncy brown hair, curvy shape, all the right accessories—you could sense a striver in the scent of her *Je Reviens* perfume. In Sandy, pretty was savvy.

"We can buy him a ticket on the *City of San Francisco,* catching the ferry to Oakland at 3:45 and the train boarding right after. But they don't have a Pullman sleeper car open. Same on the boat, third class. So, you can see why I need in there."

"That itinerary will work. Mr. Zimmer's already booked a Pullman drawing room and cabin class on the *Queen Mary.* These aren't for him. They're fine."

Her right hand shooed me off.

"He's already got his tickets?"

"Made his plans a couple of weeks ago." Sandy smiled, pleased.

"Well, will the person traveling coach by rail and third class on the boat—"

"Ship."

"What?"

"It's a ship, not a boat."

"Right. Will the other person mind no sleeper car and third class on the *ship*?"

"It's for Mr. Zimmer's college roommate's son, Pat Shea. He's young. He can withstand the hardship."

"Why's Zimmer buying tickets for him?"

"Pat's going to be the new gossip columnist."

I SULKED AT the Mission Street entrance, smoking a Lucky, ignoring lunch hour accountants, dockworkers, and factory men rushing by, the usual smell of urine rising from the sidewalk. Today I thought I might lose my breakfast all over the pissy pavement. I'd been out there ten minutes, waiting for tobacco to settle my head and stomach, but it hadn't done its magic. Zimmer was giving my job to somebody else. *My* job. And my nose hurt.

The *Prospect* doors creaked open and Wally sidled over.

"You're wanted. Something's going on. Better get back in there."

I dropped my cigarette, leaving it to burn in the gutter, following Wally back in the building, past the chichi reception area, up the spine to the second floor, where Mac was yelling at Sandy and Zimmer was yelling for me.

Jacket thrown over one shoulder, Zimmer hefted two bags, one dark leather, the other flowery. "Where'd you go?"

"Smoke break, sir." The most I could muster.

"Barry picked up your slack! Reserved the Southern Pacific tickets. Western Union's delivering 'em now. So, you need to call Pat Shea, here." He handed me his business card, with a telephone number scribbled on it. "Tell him to meet you at the Oakland station. You can use his ferry ticket, give him the train coupon book, *Queen Mary,* and Wimbledon passes in Oakland. He won't need the ferry. He's in Berkeley. Call Pat, collect his tickets, make sure he's on that train. Got it?"

"Should I ask a copy boy to handle it from here, sir?"

Zimmer stared at me with bugging eyes. What kind of girl second guessed his orders? But why should I in particular help this so-called Pat steal my job?

"I'm sure you have a lot to do, Jane, a *lot.* So much. But go ahead and figure that if your publisher asks you to do something, you probably ought to do it. Understand?"

"Somewhat, sir." I may have been acting on a death wish at that point.

Zimmer grinned like a criminal. He set down the bags and gripped my shoulders, his nose very close to my swollen own.

"There are certain elements of these arrangements that are delicate. Something that maybe is better for an ambitious cub reporter than for a copy boy."

Ambitious was the magic word.

I was used to everybody discounting me. My last English teacher before I dropped out of high school used to look at me like she'd be shocked if I ever arrived ready, like she *expected* me to come to class without homework.

I always intended to do my work and turn it in, but often enough picking went long because we needed every extra penny and by the time I walked back to camp, the sun had set and we had no electricity. I couldn't see well enough to do the reading and writing by firelight. If there was enough light early to do homework in the tent, that didn't help either because early light just increased my morning picking hours.

One way or another I usually showed up unready for class, musty from picking, dirt under my chewed-up nails, no journal entries or book reports in my satchel. Heck, no satchel either.

So, when somebody important acted like I was worth the time of day, if they saw and accepted my ambition, it was flame to my pilot light.

"Yes sir. I'll call Pat and deliver the tickets to him in Oakland."

Zimmer rubbed the top of my head. I fought the urge to smack his hand.

Sandy said, "Car's here, Edward."

Edward?

She dimpled at the publisher, no doubt thinking herself some *Mademoiselle* model in her navy-blue coat and hat and stylish calf purse that matched her shoes.

"You'll love the shops." He picked the bags up again and wound his way down the spine, Sandy right behind him. "It'll give you something to do."

Mac slammed his office door.

Our moods appeared to match.

I returned to the cub table with the card Zimmer had scribbled on, pulled up a telephone and asked Meredith to connect me. "I need Pat Shea, at Berkeley-2-2300."

Right away somebody answered. "Hallo!"

"I'm calling for Pat Shea," I said.

Something rustled, like the fella had his hand over the mouthpiece while he called out, "Pat! Some dame with a scratchy voice."

Thanks. My voice was rough from a childhood spent coughing with Valley Fever, same as a lot of farmworker kids I knew. I never saw a doctor about it, no money for that. But I kept a ripped encyclopedia page that explained the fever "colonizes the body of the weak" in my hope chest. I would think about that whenever I wanted to make myself try harder. The grainy voice got me the job as a copy boy, anyway, so there was that.

"Oh, hey, Pat is . . . indisposed," he said, insolent. I heard guffaws in the background, and swing music, too. Did he live in a fraternity house?

"What's your name, please?"

"Yeah, I'm Peter."

"Peter, I need you to deliver an urgent message to Mr. Shea." I put on my most superior attitude. "The publisher of the *San Francisco Prospect* has purchased Mr. Shea's railroad tickets leaving Oakland, heading for New York and passage on the *Queen Mary* for England, to attend Wimbledon. Mr. Shea needs to be at the Sixteenth Street Station in Oakland to board his train by 4:11 or risk missing his trip. Do you understand, Peter? Are you able to deliver this message?"

"Shit," he said. "Yes, ma'am." He slurred a little.

"I'll meet him at the station. I'll be the woman in a fedora." I hung up, gratified to make somebody else anxious.

Now Rivka.

I picked up the telephone again and told Meredith, "Tuxedo-5-9267."

When Rivka picked up, I could hear Elsie in the background, not full throated but crying, all right.

"How you doing?" I asked.

"So, your plan's not going to work, is it?"

"Why do you have to—"

"Just admit it. You did not get the job."

"You always jump to the worst thing—"

"Tell me!"

"No. Nothing. I was calling to see how you're doing."

I slammed down the telephone. I'd meant to tell her but she

blocked me. It didn't matter. We'd talk tonight. I'd tell her then.

"Jane, the tickets!" Wally hollered.

I put on my jacket and hat, grabbed the train and boat tickets from the Western Union delivery boy, calling "Somebody pay him!" Then I snatched the Wimbledon tickets from Wally, and headed out to make a delivery to the frat boy stealing my job.

———◦———

CHAPTER FOUR

Southern Pacific Ferry
San Francisco, California

I slumped on a bench, back against windows vibrating with the engine as the ferry chugged across the bay. Out on the deck was best, even with the wet and the gray and the wind, a typical late-summer afternoon in San Francisco. I couldn't stand smelling the flowery cologne, sour fish sandwiches, and cocktails inside the cabin. Not today.

A couple near me talked loud about stupid things, what Herbert said, what Hazel said back to him, whether they'd been drinking rum or beer in the Tonga Room.

I moved off to the rail, at the brink of the water, breaking my rule never to stand there the way I used to. The wind and the bay had claimed three fedoras before I figured that out. Tipping my hat to the little whitecaps, I tucked it tight under my arm.

Shea's train coupon booklet was in my right pocket, with the wadded-up apron I'd bloodied that morning, his *Queen Mary* passage and Wimbledon booking in my left.

Shea's going on a boat to England. Big deal. I'm on a boat.

I pulled out the booklet and saw my fingers had rubbed the print red from the bloody apron in the same pocket. I tossed the apron into the bay.

I flipped through the booklet to see all the parts of the complicated route, a coupon for each leg of the journey, even bus transfers, everything to deliver a reporter from San Francisco to New York.

Under the blood on the cover was this picture of a life preserver with the words, *City of San Francisco, Streamliner*, running all around it, like such a significant thing, some kind of prize Pat Shea was winning, my prize.

I needed more money to graduate out of Rivka's place and I needed to do it *now* to avoid a huge fight. I couldn't keep asking for her help at home when she had work she loved at the symphony.

She'd been good to me. She took me in off the street when I showed up at her door, lump on my head, beat up by Daddy. She fed me, introduced me to Mac, made me into a boy so I could find work. Accepted me at my lowest, thinking I'd lost family forever, and helped me rebuild. I *definitely* owed her.

The spray coming off the ferry's wake plastered my brow.

But this bossiness now, about Elsie? Rivka wasn't a mother. She had no experience taking care of babies, and yet she criticized me, saying Elsie needs Momma. Most kids probably need their mothers, but Kate Hopper Jones wasn't most mothers.

After delivering me and my brother Ben, she put him in a cotton sack and laid him on the edge of the potato field. A little, living newborn. In a sack on the dirt.

"You were the strong one, he was the weak," she claimed. "He was dying at birth." Well, big surprise, he *did* die out there, stuffed in a bag at the side of a field in the month of November. I wasn't the strong one. I was just a baby. How'd she know who was strong, who was weak? She didn't. She just decided and it became true. The injustice of that fired like a volcano, forming a rock that sat heavy between my lungs.

She'd made excuses—"I was fifteen, alone, sick with infection."

But my whole life before that confession, she insisted I killed my brother by taking up too much space in her womb, blocking him from coming out of her body.

There's not one thing about that history that says, *Here's a good-enough momma for Elsie.* Not one thing.

Usually, when I reflected on this, Ben would speak up in my head. First, I'd hear a sizzling, untuned radio kind of static and I'd wait. Then the station would come in and I could hear him telling me what things meant and what to do about it. I wasn't stupid. I understood some people might think I was crazy. That didn't stop me listening to him.

But I couldn't hear him today. *Today, I'm on my own.*

Even so, I could see things weren't right. I wasn't the best substitute mother. And Elsie wasn't acting normal, all her crying and screaming and fits. I wouldn't ask Momma, couldn't let her know about this trouble. Thinking about it made me sick and angry with doubt—what to do about Elsie.

I had to make more money and hire a better babysitter.

But this stupid frat boy and this stupid publisher.

I lifted my hands to rub the base of my skull and make the headache go away, forgetting about the hat under my arm, so of course it blew right over the rail, into the water. Fedora number four.

Freezing mad, I turned and saw the annoying couple had gone back into the cabin, leaving a rumpled newspaper behind. I returned to the bench and picked up the front section of the *Examiner.*

Just under a story about Neville Chamberlin loomed a huge, glamorous picture of Tommie O'Rourke. Platinum hair curled around her face, framing sparkling eyes and a sly smile, features perfect as a model's. She held a tennis racket, laughing at something Clark Gable was saying—I mean, Clark Gable—and on her other side, Carole Lombard twinkled at them both.

And yet that wasn't what you noticed.

It was Tommie's trademark shorts.

They showed her whole dang legs. She scandalized audiences everywhere she played, until the locals fell in love and the fashion writers followed suit. Every teenaged tennis player in every city she visited started wearing those shorts. Tommie knew how to reveal just exactly what could be quickly accepted.

I read the article's first couple of paragraphs, all about the tournament, not the tennis part at all, but how this event in England would be the most riveting San Francisco scene of the year, the chance to hobnob with the chic people around the beguiling Tommie O'Rourke. That's why Zimmer wanted Shea at Wimbledon. It'd be the perfect chance for anybody interested in San Francisco gossip.

The ferry horn blasted as the boat closed in on the Long Wharf. I put my hands in my pockets, rubbing Shea's ticket booklets between the fingers of both hands, hair blowing around my head, wild as bad ideas.

CHAPTER FIVE

Sixteenth Street Station
Oakland, California

Right away there was a problem, which wasn't my fault.
I'd told Shea's friend, Peter, I'd be the woman at the depot in a fedora. A fedora now bobbing somewhere on the bay.

Travelers clattered around me in the cavernous Sixteenth Street Station. Some were dressed to the nines, heading east to visit relatives, have an adventure. Others had just arrived, loaded down with baggage, suitcases, trunks, and gifts. Dark skinned porters in uniforms like cops rolled contraptions carrying luggage from train to wharf, for the ferry.

My family staggered into California in a caravan of top-heavy clunkers bearing mattresses, stoves, farm tools and hope chests. We'd been our own porters.

One group rushed by, smelling like they'd spent their train time drinking whiskey, their loud voices bouncing in the stony, high-ceilinged room.

"World's Fair, here we come!" said a blowsy lady.

"Sally Rand, here I come!" said the man draped around her shoulders.

She swatted him. "Bad boy!" And they dashed by.

The Golden Gate International Exposition—the World's Fair—was a short ferry ride from the *Prospect*, but I hadn't managed to go in the four months since it opened. I never saw anything, never did anything. I was at work, or I was at home with Elsie.

It was 4:00 p.m. and the train departed at 4:11. I scanned the station but didn't see anybody who might be Pat Shea, spoiled college student. What *would* he look like? Would he be wearing some letterman's sweater? A suit? Would he have a ridiculous mustache? Would he be old enough to grow one?

I walked the length of the station, from the dark brass-framed counter surrounded by ticket buyers, down the middle of the aisles of benches, full of waiting travelers.

When I squinted back at the other end of the station, I caught a glimpse of Zimmer and Sandy walking toward double doors that led outside to the tracks. It couldn't hurt to follow them at a distance, so I did, staying just inside the building, staring at them through the window.

Zimmer handed their bags to a trainman, who loaded them onto the luggage compartment. He put his hand at the base of Sandy's spine, just barely above her rump, encouraging her up the train steps. On her way up, Sandy glanced back, over her shoulder, as if she felt me glaring. I shrunk away from the window.

Sandy was going with Zimmer to New York. Then to England. On a boat. What did she do to earn this? *Well, I'm not doing that. I'm better than that.*

I surveyed the depot and saw somebody who might be the right age and walked up to him, nodding my head.

"Pat Shea?"

"What? No," he said, giving my nose a look.

"Sorry." I turned and headed the other direction.

Back near the ticket counter, I spotted couple of likely-looking guys, one of them passing the other a cigarette.

I patrolled the length of the depot to them now, tugging at a buzzing in my ears.

"Pat Shea?" I asked.

They glanced at me and at each other and laughed. I was laughable. I didn't look right. I couldn't stop my hand from going to my nose, as big as a potato, a painfully sensitive potato.

"No, ma'am," the shorter of the two said, emphasizing *ma'am*.

I retreated. That buzzing sound. I was hungry.

I decided to check out front, to see if Shea might be waiting there. The cool air and smell of trees lining the street soothed my inflamed nostrils and nerves.

A yellow cab pulled up to join a line of them. I knew it would be Shea. A lanky fellow unfolded out of the back seat and leaned into the front seat window, handing money to the driver. A stouter one bounded out of the street-side back seat door, and around to the sidewalk. Which one was he? Lanky Guy leaned back into the car and pulled a third guy out, got him sitting on the edge of the seat, feet pointed at me.

This had to be Shea.

He presented quite a picture. Feathery blonde hair flopping on his forehead, disheveled suit, tie askew, skin so fair it seemed to have no blood in it. His friends each grabbed an elbow and pulled. The driver popped the trunk and removed a suitcase.

Lanky Guy waved to the driver, who pulled forward in line. Shea's two friends wobbled quite a bit themselves. Stout Guy said, "Pal, this is your break, eh? Hitting the big leagues. Just get to your goddam berth and sleep 'er off!"

"Then get your ass to the bar car and fill 'er up again!" said Lanky Guy, somewhat less drunk than Stout Guy and considerably less so than Shea, who, in spite of being upright, appeared to be unconscious.

All the reporters, the cubs, and most of the copy boys, were drinkers. But we weren't like these guys. We weren't awful.

A voice over the loudspeaker announced, "Board now, please, for the *City of San Francisco*, bound for Chicago. Train will depart in three minutes."

Lanky Guy said, "Where's the dame with the tickets?"

I'd met so many pompous people since moving from the tomato fields to The City. But these guys? I hated everything about them. My age, acting so superior to me.

I fingered the train booklet in my right hand and the boat booklet and Wimbledon pass in my left.

Shea had no clue at all.

"That's her!"

Stout Guy looked at me, a girl in a suit who might likely wear a fedora.

"Hey, you! You're here for us!" Lanky Guy yelled, pointing one finger at the end of his very long arm at me.

This wasn't my fault.

I wheeled around, back into the depot, crossing the vaulted space, and opening the same double doors Sandy had passed through.

I walked straight up to the train, painted in a shiny leaf brown and gold, with scarlet striping and lettering. A trainman asked, "Can I take your bag?"

"I don't have a bag," I said. "But I have a ticket."

———○———

CHAPTER SIX

City of San Francisco Streamliner
Oakland, California to Ogden, Utah

I crossed boundaries. If a gate was locked, I'd climb over. Sometimes I'd get cut up, rip a jacket. No matter. Someone like me doesn't get there if she doesn't trespass. Don't clutch your pearls. This is how it worked.

So, here I sat on the *City of San Francisco* with no luggage, a few coins, Pat Shea's train tickets, Pat Shea's sea passage and Pat Shea's Wimbledon pass. I was here because I climbed over Pat when he passed out.

Now I had to figure out how to make things right with Mac back at the *Prospect*. And with Rivka at home. And I had to figure out how to use this time on the train to convince Zimmer I was his girl for the column. And what to say about Shea. And what to do about my sister.

That's all I had to do. God, I felt sick.

Setting up camp in the seat next to me was a grandma type, not somebody you might remember, black hair streaked with gray, chopped off straight at ear level, about the same length as mine, beige cardigan, black skirt. Her body was short and lumpy, but of a shape that said maybe she used to be athletic. Through her rimless glasses were critical black eyes, like she was the kind of person who sees things and reports them.

"Miss?" The conductor nudged me and held out his hand. I gave him my bloody booklet. He raised his eyebrows, pulled out a coupon, punched it and clipped it to the ceiling over my seat. "Anything I can help you with?" He returned the booklet.

"Is there a telegraph on board?"

"Yes, but it's out of service. Attendant called in sick. I can provide you some stationery, mail it at the next stop?"

"That won't do."

"Well, you can detrain when we come to Ogden, go to the Western Union next door to the depot, hop right back on to go the rest of the way to Chicago."

"When will we be in Ogden?"

"Eight in the morning."

He moved on to the next row.

I rubbed my hands on the fabric of my seat.

"You look a little off," said the grandma, in a flat, harsh voice. Her glasses magnified the papery crinkled skin around her eyes. "Did you bring food?"

I shook my head.

"You better go down to the cafe car, order something to eat. They'll be open now. Beat the dinner rush."

I hadn't seemed right since Elsie bonked my head this morning. I nodded at the grandma. "Yes, ma'am."

I walked through three coach cars, grabbing seat backs for balance, until I came to the cafe car diner. The waiter seated me at a Formica table and handed me a menu and a notepad and pencil. I marked off my choices, ham sandwich and coffee, after checking the coins in my pocket.

He took my written order. "Coming up."

"Hey, where's the ladies'?" I asked.

"Every car has one." He pointed east.

I headed that way, leaving my ticket on the table to save my spot.

I touched the bathroom door and checked to the right. Visible through glass separating cars was a dressy lounge. On the glass was a sign, PULLMAN CLASS ONLY, in gold. Beyond, at a table with a white cloth and flowers, Zimmer sat with his back to me and Sandy sat opposite him, staring right at me.

I ducked into the bathroom.

A few seconds later, the door opened and Sandy entered.

"If you're here to mess things up for me—"

"Why would I care—"

"I've been working on this—"

"Oh, yeah, *working.*"

"Yes! Working!" She took my collar in her hand and squeezed it under my chin, pressing me against a gold framed mirror as tall as me.

I pushed her hand off me. "I get it. You're working." I did understand. Girls did what we had to. I wore pants to do it. Sandy wore a dress.

"What are you doing here?"

"Shea was plastered. Couldn't even stand up."

"You're incredibly manipulative."

"Not you?"

"You just want that column."

"You just want that man."

"Not just the man. Lots of things. It begins with the man."

"So, you've got a plan."

"What do you think you're gonna do about Mac, missing work?"

"I'll send a telegram from Utah."

"Saying what?"

"I'm doing a job for Zimmer. I'll be back in by Friday."

"Don't be an idiot."

"What then?"

Sandy tipped her head up, looking at the ceiling. Then down again.

"Send it to Wally or Barry, tell them to report you're out sick. You're vomiting buckets. Your telephone at home's out."

"I don't feel great."

"That's what I'm saying. You've looked like a ghoul all day. So, ride to Chicago, talk to Edward—"

"*Edward?*"

"Grow up. Talk to him in the lounge car, before dinner tomorrow. We take dinner in our drawing room." She tilted her head up, haughty, when she said that. "Try to cinch it at drinks tomorrow. When we arrive in Chicago, turn around and ride back. There's your plan. You're welcome."

I was coach class, they were Pullman. I wasn't even allowed in the lounge.

"That'll work fine," I said. "Thanks."

I wanted to ask her what I should say to Rivka, too. I wasn't as good about making plans today—my head.

"But don't mess me up, you hear?" Sandy said.

"You neither." She could mess me up easier than I could mess her up.

We shook on it. Sandy returned to her drinks with Zimmer and I returned to my ham sandwich and coffee, wondering if she'd be sipping something fruity, with a little umbrella on a toothpick.

CHAPTER SEVEN

TUESDAY, JUNE 27, 1939

City of San Francisco Streamliner
Ogden, Utah

"Pulling into Ogden, 7:40 a.m."

I blinked myself awake, trying to recall what the trainman was talking about. A quilt spread from my lap to that of the grandma next to me, whose name I'd learned was Mrs. Lee. She opened her shade, letting morning light flood our seats.

I remembered. Buy time by sending telegrams. Persuade Zimmer by getting to him in the bar before dinner.

I asked the porter, "How much is a telegram?"

"No idea, miss." He moved on to the next row, as the conductor's voice announced over the speakers, "Coming into Ogden, Utah. Prepare to exit for Ogden."

I didn't have telegram money left after the ham sandwich.

I glanced at Mrs. Lee's purse. She followed my eyes, then stared up at my face.

"Is this some kind of emergency or something?"

"Yes, ma'am," I said. It felt like an emergency.

"It's about a man, isn't it?"

I thought of Zimmer.

"It is," I said, honest enough.

She nodded, like she knew it.

She pulled her bag to her lap and took out a coin purse with

Shangai Low, 532 Grant Avenue, printed under the snap. She had photographs in her bag in an envelope, paper-clipped together. The one on top pictured a little girl on a swing, laughing. I thought, *Mrs. Lee has her own story.* She retrieved a quarter and a dime from the coin purse and dropped them in my hand.

"Secure your future. More important than dignity. And keep the message short."

With the state of my head and the state of my life, these seemed like words from the oracle, principles to live by.

"Thank you, Mrs. Lee. I'll heed your advice."

I walked toward the exit while the train slowed, and asked the man standing next to me, "Where's the Western Union?"

"How would I know?"

The train jerked, and the conductor announced, "Ogden. Ten minute stop."

I jumped out and scoured the buildings, sun in my eyes making it hard to see. I ran to the right of the depot and found a newspaper shop.

I ran the other way to the building on the left of the station, where a blue metal sign read, WESTERN UNION TELEGRAPH & CABLE OFFICE.

Inside, a middle-aged man in overalls and a tattered hat stood at the counter.

"Go on," the uniformed attendant said to him, his black-billed cap sitting too far forward, shielding his eyes.

The customer glanced over his shoulder at me, his freckled skin patchy, blushing, then back at the attendant. He sighed, real slow, and whispered to the attendant in the cap.

The attendant repeated in a loud voice, "I'M SORRY STOP COME HOME STOP SHE'S GONE STOP." He grinned maliciously at the customer. "That it?"

The customer nodded, drooping with shame.

"Six words. That'll be fifty cents."

I had two coins. I needed to send two telegrams. Was it fifty cents a telegram? Fifty cents for six words? I earned fifty cents an hour at the paper.

The other customer left and I stepped up.

"How can I help you?"

I set my two coins on the counter. "I need to send two telegrams."

"Destination?"

"San Francisco, both of them." I gave him the details.

"Three words, two telegrams, thirty-five cents," he said.

"That won't do it. I need more words, at least five."

"You need more words, you need more money." I didn't see his eyes but the shape of his mouth made him look mean.

"I'll be right back," I said.

Outside, people were getting back on the train. Time was almost up.

I ran to a porter in a Pullman uniform helping a lady up the stairs.

"Please sir, I need fifteen cents."

He smiled at me, not unkindly, but with surprise.

"Bless your heart, miss. You're new at travel, I see. You don't understand. I'm not able to help you. Certainly not in that way."

Maybe I didn't understand how things worked. But I still needed fifteen cents.

A man with thick pomaded hair watched me, as he finished his cigarette.

"Here you go, kid. Buy yourself an ice cream." He flipped a quarter at me. It landed on the dirt and stirred up a little storm of dust.

"Thanks sir!" I snatched it and ran back to Western Union.

"Got it!" I slammed the dirty quarter on the counter.

The attendant smirked.

He doesn't matter.

For Wally at the *Prospect*, I dictated, "HOME STOP SICK STOP."

For Rivka, I said, "HOME FRIDAY STOP SORRY STOP."

"Keep the change," I said, and left.

Outside the Western Union door, bloomed a pot of zinnias, orange, red, yellow, pink, crazy, unreasonable colors in this flat, dreary place. Flowers that grew without help. Momma had them in Tumbleweed, the Federal work camp where we used to live. She just threw down seeds on hot dirt and they grew. I plucked a handful and jogged to the train as it started to move.

Mrs. Lee had freshened up and folded away our blanket.

I gave her the zinnias and said, "Thank you for everything, Mrs. Lee."

She put them in her water glass. "Did you set things up?"

"Yes, ma'am."

"Good girl," she said, making me feel warm and approved.

CHAPTER EIGHT

———◦———

City of San Francisco Streamliner
Rocky Mountain National Park, Colorado

I slept fitfully in my reclining seat most of that second day on the *City of San Francisco* as it passed the Green River and Rocky Mountain National Park. I didn't see any of the view, though Mrs. Lee had traded spots with me, letting me sit next to the window. I kept the blind drawn, her blanket on my lap. Sometimes I heard her shushing people who talked too loud.

I asked her to please wake me up at five p.m. My only job now was to be in the bar before dinner to talk to Zimmer.

But when she woke me at just before five, I was stiff from ears to shoulders. I could barely turn my head.

I made my way to the ladies' room to wash up. In the mirror my face was chalky and there was some dark red coloring under my eyes. My nose was even bigger and more tender.

A memory rose up of Daddy, coming home from a bar fight with a bleeding nose, saying nothing about it the next morning as it swelled, coloring up his eyes. He just headed out to the fields, as if nothing had happened. He only revealed things through liquor, fights with Momma, and singing. But sometimes a daughter needs information in the sober light of morning.

I still hadn't heard from Ben. No familiar, sarcastic whisper about what a fright I was or what I ought to do about it. Perfect head silence since yesterday morning.

I washed my face, wet my hair, and pushed it behind my ears. I used one of the folded towels to clean under my arms, and another to rub my teeth clean.

This was as good as I was going to get.

I stared straight at my reflection and asked, to be sure, "Ben, are you still in there?" But he didn't answer.

He'd been living in my head from the day I fought Daddy to protect Momma.

Had he been driven out now by the head butting? Had Elsie replaced Ben? Would I miss his voice?

I'd figure that out later.

I passed into the bar car.

There they were, at a little table in the corner, hunched toward each other over flowers and a candle. Sandy caught my eye and nodded.

I walked up to the two of them, an intimate pair, so not in need of my company. *Same as always.*

"Looking snazzy, Jane," Sandy said, smirking. She raised a martini glass.

Zimmer swiveled. "Appears we've got a stowaway."

A response formed in my head but didn't make it to my mouth.

"Where's Shea?" he asked.

"He didn't make it."

"Didn't make it?"

"Right."

"Why not?"

I wanted to say how drunk Shea was, how irresponsible, how arrogant, but those words didn't come out now either. I shrugged. This thing that had happened to my head and my nose seemed to have spread to my tongue.

"So, you took his seat?"

I indicated yes with my eyes.

"You climbed aboard in order to tell me Shea's a no-count no-show?"

"That," I said, thinking it conveyed enough.

"I knew that already, obviously," Zimmer said. "Good God, his father was my college roommate. Of course, Pat would be drunk and miss. I had to make him the offer. I owed Pat senior. Now my debt's paid, whether or not the check's been cashed. Cheers!" He raised his glass to Sandy.

"Oh Edward," Sandy said, giggling. "You rogue."

She raised one finger to the bartender, who nodded and started to assemble another martini. Bourbon was my drink. It was good for me, in my opinion, as compared to martinis. Bourbon made me smarter, wittier, I thought, the fire of burnt orange both numbing and igniting something essential in me, granting me admission to the *Prospect's* world of hard-drinking, talented men. I wanted to correct my order but couldn't make that happen at the moment. I sat at the third seat at their table.

The bartender brought my martini. I lifted and swallowed.

"So, Sandy tells me you want the gossip gig, assuming there'll be one." Zimmer said this just as the gin burned its way down my throat. Sandy's right hand, palm down, flipped over and made the *go on* motion.

"I was thinking," I said, and stopped.

"So, you do think. Good to know."

I thought the right words were coming up to me, from my gut, through my throat, to my mouth, but something else came instead.

I pushed back from the table, knocking over my drink.

Sandy cried, "Oh!" as my martini wet her pale silk dress.

Then the contents of my belly came up, all over the table.

"What the hell?" Zimmer yelled.

I staggered away, through the bar car and the cafe car, to the bathroom.

I slammed the door and locked it, holding off until I got my face over the toilet before vomiting up what little was left in my gut, fiery with gin at first, then bits of cracker from earlier, and then just clear fluid. Then I kept retching, though nothing came up. So the thing that had happened to my head and my nose and my tongue had now spread to my gut. It was systemic.

I heard knocking after a while, but ignored it.

Finally, I rinsed out my mouth in the sink and slouched back to my seat.

"What?" Mrs. Lee asked.

"I'm sick," I said.

She pulled the blanket out again and tucked me into my seat.

"Secure the ring, girlie. Put in the work and secure the ring."

CHAPTER NINE

AUGUST 1928

Rotten Egg Hooverville
Sacramento

I wobbled a few steps to the cleared-out patch between seven tents, three cardboard lean-tos, four trucks and two cars spread out along the highway.

My best third-grade friend, Lula Stillwater, sat cross-legged on the moonlit dirt doing science homework in a notebook on her lap. Lula rubbed the edge of her sock, trying to get rid of a red smudge, focusing on the mess she could fix, not what she couldn't, which was what I liked first-best about Lula. The thing I liked second-best was that Lula actually wanted to be my friend, a job she didn't have any competition for.

"Teacher's pet," I said.

"You must feel better. Got your mean back." Lula closed her notebook.

She bunched up her lips and wrinkled her eyebrows in sympathy for all my coughing and Momma's criticizing about my coughing. Momma might have been a field boss if she'd have been a man.

"Let's make that fire," I said, pulling a matchbook out of my pocket and waving it next to my face.

Making and explaining a fire was my plan for improving my

failing science grade and I'd spoken of it regularly to Lula, who liked its potential.

We didn't need a fire that night, given how warm the air and full the moon, but the science report was due tomorrow. I hated the humiliation of doing poorly at school when I knew I was smarter than most everybody else.

Our roadside camp had slack to no rules but neither of us had ever been allowed to build a fire. Our daddies thought girls were supposed to tend fires, not build them, though our mommas were evidently supposed to build them in order to make dinner.

"I can do it. I watch y'all every morning and I've read the official, right way to do it in the almanac, least a dozen times, Daddy," I had pleaded. Daddy smiled like I was feeble and shook his head.

"Oh, you studied the right way? You go collect the leaves, Jujee. Get me some dry ones." Then Daddy returned to his strumming, while Momma carried wood.

If Highway 99 had a face, it would have been Daddy's. It was a long, thin, tiny-lined, sunburnt face, a face proud under the first rough layer of skin. The wrinkles like worms crawling up between his brows and one snaggletooth disturbing the straight-marching lineup and a scar on the left upper cheek, matching the curve of another guy's shovel. But also the long straight nose pointing down at the folks below him in the cotton row—and they were all below his six-five height—and the wry twist of a chapped mouth about to cut the boss down with just so lyrics, and the clear, clean ice of eyes so blue they might belong to a prince, not a picker. It was an attractive, off-putting face, especially if you didn't understand how such things could combine in one person so poised to disappoint.

Daddy wasn't the sort of person I could rely on, even if he was the sort of person I could adore, partly because of the way he would talk to me, like I was worth it.

"Janie, the boss man ain't got no idea what it's like for his workers out there. He simply ain't got no idea and it's more than a *not gettin' out there* kind of thing. He cannot begin to understand what it means to be chained to the yoke, what that does to a man." Daddy squeezed my shoulder hard.

I pictured Daddy in the field, singing and talking, distracting everybody from work, most assuredly not chained to a yoke.

"My teacher's like that, Daddy. She don't know nothing 'bout the way things work. She acts like I'm sleeping in before school!"

"Huh." Daddy's eyes clouded, his thoughts momentarily derailed by my interruption. He stared at my mouth, so like his own, wide, full, curved over what seemed like an excess of teeth. Then he got back on track. "It's what happens when you become the boss man. It changes the regular man, the sensitive man, into someone who can no longer understand, because that little increase in distance ruins his vision." Daddy patted his back pocket, square with a worn paperback political screed.

Daddy got revved up talking about such things, his eyes sparking and throwing off bits of light that made me feel colorful and sharp-edged. I craved that feeling but I was beginning to see this was an effect he practiced on quite a few people. I'd seen the glow on Elthea's face at the donut shop as she laughed like a donkey at one of Daddy's jokes. I'd also seen it in a farmer's wife leaning out a truck window at the curb, rubbing lotion on her big dry arm while her husband negotiated in the feed store. She winked a meaty eye at Daddy when he smiled at her.

I understood how good it felt to have Daddy's attention.

But time had passed and Daddy didn't recognize I longed even more now than before for his attention. I was so in-between places. I hadn't gotten my first blood yet but I was taller than Momma and my head came all the way to Daddy's chin when I stood up straight (which was almost never). In the first week of school, Jimmy's big brother had hollered out the window of his truck as I was entering school late, "Same as last year. All stalk, no beans." I closed off the spigot of ideas that used to gush out my mouth at school about that time. I wanted Daddy to see me.

You don't know what I can do now, I thought but did not say, because after all I did love him. And I knew he loved me back but I was beginning to see he loved me as a kind of ideal audience, rapt and uncritical.

I had a pent-up store of ideas. There should be the exact same number of musical notes as colors in the rainbow so music and painting could say the same thing, and they should officially chop the end off every verb since nobody used the ends anyway. Daddy used to be interested in my ideas, or at least interested that I had them. But he wasn't anymore.

So, I was going to fix that. I would start by bringing up my grades.

I dictated to Lula what I would need for my save-the-grade homework fire and where we would get it, while Lula recorded the list in her smudgy notebook:

1) *Ignition (matchbook)*
2) *Tinder (five tumbleweeds, up against the smoke house)*
3) *Kindling (cardboard walls of old lean-to)*
4) *Fuel (dried cow patties)*
5) *Pit (chunks of concrete and rocks)*

Gathering it all took some time and Lula got tired and pissy. She thought it was fun to talk about how we would sneak and make a fire, but with all the hunting and gathering, the shine was off that apple.

"It's a school night," Lula complained, cradling two whitish-gray cow patties in each of her newspaper-draped arms. "Not to mention we have to pick in the morning."

"One night of beauty sleep ain't gonna fix things."

Lula dropped the cow patties and newspaper and shoved my shoulder, not hard, just enough to remind me who was who and what was what.

"Look out, beanpole. I ain't the ugly one." There were certain lines you didn't cross with Lula and implying she was ugly was one of them, even though she *was* ugly as a bullfrog.

"Cut your peaches, girl. We're done."

We took the patties and other items to a spot about ten truck distances behind the circle of tents and tilt-ups, off between the canal and the train tracks, where none of the others would hear us at work.

I showed Lula how to arrange the concrete in a circle about four feet across. Then we ripped the cardboard into strips and spread it around in the circle. We broke up the tumbleweeds, scratching our hands, sprinkling the dry bits on top of the cardboard kindling, and lit the tinder, blowing gently until the weeds began to ignite and spread to the cardboard. My heart beat faster as I saw it was working.

I felt warm and jittery, invigorated at doing something hard I wasn't supposed to do. The light from the starter blaze made the circle of trees around us look complete and safe, like the walls of a cave.

"I'll finish it off," I said, adding cow patties dramatically, fully extending my long, bony right arm, the shirt sleeve ending a good four inches before my wrist, adding patties to the crooked, steaming tower of cow shit.

Finally, I sat back to enjoy the burn. Flames licked up the sides of the tower, dancing like Indians in the movies. Great puffs of smoke filled the air in the circle of trees and then flew out to the canal, to the fields, to the campsite.

"I ain't no baby no more," I said.

I threw a broken-off chunk of patty into the fire and it hissed and spit up sparks in Lula's direction.

"Dang it, Janie!" Lula scooted backward on her butt, grinding a thick layer of grit into the backside of her legs. "You ain't got a spoon of sweet in you!"

I laughed, which caused a cough fit.

"Janie?"

I turned and saw Momma, breathing hard, black hair frizzy, white nightgown clinging, carrying a water jug in one hand. She looked like a vengeful ghost.

"Criminy!" Momma shrieked and ran to the fire. She emptied the water on our flames, causing even more smoke to rise. "What's wrong with you? Ain't we got enough to choke on?"

She dropped the jug and rubbed the sweat off her brow.

"Sorry Missus Hopper," Lula rose to say. "We was just . . ."

"Not now," Momma snapped.

Lula's smile faded.

"Come on and get to bed. We're driving up the highway in the morning for a big two-day pick in Stockton."

"I got school tomorrow, Momma. I got this report due—"

"It'll wait."

"But cain't you and Daddy—"

"He's gone. He cain't help. He's got an *opportunity*, he says.

He's aiming to get a singing spot at The Blackboard, down in Bakersfield. Your fool daddy never recognizes a real opportunity because it shows up sweating, not singing."

"But my grade."

"Tell it to him when he gets home. Maybe you'll teach him something. His daydream's causing you to fail out of school. He's gonna ruin your future."

———◦———

CHAPTER TEN

WEDNE/DAY, JUNE 28, 1939

City of San Francisco Streamliner
Chicago, Illinois

M rs. Lee pulled down a faded brown duffel and a shopping
bag with a yellow ribbon sticking out the top.

"Is Chicago your final stop, Mrs. Lee?"

"Yes, I'm here to see my daughter. Wish I was on the *Fifth
Avenue Special*, like you, Pat. I like New York, so many people."

I pictured Mrs. Lee slipping a cunning hand into my pocket,
lifting out my booklet, riffling through it, finding my fake name
and the train I'd be taking. She'd been snooping but I didn't care.
My mood dipped at the prospect of our parting ways. I didn't
care to judge a sneak who mainly treated me right. Besides,
something about her made me feel solid. I trusted her.

She settled in again and handed me some candied ginger,
which made a nice breakfast to go with the coffee she bought me.

"How old's your daughter?" I asked.

"Twenty-two. She has a new baby."

I tried to imagine myself with a new baby of my own. Of
course, I could picture me with my toddler sister, but me with a
baby in my body? That would be a whole other order of disaster.
Or maybe not. For a minute I thought, *A different baby wouldn't
be so impossible to make happy. I'd make a better mother of my*

own. Or then again, maybe everything would be the same. Maybe I was the problem, not Elsie.

"I'm staying for a couple of days to set my daughter straight before I go home. She's not a girl who understands how things work."

"How babies work?"

"She'll need me to show her how to do things right. I'll be home before my husband misses me. He likes to eat every meal at the restaurant anyway."

"Will your daughter have a babysitter?"

Mrs. Lee glanced at my flat belly, no doubt imagining a sprouting peanut. "A babysitter's a good idea. My own mother moved in when each of my five kids came. She stayed in our house for a few weeks after each one. Then she walked back and forth every day to watch them while my husband and I ran the restaurant. That worked. I can't do that for my daughter. I've got the restaurant."

Momma wasn't going to come babysit Elsie at my apartment. She had the roadhouse. She wouldn't serve someone else unless it served her, too. She wouldn't take care of Elsie without *owning* her.

I opened Shea's coupon booklet to all the rides that had been paid for—a transfer from the Chicago North Western Station to the La Salle Street Station, a coach seat on the *Fifth Avenue Special* to New York, a transfer to the pier where the *Queen Mary* would launch.

I had to get back to Elsie and resolve matters. I missed her soapy smell, the warmth of her scalp, how fine her soft strawberry hair was up against my cheek, the sound of her throaty, babbling conversation, things I'd noticed in the small meadows of time between her tantrums and my rushing out the door.

I'd thought this train ride would help me do the right thing. Now it had become the absolute worst combination of failures. I'd left Rivka in a terrible situation. I didn't want to think about what Elsie might be feeling. That would make me cry right here on the train. I immediately felt the risk of that.

"I'll be right back," I said to Mrs. Lee, and headed to the ladies' room.

Zimmer came out of the next car's men's room, three yards away from the ladies'. I steeled myself, passed through those doors and tapped him on the shoulder.

"Sorry about last night, Mr. Zimmer," I said. "I was sick."

"Evidently. Should I throw on a tarp?"

"Not on my account, sir."

He put both hands in his pockets and rocked up and back. "You've got Shea's passage? All the travel documents?"

I nodded.

He shook his head. "Listen, I've seen what you've written before—sure, all the police blotter things, the city council stuff. I don't mean that. I'm talking about that article you wrote a year and a half ago, with somebody else's byline on it. The scandal thing with the photographer and the dead girl."

I winced. Vee hadn't been *the dead girl*, but a kind of shadow to me, my age, an Okie too, trying to come up in the world, working for a famous artist. A girl killed while waiting for me at a bar because I didn't show up when I said I would.

I'd thought her so *off*. Strange, poorer even than me, on the verge of something really destructive. She was not the kind of person I aimed to associate with. Not when I compared her to the switchboard girls and receptionists and typists at the *Prospect*, with their tidy, healthy appearance, their pink skin and curled hair, their giggling secrets.

I'd escaped from Rotten Egg Hooverville to reinvent myself in The City. I couldn't be associated with *off,* I thought. I'd felt so at risk myself, I hadn't summoned the minor generosity and courage it would have taken to be kind, to be bigger than my insecurity. Also, I was seventeen.

So, I'd skipped out on Vee and she'd been killed outside the bar where we were supposed to meet.

Yes, as Zimmer said, I wrote about it under someone else's byline. I'd spent so much time on that, driven to receive the blame. But the blame never came. Now this recognition. Things rarely worked the way I assumed they would.

"Listen, the trip's paid for. There may be something in you, though you're a damned odd girl, maybe too odd for anything important at a place like the *Prospect.*"

I could be less odd. I could be normal, better than normal. Talented.

"There *is* some kind of *oomph* in you. We'll see. I'll have Sandy wire Mac, tell him I'm giving you a shot, at something."

Zimmer seemed like a redwood before me, the worldly height of him making me dizzy below. This was what I wanted, to be chosen, to be elevated. I could move up, move out, hire that babysitter for Elsie, everything. I felt the whoosh of open sky all around me up there.

I'd sent a wire to the *Prospect,* saying I was home sick. That was okay. Zimmer's would override that one. I'd also sent a wire to Rivka, saying I'd come home Friday. What would she do about work? I stopped myself going down that path. I could send a new wire. It would be worth it to her if it got me and Elsie out of her flat. This was about more than a couple of weeks. I aimed to fix the long term, for all of us.

"Yes, sir," I said.

"What kind of writer would say no to this, eh?"

"No writer at all."

"See you in England. Sandy says we're on different trains this leg, different parts of the boat."

Zimmer said boat, not ship. That gave my mood a little party.

"Thank you, Mr. Zimmer. You won't be sorry."

When we pulled into Chicago, Mrs. Lee handed me a card with *Shangai Low* printed on it, underlined by chopsticks. She'd written, *Mrs. John Lee, CH8-4203* in loopy cursive below the restaurant's address. "Call me there if you like."

"I'm headed to England," I said.

She tapped her forehead with her finger, "There are more ways than one to skin a cat," which I thought made an excellent goodbye.

———————o———————

Chicago and North Western Station
Chicago, Illinois

There was still a big fat fly in the cup. I didn't have a passport. They weren't going to let me on the boat without one.

In the station, I found Sandy waiting with their luggage while Zimmer ordered pretzels. I rushed her, figuring I had only a couple of minutes.

"I need a favor," I said.

"How many will there be?"

"Well, at least two more. First, I need your help with a telegram."

"I know. I'm sending it from the next train to Mac."

"I need another."

"For crying out loud."

"I owe you. A lot."

"We're not even friends. You never talk to me unless you want something from Mac. You act like you're above me."

I hadn't considered talking to her the way I talked to the switchboard girls. Somehow I hadn't thought of her as a worker. Why was that?

Was it something about her type of ambition? Was I disrespecting Sandy because of her matching skirts and purses and shoes, because of the lipstick she wore as if she liked it, as if liking it made an ambitious girl less significant?

Though I could hardly claim to be above *anyone* as an Okie tomato picker, I guess I did feel kind of superior to her. I'd gotten myself a writer job. I *was* above her in that way. Confusing.

I had to admit, there was something extremely competent about Sandy, more competent than me, if I was honest, and far more connected to power than me. I ought to have seen all that earlier.

"I apologize. Really." That was all I had.

She blew a puff of air out the side of her mouth. "What's the telegram?"

I scribbled the particulars on a page from my pocket moleskin and handed it to her. "I appreciate this. Really." I thought of something I could give her, a little bit of the truth to prove our new friendship. "I need the columnist gig for the money. My roommate's very mad at me. I may have to move out but I can't afford to." Did Sandy see me the way I'd seen Vee, as contagiously at risk?

Sandy slipped the paper into her purse. "You appear to breed trouble everywhere."

"So they say. There's something else too."

"What?" Her eyes jumped over my shoulder impatiently.

"I don't have a passport."

"Jehoshaphat."

"Is there anything you can do, somebody you can call?"

"Okay, okay, okay. I'll try. I'll see you in New York. Maybe we can fix this. You're a wreck, a regular Titanic."

As she hustled off, heels clacking, I sensed not only that she would fix this, but that she'd enjoy fixing it. And I thought she didn't wear those heels just to look stylish but that they were a subtle tool for getting things done.

---○---

CHAPTER TWELVE

SATURDAY, JULY 1, 1939

Cunard Pier 90
New York, New York

I arrived in New York with almost no assistance from anybody, other than the *Prospect* paying my way, a kind stranger flipping me a quarter, Zimmer saying yes to the column, Sandy sending the telegrams, Mrs. Lee giving me money and nursing me through the trip to Chicago, and Rivka caring for Elsie.

Other than that, nothing.

I felt exposed and alone standing there on the dock, waiting to board *RMS Queen Mary*, New York to Cherbourg to Southampton. Anxiety pressed, not just because of everything unknown about this boat passage itself but also having no passport, a literal, official barrier.

I stood near the signs that read CABIN CLASS PASSENGERS, looking like anything but that I belonged there, huddling in my filthy, thin suit jacket, wind whipping all around me, surrounded by thousands of people on the rocking dock near the boat.

The *Queen Mary* dwarfed me, as tall as the Empire State building, wide as a football field, long as four New York City blocks.

Behind me I found Sandy in a cheery blue and white suit, like she dressed to sail every day, like her closet was full of just the right things for such a trip. Her arm was tucked neatly into

Zimmer's, as if she thought it had a right to be there. I was beginning to think it did.

I waved as I approached to interrupt their lovebird preening.

"This is the cabin-class line," Sandy said.

"I know, just . . ."

"Girl talk," she said to Zimmer and pulled me away to the side. "So, I solved your problem. Here's your passport." She glowed with pride.

I opened it to my picture ID from the *Prospect*, cropped to the right size. And a new birthdate, making me twenty-one, not nineteen.

"This is amazing. You did this official thing. . ." I said.

"Well, not *exactly* official. Look at the name."

It read, *Pat Shea.*

"I graduated from the Katherine Gibbs Secretarial School right here in New York, so, in spite of what you might assume about me, I'm not just a pretty face and a fantastic figure, with a tremendous sense of style. I actually know what I'm doing. You'll want to procure the real thing later. This is what you need for now."

She knew what she was doing. Why hadn't she found me clean clothes? Maybe I should have asked for them. Had she thought about doing that and rejected the idea? I would consider that later.

———o———

Third Class
RMS Queen Mary

I craned my neck, taking in the double-wide staircase of shin-
ing silver oak, rails accented with metal speed bumps to keep
third-class kids from using them as a slide. I would have given in
to such a temptation if I'd been the kind of girl from the kind of
family that would sail in a boat across the ocean.

The third-class rooms were arranged around this central
core, blocking us from tourist and cabin classes. *Three different
worlds on one boat*, I thought. I remembered the workers and
corrected that, four worlds, one boat.

They had a huge space for third class to gather and socialize,
portholes for a view of the sea, wicker chairs and fresh flowers
everywhere. They offered us movies and a library, even a children's playroom. I'd never seen anything like it. Much grander
than I'd expected, which confused me. I'd thought *third class*
meant tacky.

I wandered the boat, looking at room numbers, until I found
Pat Shea's stateroom, entered, and discovered my bunkmates,
three brothers speaking another language. I guessed they were
Italian.

They were friendly enough, shocked and delighted by my
arrival, like they didn't know what to make of the gift of a girl in
boys' clothing.

I rushed out Pat's door, flagging down a maid in the hall to tell her I'd been booked in a room for a male Pat Shea, when I was clearly a female Pat. She nodded sympathetically, and led me to a uniformed boss lady who was empowered to fix this. The woman looked exhausted, not pleased. "We'll collect your luggage and move it to another room," she said, sighing.

"I don't have any luggage."

That confirmed I was suspect. She appeared to be working hard to keep her eyes from rolling on their own volition.

"Follow us," she said. The maid got in line, dangling keys. I had to rush to keep up, hard to do with the pounding in my head. "All the existing beds are taken, but we'll move a cot into a four-berth ladies' room."

We arrived at my new boat home and the boss lady knocked lightly and the kind maid unlocked the door, admitting me to a narrow room with four mahogany beds, the two uppers of the Pullman type, which folded into the wall.

There were four ladies dressed in the style of secretaries on holiday (according to an issue of *McCall's Magazine* I'd picked up on the train). They interrupted unpacking festivities to gape, bewildered.

"Our apologies, but we have an extra roommate for you, ladies. Meet Pat Shea. She'll be staying on a cot, which we'll have wheeled in here shortly."

A skinny redhead in a fresh green dress said, "But this is *our* room!"

Her friend with round, dark eyeglasses chimed in. "We've planned this passage for a year. You can't just—"

"The *RMS Queen Mary* is happy to refund you twenty percent of your passage for this inconvenience." The boss lady tilted her head at me, the inconvenience.

A cloche-hatted girl pouted and a pocket-sized brunette put her arm around the hatted girl's shoulders.

The maid left as the room was unpacked, and a bellboy rolled in a metal cot, the girls harrumphing as they returned to unpacking around him. The only free spot for the cot was in the middle of the room, where it blocked the washbasin and mirror, a development that amplified their disappointment. The bell-boy said before leaving, "If you find the cot blocks the mirror too bad, the ladies' room is down the hall."

The little brunette drooped like she might cry, as though having a sink and mirror in their room had been the trip's selling point. I was clearly going to ruin their vacation.

The trip wasn't looking so good for me either. In addition to my throbbing head, the contractions of my gut announced the approaching arrival of my monthly curse.

I refused to ask these girls for help, so I slipped out the door of our room and into the shared restroom down the hall, where I found the kind maid scouring sinks. "I'm sorry," I said. "I have no luggage—long story. But I've got my monthly visit and I need help, please."

"Oh, Miss!" said the maid, whose name tag read Yvette. "I'll fix you right up. You wait here." She came back in a few minutes with a brown bag filled with sanitary pads, deodorant, a bottle of aspirin, and a laundry bag with hand-me-down clothing.

"These aren't exactly your style," she said, looking at my suit. "I found 'em in the lost and found. But they'll give you something to sleep in, something to change into."

I saw her through a wet film. I stared at the linoleum instead of talking.

"Miss Pat," she said, "you don't need to stay in that room with them girls all day. Even if you're too poorly to meet other passengers, you can settle on a deck chair with blankets and enjoy the view. Nothing like the Atlantic. I could stare at it day and night. You can find yourself in that sea."

"Find yourself?"

"Oh, forget I said anything, Miss. You don't need finding."

I wondered at her observation, where she came from, what brought her here, scrubbing toilets and sinks in a bathroom on this boat, helping me so graciously.

"Thank you, Yvette."

She nodded and returned to her work.

I cleaned myself up and swallowed three aspirin to dull the pain of my injured head and my cramps.

I donned one of the dresses in the bag, too short and too loose, but otherwise not bad. I gave a passing grateful thought to the shorter, wider woman who'd left it behind, then took Yvette's advice and settled myself into a deck chair, next to a dormant old man, a spot I claimed all day, all five days. The old man snored but it didn't matter because the ocean roared louder. I lay there next to him, sick in varied ways, in varied regions of my body.

Gazing at the unrelenting gray of Atlantic sky and sea, I relived my butting heads with Elsie, trying to figure fault, deciding neither of us was to blame.

I tried to tell if the spots that were sore from the collision were different than the parts paining me now. They were. The pain had migrated. Or was this pain new?

When I woke for meals, I took my seat at an assigned table at the edge of the third-class dining room with a large family who didn't speak English and, as a result, didn't expect me to talk. I couldn't taste the food. I could scarcely see it.

Only my sickness mattered. My neck ached with tension, my

head spun like a dying top, my belly cramped, and I didn't want to talk. This was all just as well, since my swollen nose and bruised eyes must have made everyone I passed worry my luck would rub off.

On the fourth day, while drifting in and out of sleep on my deckchair, I was sure I heard Sandy's flutelike giggle and the rumble of Zimmer's own laughter from the deck above.

I strained to hear more but the ocean drowned them out. What was he saying? What did she think? Was Sandy securing her future, as Mrs. Lee said, getting the ring?

The sound of her voice was the only reminder that week that I was on the same boat, going to the same tournament as Zimmer and Sandy. My first Atlantic crossing was like sailing through a delirious dream.

But just the wisp of Sandy's voice, maybe a memory and not a real sound, provoked the most solid fact of that week. Sitting on that deck chair, belonging nowhere, I wanted to be up with Sandy and Zimmer.

As comfortable as third class turned out to be, I wanted to be first class, cabin class, whatever they called it. I wanted up there.

But how would a third-class girl like me accomplish such an ascent?

I would do what I'd always done. I would study and learn and change. I would become who I wanted to be. And until I'd learned enough to be that person, I would act like I already was.

Pretending would make it so.

CHAPTER FOURTEEN

JULY 7, 1939
All England Club
Wimbledom, London, UK

Though my nose was no longer red and swollen, I could see it
had changed, with a sharp bump and a slight cant to the
right. My eyes resembled those of a drunk, slightly unfocused.
The shade underneath them had gone from red to blue-gray. I
washed a few spots off my shirt and my jacket cuffs, and exited
the bathroom at Wimbledon, ready.

I'd arrived two hours before the ten o'clock start to get the
lay of the land before the match officially started. I needed to
learn how this thing worked before I could concern myself with
who wore what and so on, what I figured the gossip angle would
be. Honestly, I had no idea about the gossip angle.

I watched a team of Labrador retrievers, a canine security
detail, racing between all the green chairs, sniffing for danger.
Watched workers trimming grass to less than an inch high, re-
painting court lines that seemed to have been painted minutes
before. Watched umpires consulting, technicians setting up
lights, cameras, microphones. Watched spectators swarming the
North Concourse. Watched the arriving crowds down rivers of
champagne, mountains of strawberries and cream, sweet fizz
rising in a mist over the throng. I wrote in my moleskin notebook, *It's the greatest carnival ever.*

I didn't even care that nobody seemed to see me. *My isolation's a secret power*, I thought, which was not the way I usually felt. On that day, I liked it.

I picked up a full glass of champagne someone had left on a table and swallowed it. I found leftover strawberries and ate them.

I heard a couple of workers, one with a broom, one with a bag—accents so thick I got only every fourth word—say something about the *players' box*. One pointed at a fence, jerking her head, so I followed her nod and that's how I found my spot, outside the stands where the important people gathered.

Leaning on that fence, I scoured the well-dressed crowd and found Zimmer right away, glowing in the stands, so dashing, those bright white teeth in a brown face, flirting with a redhead on his left. Sandy sat on his right, sulking. Maybe the trip had proved less productive than Sandy had hoped.

Everybody sitting around Zimmer had the arrogant look that pained me. The girl at his side looked like a starlet, I thought, as she had a movie magazine face. Next to her was a tall, fair young man, thin as a willow, with Tommie's profile, probably her brother. And all kinds of other people wearing costumes I couldn't decode.

I'd become clever at the details of San Francisco uniforms, worn by bankers, accountants, salesmen, bar men, debutantes and secretaries, passing on the street. But the fact that I was in Britain, where the uniforms differed, diminished my skill.

Now Zimmer's crowd rustled in a new way as an elegant woman glided toward her seat, spine straight, long arms taut in a capped-sleeve, dove-colored linen blouse, and straight navy skirt, ankles tan and bare above smart polished heels.

Her wavy hair was pulled back and up away from her face, so I couldn't help noticing her cleft chin, her arched brows.

The crowd murmured as she passed like the most significant float in a parade.

She had enough silver woven through the gold of her waves to show she was of a certain age, though not old. She made the glamor and power of mid-forties look greater than that of twenty-five, at least for someone with no apparent bulges or folds.

She may have been ideally seen from this distance as her cheekbones were so high and round they pushed her eyes into a squint, suggesting a judgmental bent, which was probably true, based on that radio interview.

The guests in the players' box all rose as she approached, backing into their seats to make room, nodding as she passed, each patting her shoulder, her back, softly, polite and unobtrusive.

They seemed to understand how this should work, responding to Coach's need, rising, moving back, making room. All except for one, the starlet next to Zimmer, who leaned forward to Coach's row as she passed, extending her hand to shake.

"Hello Coach Carlson, I'm Leena. I've been so eager to meet you," she chirped, apparently not perceiving her failure to submit to ritual. Even I could see that Leena was breaking the rules.

Coach didn't accept Leena's hand. Instead, she shivered, signaling alarm, and moved toward her seat down the row, on her way again. There was a strange kind of panic in her face, which seemed too white, even sweaty.

A man in Coach's path, turning to glare at the offending Leena, accidentally, unbelievably, elbowed Coach, knocking her backward. I caught my breath as I watched her topple, like a slow-motion scene from a bad movie, over the row below. Those marble muscled arms slashed the air as if on the verge of flight, while she shrieked "Ohhhhh!" all the way over and down, filling the stadium with her cry.

It seemed forever that the crowd froze in silence.

Then Zimmer barked "Imbecile!" at Leena, who burst into tears. I wrote her name in my moleskin.

Because Tommie and her opponent were not yet on court, the reporters and their cameras below had still been trained on Coach, probably discussing her clothing, her purse, the sunglasses perched on top of her head.

So, when she fell backward and down, they were ready to record the worst bad-luck entry to any event ever. Bulbs flashed, pencils scribbled, microphones hissed.

Coach landed on her side, her elegant skirt hitched over her knees, her purse three feet away.

For a split second she took in the hundreds of faces gaping at her, some contorted in horror, others in glee.

Her sunglasses had slipped to a cockeyed angle in the fall. Now she pulled them over her eyes as she pushed herself upright, moved past the offenders, climbing over the wrong row to take her official seat, and brushed her skirt of wrinkles.

A young, forgettably ordinary woman in the seat next to Coach tucked her left arm into Coach's right, and gripped her upper arm, whispering in her ear. Coach grimaced and pushed her off.

Mad as a wet hen, I thought.

I'd read in the papers on the boat about Coach's required behavior in the stands. Everybody was supposed to stick to almost religious rules—step back, nod, allow her to pass to her seat last, sit in dignity and focus on Tommie on the court, no one or nothing else.

There was supposed to be magic or luck involved in winning, no matter how hard you prepared. You had to manage the luck as well as the preparation. Luck was *part* of the preparation, she'd said in the article. I scribbled this in my notebook.

A roar rose up from the crowd.

The linesmen marched on court in silly official uniforms, buttoned up nearly to their chins. Clouds parted as the tarp was rolled back and net posts hammered.

Tommie and her opponent, the British favorite, Beryl Davis, came onto the court, waving at the audience, bowing at the royals' boxes. The Queen nodded her head.

While Beryl wore the expected ladylike skirt, Tommie wore her shocking trademark shorts. I thrilled at the sight of another girl dressed the way she wasn't supposed to dress. Beryl clapped her hands three times and wiped them on her skirt. Tommie's hands made the strange motion I'd read about—left hand extended, right hand strumming an invisible guitar. Beryl blew a kiss at someone in the crowd. Tommie dipped her head in a half neck stretch.

With everyone else in the stands, I watched them warm each other up for ten minutes, umpire keeping time, my heart thudding with every thwack of the ball, as if this had something to do with me.

I watched the coin toss, thrown by a knock-kneed girl who smiled ear to ear at the honor.

Tommie bent, shaking her arms like ropes. She rolled up, one vertebra at a time, turned her head left and right, took a head band off her wrist and pulled it up around her thick wavy hair.

The band burst off her head, flying up into the air and down onto the court at her feet, leaving her hair hanging loose in her eyes, the very worst place for her hair. The crowd murmured.

Coach craned her neck all around, panicked. "Does anybody have a hair band?" she shouted, setting off a flurry of purse searching in the stands.

"Here!" called the starlet Leena, waving her arm in the air.

"Please," Coach said.

Leena tossed a green band—green, not white, as the original had been. Face ashen, Coach tossed the band down to Tommie, who caught it, registering shock, yelling, "Green?"

Boy howdy. I gripped my notebook. Something strange was happening.

Coach remained perfectly still, once again under total control, hidden behind her sunglasses. She breathed in deeply through her nose and blew it out her mouth and smoothed her skirt again. With the tips of her fingers, she wiped sweat from her brow.

The players curtsied to Queen Mary and the umpire announced, "Play!"

Tommie bounced the ball four times, made a slash with her body, and play began.

Below me, a British reporter said to another one next to him, "Let's see what she does. She's a trickster, this one."

Tommie was riveting, at the same time beautiful and frighteningly powerful. I moved down closer to the court, where the radio reporters hunched over tables narrating the match, and I listened, taking notes.

One American radioman caught me with the fervor of his voice. "Hitting groundstrokes, back and forth. Beryl hits a hard backhand, pulling Tommie out wide." He spoke at machine gun pace, with authority. "Tommie gets there but slices it short, two feet past the service line. Then she reverses, back to center. Beryl moves in to take the short ball and smacks it back to the same corner. Tommie runs toward the centerline, ball heading behind her. No time to turn. Beryl follows the shot into the net at an angle from the backhand side. Tommie reverses, skipping backward, one, two, three, and hits a forehand out of her backhand corner. Tommie fires her topspin into the equivalent of a two-inch cervix with no setup time. Beryl lunges and misses!"

My head spun and my heart pounded.

The British reporter said to his friend, "I can't say if it's God or painkillers but that girl's got something extra."

I'd never seen a woman like this, a woman of such undeniable power, who the world actually appeared to approve of. She pulled a crowd of thousands out of their seats and onto their stamping feet, made them call her name in adulation—*Tommie, Tommie, Tommie.* She electrified everyone who witnessed her.

Tommie went on to ruin Beryl, the beloved Londoner, 6-2, 6-0.

The reporter below said, "She's a cyclone. No woman's ever played like that. She's a monster, a perfect American monster."

A monster? Because of how hard she hit? Because she didn't let up? Because she aimed to win? *He thinks she's unnatural.*

The two athletes met at the net to shake hands, Tommie beaming, sweat misting off her, in a picture that would be sent round the world. Beryl hugged Tommie and they both walked to the stands to meet the Queen, sitting next to US Ambassador Joseph Kennedy. The Queen leaned down to say something to Tommie, who smiled demurely—the opposite of monstrous—and nodded, then backed away, toward the players' box.

I inspected the crowd for Coach, wanting to see her finally smiling and relaxed now, on what must be her most triumphant coaching day, but I couldn't find her through the standing crowd. I buzzed inside, like I was a part of this, not just a part of the jubilant crowd, but connected to Tommie's own electricity.

From my spot on the other side of the fence, the box crowd appeared to swirl like water in a drain, cycling inward, down to where Coach should have been standing.

Leena the starlet screeched like a hawk.

The cameras all pointed and flashed at her, though the relevant action was taking place outside their camera sights, in the center of the vortex, where Coach Carlson had crumpled on the ground in front of her seat.

PART TWO

———o———

JULY 9, 1939

Southampton Docks
Southampton, UK

The *Queen Mary's* berth at Southampton's Western dock was cold and drizzly as the eye of a sneeze.

My plans had come to nothing. Everybody who'd traveled from San Francisco for Wimbledon was trooping home now, party over, Tommie departing in tragedy. Coach had fallen dead in the stands at the peak of Tommie's triumph. The bad news wrote itself.

I had to admit to selfish disappointment. I'd worked hard to get there, putting everything at risk, and now my plan had gone rump up, my having neither met nor impressed anyone. My column would have to turn on what I wrote, with no relationships to bolster it.

I stood once more in a third-class throng to board the *Queen Mary*, the cabin class on my left, tourist class on my right. I gazed longingly to my left. Thousands of people lined the docks to send off the boat. A band played *Anchors Away*.

About forty people to the side and behind me, stood Tommie. She wore a brown gabardine suit, which draped her frame loosely with its sculptured bust, jacket cut long at the hip. She seemed dressed to soften her frame. Maybe, off the court, she tried not to emphasize her power.

I understood. Back when I was Benny, I had to work so hard to stand up straight, to claim my height, to fight my learned tendency to take up less space.

The grief on Tommie's face unnerved me, the red rims of her eyes, puffy lips and nose. She seemed to have been crying for hours.

I couldn't stop staring.

Was it literally something about her appearance? Or was it knowing she centered her world, everywhere she traveled, was always the most famous, most talented person?

Or maybe I couldn't look away because I blamed her—the social scene around Tommie after that match was supposed to be the source of my story. I may have been that heartless, resenting a mourning woman because I wanted her to give me gossip.

She folded into herself even before I heard the men yelling, their pounding footsteps stampeding toward her, cameras flashing, microphones thrusting into her face.

"Tell us what really happened, Tommie!"

"Does this diminish your greatest win?"

"Was it unnatural causes?"

"What was your relationship with Coach?"

"Is it true you were on the outs?"

"Did Coach disapprove of your love life?"

Shame bubbled in my gut because I aimed to be counted among that crew, writing the nasty headline, clicking the unflattering photo, finding the tiny, incriminating tidbit. I knew what they were doing—their job! But its effect played out on Tommie's face. Those fine features seemed to collapse into themselves, as if her face might implode in a sinkhole of emotion.

The guy who matched Tommie in the stands rushed to her

side, upending one of the reporters and sending his camera clattering into the crowd. A kid in dirty clothes grabbed the camera and ran off with it, as the reporter on the ground called, "Bobbies! Bobbies!"

Tommie cried, "Frank, no!" as he swung at somebody with a mike.

Frank was the wiry type who could apparently land a punch. About six-foot-three, he moved like an athlete.

Bobbies descended, pulling Frank back, hauling him away. He wrestled with them, trying to break free, to protect Tommie, but the men in black surrounded him, one raising a club.

Tommie screamed, hands at her face, desperate and seemingly unmoored with grief and fear. Something surged in my blood and I wanted to protect her, but I'd seen what happened with Frank and I wasn't going to have that.

I yelled as loud as I could, "Hey, that's Johnny Weissmuller with Leena! They're swinging again!" I pointed at the end of the line.

A couple of photographers pivoted and ran, having gotten their fill of screaming Tommie photos anyway, and then the others did too, making the same calculation.

Tommie stared at the departing photographers, dumbfounded.

I ran to her side and took her arm. "To the front."

Either the other cabin-class customers were too shocked to react or they figured it best for them too to rush her onboard, and they backed away, leaving space at the front of the line

The rope attendant said, "Let's get you away from that."

I said, "Your passage," and Tommie pulled it out of her purse and handed me her booklet and her passport. I passed them on to the attendant, who asked for mine.

I could hear the mob running back to us, their storming feet on the dock, someone yelling, "There they are!"

I pulled my booklet and passport out, looking behind us at the press, who'd want to thump me for the ruse.

"Sorry, I'm third class."

"That's fine, Miss Shea. Just go!"

We rushed up the ramp, me behind Tommie, who craned to the side to see the bobbies releasing Frank, fuming as he headed back to his line.

On deck, Tommie straightened her jacket, pulling her sleeves down to cover her wrists, still breathing heavy. "I owe you for that."

"Oh no. I mean . . ."

"Really, I had to escape that mess, and Frank's fix made everything worse. Now the news is going to be full of that fight, too, my screaming. Just, everything . . ."

"It's not his fault. Who could blame him?"

"Well," she pouted, "his sister could. If she's put up with enough of it."

I shrugged and said, "Family."

Around us, passengers crowded the deck, waving, streamers dropping. Propellers turned in a roar, and ropes holding the boat to Great Britain were hoisted. The captain sounded a horn.

"Right, family," she said. "You're Shea. What's your first name?"

My chest tightened. It was exhausting, having always to lie about everything. I'd lived so much of the lying life, pretending to be Benjamin before. It felt good to be Jane again. I didn't want to be Pat Shea now. Tommie's face was so open and I did understand the power of revealing secrets in making someone trust you.

But I had to protect my interests and sometimes that meant pretending.

———o———

SEPTEMBER 1937

Rivka's Flat, 3528 Clay Street
San Francisco, California

I patted my hair, newly shorn, an inch long and gummed up with pomade. Running my hands over my shoulders, arms, hips, legs, I understood why Rivka had mocked me when I rose from the bath the day I arrived, a beaten-up girl, oddly tall, with bone-shaped limbs, a concave chest.

This was how Ben would have looked, like me. If he were alive, we'd be a matched pair. Rivka cutting my hair felt like letting that happen.

But still, he wasn't standing there with me.

I'd lived and he had died. *Not my fault,* I comforted myself.

I straightened up taller, less dangly.

I pulled on the snug, stretchy boys' underwear Rivka bought me. These were nothing like my droopy, homemade panties. Nothing like dress-up hose and garters attached to a girdle, making me feel sucked in, breathless, jury-rigged, as if the snaps might break, giving me scarcely any inclination to think what I thought, so aware was I of the rayon pattern scratching into the skin of my legs.

From this very first layer, I was comfortable being Ben, for Ben, for a while.

I pulled on wool pants, my bare skin slipping into baggy, slippery-lined legs, pulled on the crisp, ironed shirt, thick socks, wingtips, all the layers of protection.

I stuffed my pockets with a beat-up wallet, a dollar in change, a keychain, a handkerchief, a pack of Lucky Strikes, a pencil, and a pocket notebook. "Ballast," Rivka called it. "A man needs weight," she said as she piled it all on the dresser.

Daddy used to load his pockets with nuts, bolts, his pocketknife, when he didn't have money to carry. He needed ballast too.

I put on the fedora, which warmed the top of my head.

Hands in my pockets, knees wide, I felt the freedom of spreading out. I'd worked hard for so long to hunch over, to hide the height that made me the butt of jokes, so that my very self was what stopped me from getting the things I wanted.

Rivka taught me to light a cigarette like a boy, how to let it dangle out the side of my lips, how to grip it with my thumb and two fingers, flicking ashes, rude, as if no one needed to sweep up after me, or as if I didn't care they did.

Wearing these clothes, acting this way, I felt the carelessness of boyhood. To be a boy was to be presumptuous, to fling open doors I would have waited behind before.

See? I told you, Ben said in my head.

"This is still me, though," I said.

Sure, it is, he answered.

"This is a costume, just for now."

Everything's a costume, everybody's acting.

"What made you so dark?"

Really? he said.

Rivka saw it the same way.

"Choose your costume carefully," she said. "Not because it

shapes the world's perception. But because it makes you. You can keep adding new color, texture, pattern, but the first layers remain underneath, shaping everything added after."

———•———

CHAPTER SEVENTEEN

Tommie's Suite, Main Deck 117–119
RMS Queen Mary

"You'll take Coach's room." Tommie pointed at a closed door in her cabin-class suite, configured of two rooms on Main Deck, 117 and 119, with a shared door between them.

I'd be sleeping in a dead woman's bed. She'd be sleeping in storage, I figured.

The drawing room walls were covered with framed paintings of tennis played throughout history, all the players in flowing white gowns, all with Tommie's platinum hair. I doubted the accuracy but respected the flattery.

"Does all cabin class look like this on account of Wimbledon?"

"No, they do things up nice for some of us. We had the same suite coming over."

All this, because of her job, because of her success.

Someone tapped on the door.

"That'll be the stewards," Tommie said. "Come!"

A uniformed man entered with one cart, followed by another with a second, each loaded down with trunks and garment bags on hangers.

"In there," Tommie said. "Same room as last time."

Both of the men rolled the luggage into Tommie's room.

"You'll need to locate Miss Shea's things," Tommie said.

"My bag was stolen." The lost-and-found duffel had been taken out from under the park bench where I slept the night before, which was not such a loss. Nothing fit.

Tommie cocked her head.

"It was a loaner. I didn't know I was coming until I boarded the train."

"You boarded with no clothes from home?"

"Two trains, one boat, Wimbledon, a park bench, no clothes, except for what I borrowed from lost and found."

"It's a ship, not a boat."

"Right."

"Aren't you unencumbered? You're about my size. I can loan you."

We *were* about the same height, though she was sturdier, with more significant curves. I was tough but thin as a stick.

She called out to the stewards, "When you're hanging those up, try to leave an inch or so between hangers. I don't want the wrinkles this time. And bring me the toiletry case, white leather."

"Yes, Miss O'Rourke."

"Have you bathed at all?" Tommie sniffed almost imperceptibly.

"A little. In the sink."

"Well, first stop, long bath. Go on. I'll find you something to wear. And if you want my opinion, choose the freshwater option. Who wants a salt bath? Yuck."

In only one hour's time, I was doing what Tommie told me. The promise of hot water was persuasive. I started the faucet, choosing what she said, freshwater.

I took off my scuffed Oxfords, dropped my pants, under-things, shirt, and jacket all on a bench, and slipped into the tiled tub. There was a bottle of bubbles on the bath's edge so I poured that in, and sunk into vanilla sweetness, rinsing my wounded scalp.

I was mostly submerged when Tommie entered, then exited with my clothes in her arms. "I'll send them out for cleaning." A few minutes later the door opened again and she hung some clothes on a hook. "These should work. Call out if they don't."

I toweled off and inspected the clothes. She'd been thoughtful. The outfit was several steps above my usual quality, not anything I'd normally wear, but something I might admire on someone else.

I put on an ankle-length navy skirt. I cinched up the belt, which caused some bunching, but worked. It had pockets, too. I put my hands in them, clenching my fists, then spreading my fingers. I wished I had the ballast to fill them. Next came a starched blouse with wide lapels, and a matching jacket. Though it cut in at the waist, on me it was loose, which I liked.

I didn't favor skirts or dresses, but that was because of the girdles and hose and high heels that typically partnered with them. Tommie hadn't delivered any of those to the bathroom, hallelujah. I walked barefoot, hair dripping, out of the bathroom, feeling good.

"Not bad," she said. "What happened to your face?"

I stared at her.

"You're blue around your eyes. Are you sick? Have you not been sleeping?"

I'd been sort of honest, but I knew not to cross this line. Tommie didn't need to know about Elsie. I'd kept her existence in Rivka's flat private for a year and a half. I didn't want my job given away to some Shea type.

"Accident. On account of a door."

"Oh yes, doors can be terribly dangerous to a girl." She

crossed to a dressing table. "There's some concealer in here. I never leave home without concealment." She laughed, puffing a big cloud of cigarette smoke around her head.

I perched on a stool at the dressing table and she stood next to me, opening the white box, revealing a wild jumble of lipsticks, eyebrow pencils, powders, all kinds of tools. She chose a little pot and screwed it open, smearing cream on her finger and rubbing it under each of my eyes. The blue disappeared. I was almost a normal girl. I traced the length of my nose with my finger, curious about the change to the bone. I thought it made me look older.

I brushed my hair, carefully, avoiding the tenderness of my head in back, flattening my waves down on the sides with my hand. It had been a while since I'd had my hair trimmed. I hardly knew what to do with its jagged line on my brow and around the top half of my face. I never had even a minute to mind my looks at home.

What time is it in San Francisco? What's Elsie doing now?

There came a knock on the door and Tommie asked, "Who goes there?"

"Frank."

She jumped up and opened the door, giving Frank a hug, arms wrapped hard around his neck. "You idiot! I love you, you idiot!"

"Yeah, right. But what was I gonna . . ."

"What do you ever, big brother?"

Tommie backed up and held her arm out to me. "Here's Pat Shea. Came to my rescue after you were bound up with the coppers."

"So I saw," he said, dipping his head and looking at me through frowning brows.

"Don't be rude," Tommie said. "After that pack of beastly jackals, I shouldn't have to deal with your surly attitude. Besides, I feel protective of this third-class lamb trapped in cabin class."

Frank crossed the room to the dressing table, his hand extended.

He looked familiar. Seemed like I wouldn't forget such a handsome face.

I took his hand and shook it.

"Hello Pat. Nice to meet you as a girl."

Does he know the real Pat?

I waited for my breath to recommence.

"I used to bartend at Jonesie's, back when you were Ben. Before you were Jane."

I got a flash memory of that face, behind the bar, on a night of many martinis.

"Bar's full of newsies, everybody talks."

He couldn't see my hands gripping the inside of those lovely skirt pockets. How many things did a person have to confess to survive an afternoon's conversation? And which parts deserved hiding for what reason? The name part? The boy part? The newspaper part? The sister part?

I didn't answer right away. I couldn't calculate that fast at the moment.

"You do realize she works for the *Prospect*, right?"

Tommie took a long drag on her cigarette and then set it in a crystal ashtray on the coffee table in front of the sofa. "Just tell me—Ben-Jane-Pat—what fresh horrors must I now confront?"

"My name is Jane. I took the tickets from a fellow named Pat Shea, who was too drunk to get on the train. I do work for the *Prospect*. I did pretend to be Ben to get a copy boy job." I glanced at Frank. "I'm a cub reporter now. City Hall and court stuff, details for bigger stories."

"Fascinating. So, is this part of some long-hatched plan to exhibit my sorrows to the public?"

"No." Not long-hatched.

"Anything else, Frank?"

"I don't know. Anything else, Jane?"

"I can go back to my berth. I just need my clothes and shoes and I'll go."

"Oh, cool your heels," Tommie said. "But no new identities?"

"No more." *Please, no more.*

An announcement came over the public address system: "Please report for the mandatory lifeboat drills. Find your cabin's drill location on your welcome packet."

Tommie said, "We never do that. That's for everybody else. You hustle over to the dining room line to reserve the best possible table for four at the Verandah Grill, 8 p.m. every night but Monday. Costs extra but it's worth it for the privacy. But get us a table in the dining hall Monday. It's the Lady Jane dinner."

"What?" Was she teasing me?

"They always find a reason for a party. July 10 is the first day of the reign of the 'Nine Days Queen,' Lady Jane Gray?" Tommie flipped through a brochure. "Too bad though, executed right after."

"That's a little discouraging."

"It's probably too late for a great table but do the best you can. I don't want to sit with anybody bad. Make sure the chief steward understands you're there for me. He'll know what to do. And name yourself and my thug of a brother, too, obviously."

I moved toward the door.

"You'll need shoes, dummy," she said. "Those over there. You all right with this, Frank, or do we need to have a thing?"

Frank didn't answer, just glowered.

I pulled on Tommie's shoes and tied them. They were both familiar and fresh. Oxford style, but made of a polished, supple calfskin, with a sturdy sole and a wide, one inch heel. Like mine but dressier. They were only a little snug on the sides of my toes.

I thought it would take hardly any time to stretch them to a perfect fit.

———◦———

CHAPTER EIGHTEEN

Cabin Class Dining Room, C Deck
RMS Queen Mary

It wasn't a line. It was a mob.

All the waiting to board the ship was nothing compared to this bruising pileup of wealthy passengers elbowing their way to the cabin-class dining room's bar so they could reserve the best tables possible for the trip, either in the 800-seat ballroom or the 80-seat Verandah Grill.

The willingness of rich people to swing a hip, blocking one another for seats nearest the window, away from the kitchen, next to the bar, middle of the room, or whichever particulars they aimed for, astonished me.

These people should have already moved through the reservation line by now, leaving almost no tables for us, but there'd been a staff problem that left everybody waiting in a bunch in the hall outside the big room's doors.

When they finally opened them, late for this ritual, my competition was ready for battle. I might have shown them just how bad an elbow can hurt except that I felt too awful for it. But I held my spot in the crowd because I didn't want to fail at my mission.

Meantime, I eavesdropped. Plenty of chitchat about dinner menus, ball gowns, anniversary parties and the like. Then I heard a relevant conversation.

"So, she's grieving, what a loss, coming when it did."

"There's something under that."

"You're buying the gossip?"

"Not gossip, I've got this first hand. On the passage over, my girl was walking down the hall by their suite. They were fighting. She never did hear two women fight like that."

"You understand this is the definition of second hand, don't you?"

"Stop splitting hairs, Felix Frankfurter. I heard from Sally, who heard it herself. Sally said this was personal. I believe her word would stand up in court."

The mob surged, advancing me beyond the others, which was good, except I didn't want to lose that line of gossip. I loaned my ears what remained of my strength.

Just then a pearl-wearing bowling ball of a lady, smelling overmuch of Chanel No. 5, leaned into me hard. "Hello, dahling, I believe you boarded with Miss O'Rourke. Are you a tennis player, too? Lawrence, come over here, here's someone I want you to meet! What's your name? Meet my American grandson, Lawrence."

Her pale heir worked his way to us in the crowd. "Pleased," he drawled, shaking my hand. He struck me as odd. Something about the way he held his frame, dangling above his feet.

"She's another tennis player!"

"No, actually, I'm not."

I could still see the lips of the gossipers flapping and I strained to read those lips.

"Who are you?" he asked.

"She's a friend of Tommie O'Rourke. That's good as being a tennis star herself."

Now the two gossips and quite a few others were looking at me.

"Is Tommie superstitious?" Lawrence asked. "Will the drama hoax her?"

"Oh, you lovely girl. What's your name? You'll have to sit at our Dining Room table. I'm dying to hear everything you have to say, dahling!" Pearly Grandma aimed to close the deal. I could see why Tommie wanted to eat in the smaller Verandah Grill instead. It was like they wanted to consume Tommie herself.

People ahead of us gawked at me and the former gossipers' faces sparkled with hope, flipping the transaction, as if I might provide gossip for them to partake.

We were nearly at the bar now and Lawrence said, "We'll put you at our table. And Tommie, too. We'll introduce you around."

I couldn't stick Tommie with people like this, even for the one night we'd be in the big room. I grabbed a sheet off the bar and started to fill it out desperately, Pearly Grandma and Lawrence yammering behind me.

I shoved the paper in front of the string bean chief steward behind the bar.

I could see him lipread my note: Tommie's name, Frank's name and my name and the words, *the Dining Room just for Lady Jane Dinner, no busybodies, no bores, not those two behind me. Tommie says you'll understand. A table for four at eight in Verandah Grill on the other nights.*

"Absolutely, Miss Benjamin." He examined me and Pearly Grandma and Lawrence and smiled. "I understand." Then he leaned in and whispered, "Why don't you use our private exit, there." He indicated where with a slight roll of his head.

I threw my best grateful smile and inched away as unobtrusively as I could, working to swallow the urge to vomit. I didn't want to abuse this privilege. I understood, special people got special accommodations.

CHAPTER NINETEEN

The Rail, C Deck
RMS Queen Mary

Fluid lapped like waves against my organs. I hung onto the rail, afraid to pitch over the side after what I'd spit up.

"What are you doing in cabin class?" Sandy's hand gripped my elbow from behind, her face too close to my own. "And where'd the clothes come from?"

Why'd she ask this now? Did it bother her I looked better? And I had so much explaining to do, all the time. *Who am I today?* Trying to remember what I could say and who I could say it to. I needed quiet. "I helped Tommie on deck at boarding time escape reporters. I tricked them into running off. I got her up to the front of the line. So, she gave me Coach's room in her suite, M119." There, done.

"Coach's room." A statement, not a question.

"She don't need it anymore."

Sandy slapped my arm in annoyance and minor shock waves moved up to my head. "Don't speak like an Okie."

"Please . . . What room are you?"

"Okay, okay, okay. We're M110. So, you were in there," she said, pointing to the bar, "reserving a table for her?"

"And me."

Sandy paced a little behind me. "Who else?"

"Her brother."

"Okay, okay, okay," she said again.

"What's okay?" Things weren't okay.

She got up close again, and turned me toward the cold gray view again, so we were side by side, backs to deck walkers. "You keep me posted what's going on with Tommie, morning and afternoon. I'm your inside person."

I was sick but not lame. "*I'm* the inside person. *You* should be keeping *me* posted on outside information."

"Can you keep up for even three minutes?"

"What's in it for you?"

"Everybody needs a team. I'm yours."

"Like I said, what's in it for you? If you think I'm gonna let you steal my stuff, write your own—"

"What's wrong with you?"

"I mean it. You ain't gonna steal my stuff." It'd happened to me before.

"I have no interest in writing a story."

"Then what's your interest?"

"Information is my interest." She raised both hands in parentheses at the sides of her face and threw them out in the air, like her brain was exploding, something I could tell her all about. "I can be useful with information."

"I don't need your information. I'm the one getting the information."

"Stupid! I can be useful to Zimmer with information. If I'm useful to Zimmer, I can be useful to you. Assuming you want to advance. Get it? Can anything pass your thick skull?"

She lightly rapped the side of my head and fireworks ignited behind my eyes. I cried out and my hands jumped to my forehead.

"What's wrong with you?" Sandy asked.

I couldn't see, could barely stand, thought I might vomit again, couldn't remember what I could or couldn't say. I'd have to say it all about Elsie, explain everything. But I couldn't. "Stop bitching at me! Just stop!"

My fingers felt the wet on my face.

Sandy's hands were on my shoulders. "We're going to the hospital, now." She wrapped one arm around my back and led me, with my eyes closed, like I ought to trust her. She knew where we were going.

CHAPTER TWENTY

Hospital, D Deck
RMS Queen Mary

I felt sick. I'd never in my life been to the doctor.

Nurse Fleming wasn't exactly a comfort. Her head covering was the most abundant thing about her, wrapping like a pillowcase around the top and flowing in the back. Her white dress had a wide collar and double rows of buttons going down the torso, keeping everything contained.

She scowled. "I'll fetch Doctor. He's finishing up in the operating theater."

I sat on the side of a bed in the ladies' cabin-class, two-bed hospital as Nurse Fleming opened a door to the next room. I wished she hadn't shooed Sandy away. I didn't know how much of it was the not-knowing what I should expect in a hospital room like this, pressing on my fear of being ill prepared for the rooms I would enter.

Nurse Fleming said, "It's urgent, Doctor."

Short and bald on top, with a ring of light brown hair circling his head, and little half glasses balanced on a bulbous, purple nose, he removed a long white jacket, revealing a black uniform like the captain's, which I'd seen in photographs in the hallway. Just before the door to the operating theater shut behind them, I caught sight of Coach laid out flat on a table, blanket to her neck, dead on a slab. At least I thought that was her. My fingers tingled.

"I'm Doctor Simpson," he said, rolling up on a stool in front of me, the smell of whiskey wafting off him. "What happened?"

"I've had an injury, two injuries."

"Go on . . ."

"I was hit here," I said, pointing to my nose, "and here," pointing to the back of my head. "I feel like vomiting. Dizzy." I stopped and waited for bad news.

He raised his eyebrows at Nurse Fleming, wobbling a little on his stool. She dabbed something on a cotton ball and gently wiped under both of my eyes, rubbing off the concealer.

He leaned in and shone a flashlight into each of my eyes.

He nodded. "So, what happened?"

"I don't understand why . . ."

Nurse Fleming said, "He needs to know what happened to your head."

They didn't know anybody at the *Prospect* anyway, so I decided to talk. "I was holding my sister in the middle of her fit, bucking back and forth. Her head slammed into my nose. I jerked back hard so she wouldn't hit me again, and I slammed the back of my head into the wall behind me. Then her head hit me again in the forehead." This sounded like betrayal, like I was setting Elsie up as the cause of my troubles. Which is how it felt sometimes.

"How long ago?" he asked.

"Week and a half."

"That would do it." Dr. Simpson stood and leaned over me, touching the back of my head. I flinched, though it didn't hurt. He returned to the stool. "You are suffering from both a nasal fracture and traumatic encephalol . . . encephalopathy."

I glanced at the nurse.

"You've got a broken nose and a concussion." She patted

my hand, and the surprising moment of tenderness alarmed me.

"So, am I going to die?"

"You are going to die," the doctor said. "But not on this ship."

"Am I in danger?"

"Yes. But only if you behave badly."

I gestured at the door to the operating theater. "Coach Carlson's in there."

Doctor Simpson hiccupped. "You'll be relieved to learn I don't discuss any patient with any other patient. Your situation is as private as hers." He sounded oddly prim, considering his drunken state.

The telephone rang in the attached office and Nurse Fleming marched off to answer it, while Doctor Simpson made some notes on a clipboard.

"I'll ask him. This is her, Doctor. Are you ready?"

"Just a minute. And I'll need you to prepare a compress for Miss Benjamin's nose." He swiveled back to me. "A concussion's a serious injury. It can become much worse if you don't treat it right. On the other hand, if you do take care of yourself, you will likely be fine in a few weeks. It partly depends, though, whether you've had head injuries in the past."

Daddy hit me two years ago, gave me a lump over my brow, waking my dead brother in my head. Dr. Drunk didn't need these details.

"No other head injuries," I said.

"All right. Sleep a lot, eat protein, no alcohol, no stimulation, no exercise, no stress. Ask your room steward for compresses throughout the day."

Sure, no problem, none of it.

They both headed out to the office, Nurse Fleming for supplies, Doctor Simpson for the telephone. The door shut behind them.

There wasn't much time.

I slid off the bed and over to the door to the operating theater, opening it. The smell of antiseptic made me weak, reminding me of Granny in the days before she died, the odor of poisonous medicine. Silver coils and tools hung from white walls all around, silver counters lined the room, with supplies in glass containers.

In the center of the room, a huge, white light spotlighted Coach's body.

Her arms lay straight at her sides under a gray blanket. They'd pulled her hair back neat. Her face was placid, though her neck was raised on some kind of black block, exposing her throat. I could see her beautiful cheekbones, her cleft chin, these high, arcing eyebrows. Classic, like a fallen statue.

I stood there, next to the body of someone I'd never once met, surprised at the stinging in my eyes.

I'd seen her at Wimbledon, in the very minutes before she died. I'd heard her on the radio, talking about what would make Tommie a better athlete, heard her being disrespected for those opinions. I touched her cool cheek. I pulled down the blanket and witnessed her bare torso, palms up, needles and tubes coming out of her arms, dangling. Buckets full of blood lined up around the table.

Doctor Simpson's voice sounded from the office: "Of course, Miss. We're closing up for the evening now, but we can discuss next steps with you tomorrow morning."

I moved back to the door, closed it behind me, climbing onto the bed as Nurse Fleming reentered with supplies.

"Do not overtax yourself in any way," she said. "Not even

with too much thinking. Make this week one hundred percent off-duty time, meant just for recovery. Totally uncomplicated, unstrained time."

CHAPTER TWENTY-ONE

JULY 1935

Rotten Egg Hooverville
Sacramento

Daddy had pleased Momma in the field that day, working harder than most, certainly more than usual, no slacking. He'd earned his relaxing time, it seemed.

He bent over his guitar, sitting on a big rock near the fire, surrounded by a couple dozen people who'd discovered his whereabouts and made their way to Hopperville, a nickname some bindle stiffs coined and Daddy approved, referring to any rough patch where he laid his head.

"Poor deposed Herbert Hoover," Momma said, proud their campsite had been elevated by their presence over some sorry old Hooverville.

Daddy sang that night for old men and women in home-made clothes, loose threads dangling at the hems, young toughs smoking grapevines, pretending they were tobacco, tired-of-school girls who'd pinched their cheeks, aiming for town, and foul-mouthed kids, running around the rest of them, throwing sticks and tripping on rocks. I'd only recently graduated from running and throwing and tripping.

Daddy played their requests past midnight, the crackling fire flashing light across the flat planes of his red-brown face, like hobo footlights. He played train songs, prison songs, whiskey songs, broken-heart songs, and hymns and sometimes they were all the same song, "railcar bucking like a coffin o'er a cliff, bucking off to Folsom, no solace for the stiffed."

He played banjo and mouth harp to make them laugh, wolves howling, babies crying and old folks making the beast with two backs, all mixed up in the Irish tunes.

He played haunting songs he'd invented himself, which made the women cry, and sometimes the men, with angry words about unfair hiring practices, about banks and boss men. Those lyrics felt smart and true.

His hoarse voice didn't hit all the notes right, but it performed history and experience, scratching on the most sorrowful words, "like honey on rust," a secretary from the radio station had said once, though after Daddy told everybody about that compliment, he failed to persuade her to help get him on the air.

"Good Lord," one fat old lady said, rubbing her hands down the sides of her hips. "Abraham could tickle an egg from a rooster."

That led Momma to sit down on the big rock, hip to haunch with Daddy, and rake her fingers through the forelock that liked to block his eyes.

Everybody watching that night knew he had the poet in him.

It's in me too.

I'd stuck a scribbled lyric in his pocket that morning, hoping it would turn into a song that night. But that didn't happen. It never did. And he never asked me to sing with him, either.

After he was done, Momma said "Janie, you look like to cough tonight."

"I ain't coughing."

"Best to sleep in the car tonight, Jujee," Daddy stepped in. "We need our rest."

So, I climbed into my back seat bedroom, leaving my parents to the tent.

The kind of singing he did that night, after working hard all day, made us all feel good. It was a real and meaningful way to recover from the work.

Trouble was that singing did not buy much in the way of beans or flour. So, Daddy had to pick tomatoes or cotton like the rest of us the next morning too. But he struggled to be regular about it. Even as regular as I was.

That next morning, he attended to the up and down effort for a full row, saying nothing, just working that back and arms and hands, bloodied by sharp cotton boll spikes, trailing a ten-foot sack that could weigh up to 100 pounds when full.

Except his sack wasn't going to bear that weight because on the second row he stopped to tell a little story to the fellow beside him, and he laughed and his wife gave him a look that said, *Don't let Abraham mess you up.*

Daddy became so distracted by the sociological implications of marriage on a man's sense of humor that he missed about half the bolls worth picking. By the time he got a quarter of the way down the third row, he was singing about humorless women.

Then he appeared to think, *Hey, that's good,* and needed to write down the lyric, and he wandered off to sit in the shade of a truck, pencil and pocket notebook in hand, his soggy cotton sack discarded near a tree stump.

Daddy couldn't make himself regular at the only paid work he could get, so he did it badly, and Momma would nag him about that, constantly, as she did that day.

He said, "You're tighter than a duck's ass, but at least you can eat the duck."

She said, "Piss in one hand, wish in the other, and see which fills up first."

The good day and the good night were done.

Daddy managed a complicated hydraulic system, consuming all he could of music, alcohol, philosophy, and sex, to fill an otherwise empty bucket. Those spigots rarely ran out. But when they did and Daddy glimpsed the bucket's dry bottom, he would lash out, scared as a thirsty dog, mean as Momma. And then there was trouble.

———◦———

CHAPTER TWENTY-TWO

Pig 'n' Whistle, C Deck
RMS Queen Mary

I needed to know more about Coach before I'd go back to my room to rest like a good girl, so I tailed Nurse Fleming after she'd turned out the lights and locked the hospital door at closing time.

Following her through stairwells and hallways, I dodged uniformed workers past dozens of separate rooms with painted signs—RIPENING, KOSHER MEAT, FISH PREPARING, EMPTY CANS, WINE & VINEGAR, ROOT VEGETABLES, KOSHER COOKING, and CREW GALLEY, and so on. I tailed her up to C Deck, trying to stay far enough back that she wouldn't sense me, but also close enough not to lose her in the throngs of workers.

We finally arrived at baggage storage, a cavernous steel space with trunks and suitcases everywhere, balanced in unlikely tottering towers. Nurse Fleming disappeared into it.

At the far end, a makeshift platform was set up in front of a pair of huge elevator doors. A sign hanging by a chain over the stage read PIG 'N' WHISTLE. Here in the belly of the ship, three musicians sang and played banjo, mouth harp, and fiddle. Others in uniforms, mostly white jackets with black bowties, but also some in mechanics' jumpers, clapped and joined the singing.

I've run with the wild herd, since I was a lad,
I've lost all that I earned, spent good after bad.

But now, I'm a changed man, with money to share,
I'll never again leave my pretty young mare.
And I'll run with 'em no more,
No never, no more,
Will I run with the wild herd,
No never, no more.

Others sprawled at wobbly tables and chairs, cribbage and checkers and beer glasses covering every surface. Light bulbs dangled from wires high above the plank floors, light flickering off steel bulkhead walls. A crowd in the corner whooped and hollered over a vicious game of darts.

This music, this "no never, no more," so like Daddy's lyrics about trying harder, starting over, began to make me feel not quite right, with its connections to my past, its questions about the worth of a person's work.

I struggled to breathe in the humid space, ears ringing with raucous noise. The compress wasn't in my hands. I'd dropped it. I couldn't see Nurse Fleming anywhere.

My breath came in sour puffs, everything swam yellow, and the floor began to rise up to meet me. A redheaded guy and another with yellow hair grabbed my elbows. "You alright, Duckie?"

"Hungry, I think."

"How about some biscuits and beer? That'll fix you up."

They guided me to a table at the edge of the room. One petted my hand while the other rambled off to fetch something to eat.

Redhead asked, "What are you doing down here, Miss? This is for the crew. You ain't a stowaway, are you?" He said that laughing, like a joke.

"I'm looking for someone."

Yellowhead returned with the beer and cookies. I remembered the doctor saying, "No alcohol," but I didn't want to be rude so I took a sip and a bite of a shortbread cookie.

The two guys sent silent messages with their eyes.

I asked them, "Why is this the Pig 'n' Whistle?"

Yellowhead leaned forward to answer, hard to hear over the ruckus.

"Comes from the navy. Pig's an officer. When men are up high, working the sails and rigging, officers care little for what's going on up there. Like a pig, an officer can't look up."

I'd never noticed a pig can't look up. Why had I never noticed?

"As for the whistle, a famous mutiny started with a sailor whistling a tune. So, whistling in front of an officer is the signal for rebellion. That's the story anyway. Pig 'n' Whistle is a poor bloke's joke against our Lords and Masters."

Maybe he meant to make me feel threatened, but he didn't understand I was more poor bloke than lord or master.

Redhead said, "Who're you looking for?"

"Nurse Fleming."

They exchanged looks again and Yellowhead stood and walked off. A minute later he returned with Nurse Fleming, whose face and neck had pinkened now. Her hat was gone and her hair was down, more blonde than the gray I'd thought before. Her two top buttons were undone. She held a tumbler of drink.

"Miss Benjamin," she said.

"If you don't mind, I have some questions for you."

Redhead rose and gave Nurse Fleming his seat. He tipped his oil-stained cap, and they moved to the dart game.

"What are you doing here?" she asked in an accusing, off duty hiss. "And you're drinking."

I glanced at her glass of whiskey. "I need some information about Coach."

"How'd you know who the body was?"

"I'm traveling with Tommie O'Rourke. I'm staying in Coach's room."

Spider veins had reddened her cheeks and I thought it hadn't taken much whiskey to make her this pink. Or she'd had a few already.

"What did she die of?" I pressed.

"I cannot, under any circumstances."

"Tommie's afraid she died of unnatural causes."

She exhaled, blowing a bitter breeze my way. "For goodness' sake, she died of heart failure. The Wimbledon doctors told us." Nurse Fleming picked up one of the cookies and bit into it. "She was diabetic. Could have been related to that. But she took insulin, little pinpricks on her belly. There was also a mark on the back of her arm. They told us she and her player each got a shot, to help with competition."

"What does that mean?"

"Listen, the doctor says nothing diabolical was going on. We didn't do an autopsy, just the embalming, because of the obvious natural causes, which were reported from London. This is something that happens to diabetics. Lucky she lived this long." Her jaw moved back and forth, grinding her teeth.

"Do you think they're right?"

"They're doctors."

CHAPTER TWENTY-THREE

Verandah Grill, Sun Deck
RMS Queen Mary

We entered the Verandah Grill at eight fifteen, Tommie and Frank already liquored up, me still fuzzy from a nap. I hadn't planned enough time to dress, expecting the clothes Tommie loaned me earlier would work for eating in the grill, as opposed to the cabin-class dining room. A grill sounded to me like a pork chop and beer after work. I got that wrong.

When I woke to join them in the suite drawing room, Frank was in a black dinner jacket and tie, Tommie in a long, slinky gown of gold, showing all of her arms and most of her back. Her light hair glowed in a halo around her face. The side of one breast was revealed near the armhole. I blushed, ashamed to witness that flesh.

"I've left something for you in the bathroom," she said, alarming me. I didn't want to show my skin.

But she'd set me up modest enough in black-and-white, full-length taffeta. It had a businesslike waistband, full skirt, buttons up the front to a high collar and short sleeves, like a secretary's shirt dress had been gotten up shiny. Once again, the dress had pockets. Tommie did important things right. It was a little loose on me so I liked that.

I thought the two, thick white stripes running from the bottom hem up over my shoulders and down to the floor on the back side might make me look like a skunk with two stripes but when I came out of the bathroom, Frank said, "Glory be," and whistled.

"Balenciaga," Tommie answered.

"Weren't you the girl always stealing my jerseys, even my socks? What did they do with my sister?"

"Keep 'em guessing, I always say." She pushed my shoulders down until I sat in front of the dressing mirror.

She slicked my hair back and twisted my short bangs into a spit curl. She added concealer again on the bruised skin under my eyes, a little kohl on the lid, and applied Tango Red lipstick. Then she put her index finger in her mouth and wiped a wayward smear of lipstick off my face.

I didn't look half bad. She handed me a beaded evening bag and a pair of black satin high heels, the only disappointment of her design. My feet were tender from her Oxfords already.

At the Verandah Grill, I saw just how clever she'd been.

I heard the room breathe, "Ahhh," when the three of us entered the intimate space. With wall-to-wall black carpets, walls and ceiling painted silver and gold, Tommie stood between us, shimmering in her gold gown and metallic white hair, Frank and me in black on either side of her. Frank and I were the winners, Tommie the trophy.

The room broke into applause. She smiled and nodded at people around us. I tried to tuck myself into the background, so as not to ruin anybody's picture, but Tommie pulled me back up into the frame.

I'd never before been someplace fancy where I actually appeared to belong. I didn't know what to say or do here but I *looked* right, and that was something.

The maître d' delivered us to a table at the center of the room, seating Tommie and Frank so they could see the dusk sky and ocean through massive semicircular glass ahead. I faced the rest of the restaurant and that was fine because I was the first to see the actors Charles Boyer and Irene Dunne rise from their table and come to ours.

They bent and took turns kissing Tommie, giving her a squeeze, shaking Frank's hand. When they finally regarded me with question marks on their faces, Frank said, "This is Jane Benjamin."

Boyer said, "Enchanted," stealing my power to speak. Miss Dunne appraised my hair and gown, then nodded. They both exuded confidence, but not more so than Tommie and Frank did. I stopped looking around the room because everyone was staring at us and that began to feel overwhelming, even though I was in the shadow of the O'Rourkes.

Our head waiter said his welcome speech, looking at Tommie, and asked if we'd be joined by a fourth. Tommie said, "Leave the setting, just in case."

Moments later, three more waiters appeared, one behind each of our shoulders, whipping down menus for us each at once. I gasped at the choreography.

The menu's cover was a watercolor painting of Tommie. Her body rose at a slant, long arm extended into its racket, right leg bent, her lean frame taut, shoulders back. The artist captured her in a white polo shirt, white shorts, white visor covering her eyes, that metallic hair, her smile and red lips, a splash of lime green behind her. The word "Wimbledon" was on the side, in the same warm peach as her flesh.

I'd seen the photograph version in London papers. It must have been painted that morning so they could reproduce it for the special people in this room tonight.

Inside, the menu listed our choices.

Hors d'Oeuvre—Malossol Caviare,
Alligator Pear Cocktail

Soups—Cream Soup a la Reine,
Consommé Double Cameran

Fish—Boiled Salmon, Sauce Moscovite,
Fried Scallops, Sauce Tatare

Special Dish Today—Larded Carre of Veal
with New Vegetable

Entrees—Leg of Venison Grand Veneur,
Omelet with Asparagus Tips

Cold dish—Coburg Ham, Sauce Cumberland

Roasts—Sirloin of Beef with Gravy, Yorkshire pudding,
Chalons Chicken en Casserole

I stopped trying to read it halfway down.

Tommie sighed. "These people try too hard. Cigarette, Frank."

He pulled one out and lit it for her.

The waiter returned to ask if we had questions.

"Bring us the best, please," Tommie said. "No repeats. We'll want to sample. Champagne too. And wine for them."

Frank gaped as he did the math.

"This is my celebration. It was *supposed* to be my celebration. Anyway, we're not paying, may as well enjoy the goods."

Frank said, "So, who are you expecting for the fourth chair?

"Don't worry, the niece."

"I wasn't worried."

"Right."

"Who made you a mind reader?"

"Who made you Nervous Nelly?"

"I was wondering if it was the wallet," he said.

"No, I said it's the niece."

"I suppose one's more convenient than the other."

Incomprehensible sibling talk. I paused my thinking to give Ben a chance to speak up but he didn't, though my head did feel kind of spinny and this was the sort of thing I could expect him to comment on. I missed his commentary. Maybe Ben wasn't in there anymore. Maybe I was really alone now.

As I took my first taste of consommé, I heard a rumbling voice in the line of table visitors to Tommie. Zimmer, of course, with Sandy hanging off his arm looking glam, all in shiny silver, setting off her glossy brown hair. She gave me a questioning look and touched her head.

I nodded and mouthed, *Thanks*.

I remembered Momma saying, "people show you who they are," which was funny, coming from Momma, who constantly showed you bad things about herself. But Sandy did show me who she was. She got me to the doctor when I needed to go, with no extra muss. I'd remember that, even if I reserved doubt.

Zimmer said, "So thrilling to see you on Centre Court, Tommie."

"Thank you, so much, Mister . . . what was it again?"

"Zimmer," he said. "Hello, Jane."

"Hello, Mr. Zimmer, Sandy."

We were all quiet for a beat and so he put his hand on Sandy's back and guided her to a table nowhere near as good as ours, Sandy sagging a little on the way.

Frank said, "Naughty, little sister."

"Girl's got to have *some* fun."

I was tucking into the roast sirloin, washing it down with a red wine with a French name, which I shouldn't have been drinking, concussion-wise, but I figured it was high quality so unlikely to create trouble, when another visitor arrived and took the empty chair.

"Tommie, Frank," he said.

"Mr. Lowe," said Frank, irritated.

"Adam," said Tommie, dimpling.

I studied the room to confirm his status—second handsomest man in the room. Frank came in first.

Thick, light-brown hair, parted far to the side, showing off its wave on the way back. Pale gray eyes, like a kid's, they were so clear, though he must have been in his forties, old enough to have seen a few disappointments.

He threw his wide shoulders back, leaning into his chair, legs crossed, foot bouncing, his hands on his knees. Seemed like his center of gravity hovered right underneath his cummerbund. Even at a table with friends in the Verandah Grill, I sensed his belly muscles clinching.

"Where's your fourth?" he asked.

"Have no idea where she's run off to."

"You haven't been unkind, have you, Tommie?"

"Who, me?" She chewed her meat conscientiously.

"It wouldn't hurt to be magnanimous. She's distraught too."

"Decimated, I'm sure. Whatever will she do?"

Lowe smoothed his jacket. "Do you have everything you need? Are your rooms comfortable?"

Tommie made a kissing motion while Frank investigated the napkin in his lap.

"Jane, this is Frank's employer, Mr. Adam Lowe, of Lowe Construction. I'm sure you've seen the signs on the railcars and ships and all along the docks in The City? He has his name on everything that stands still long enough to paint."

"Pot, meet kettle." Lowe waved the menu with Tommie's picture on the cover.

"Nice to meet you, Mr. Lowe," I said.

"And who *are* you, Jane?"

At first I thought he asked *how* I was but, no, he wanted to know *who* I was.

"I'm a cub reporter at the *Prospect*."

"Tommie, I'm not familiar with you getting familiar with reporters. New?"

"First time for everything." She blew a puff of smoke. "Jane saved me from scandalmongers. Saved Frank from the hoosegow too. She's staying in Coach's room."

Lowe frowned and Tommie's eyes sparked, seeming to enjoy his displeasure. Frank projected a bone-deep loathing.

"What's your beat, Jane?" Lowe asked.

"City Hall, police blotter. Kind of a gopher. Working on moving up." Why'd I say that? I didn't want him to think I was a loser. I needed to check that instinct.

"Up to . . . ?"

"Unsure right now."

"Let's see. What would a cub reporter aim for? A big story, I guess. One that garners a byline, fat headline, wide distribution, offers by finer newspapers than the *Prospect*? Is that right, Jane?"

"The *Prospect's* a good newspaper."

"Of course it is. I was speaking of circulation. But what a unique opportunity for you, to travel across country and across the Atlantic for a tennis championship as a cub at the *Prospect*. And to be actual suitemates with a star, like the champion? An experience money can't buy. Though, I guess, sometimes it does."

"I'm a lucky girl."

"I hope it holds out for you. Jane Benjamin, wasn't it?"

"Give it a rest, Adam," Tommie said. "How about you join me for a drink at the club afterwards? Save your place in line to twirl me around the dance floor?"

His face briefly flamed. "I've two or three crises to manage. If I don't do it, who will? Right, Frank?"

Frank glared in what was beginning to look like his default expression.

"You're always working. That's your secret," Tommie said.

"It's no secret at all. Everybody knows it. But do they do it? Right, Frank?"

"I assume these are rhetorical questions," Frank answered.

Lowe rose and smoothed his jacket. "Tommie, do speak up if you need anything at all. Jane, I'll be looking for your headline." And he walked off without saying anything to his employee.

"Nice boss," I said.

Tommie laughed. "Rhetorical questions. Frank, you kill me."

———○———

CHAPTER TWENTY-FOUR

Sun Deck
RMS Queen Mary

"Must be nice and warm back in the suite," I suggested. Tommie and I reclined on deck lounges in our evening gowns, looking up into an inky sky. Or rather she did the star gazing. I just shivered. Rich people loved the great outdoors, I noticed. When you'd lived in a tent, the outdoors wasn't so magical.

"They're converting the grill to the club. We can't miss the music and dancing."

I could miss it. Dinner had been so rich, but I never said no to food set in front of me. I'd had the champagne and wine too —bad idea. Now I was freezing, my neck stiff, smoking. Doctor Simpson hadn't said anything about smoking. Seemed like it could be a no-no.

"I may go back now. I'd rather have peace and quiet."

"Ingrate. Who wants peace and quiet on a ship? Stay with me until the club opens, then go to bed. Steward! We need blankets!"

I clenched my shivering jaw.

"Three questions," Tommie said. "Let's play three questions."

The steward returned and spread a couple blankets over each of our laps.

I said, "How about I just ask *you* three questions."

"Cheater. That's not how it works. I go first."

Naturally she'd go first.

"Number one. What happened, with your eyes and nose?"

I'd already spilled the beans to the doctor and nurse but hadn't given away the part about raising Elsie, the secret part, though I'd sort of lost track of why it was a secret. When you lie a lot, it gets to be like a knotted necklace. Sometimes you leave it in a drawer that way, never wear it again. Sometimes you sit down and work it out.

"My little sister pitched a fit, hit me in the nose with her head, then I banged my head against the wall."

"Ugh! She must be awful!"

I winced. "Elsie's not awful. She's difficult. And a toddler. Not awful."

"God, sisters. I have five of them, and just the one brother, Frank. They're all proper girls. A nurse, two teachers, a secretary, and a mommy. They came through all that poverty the way they were supposed to. I'm the odd one out, so I do what I want." The question-and-answer format had taken a turn. "We had some awful fights, too. We were all scrappy, even the conventional ones, *especially* the conventional ones! Hey, how'd you make me talk instead of you?"

"Some people would rather go on about themselves."

"Cheeky."

"My turn. Question one: why'd your parents name you Tommie?"

"Oh well, let me introduce you to my authentic self, Theodora Shannon O'Rourke." She made a little bow from her deck chair.

"I guess that's hard to cheer from the stands. Go get 'em, Theodora!"

"No, not that. I was starting pitcher, team captain, on the Poly High Parrots. Only girl on our high school team, only girl ever on the field! I also played basketball and ran track. It bothered Frank I was so good. He played baseball at Berkeley, two years ahead of me, but was never a natural like I was."

I thought hardly anybody anywhere was a natural of her caliber. Must be hard to have a sister like that.

She continued. "I actually may have bothered everybody in my family with my sports. Probably especially my father." She tipped her head back, exhaling a ghostly tobacco bloom. "So, Frank bought me a tennis racket. He might have stolen it. I imagine he didn't have money to buy it. He said I should play a sport for girls. He said, 'Time to stop being a tomboy.' Everybody called me that. But he said I could be who I was, more or less. I could find a way to make it work. So, I learned tennis at Golden Gate Park, picked it up fast. Anyway, he stopped calling me tomboy and started calling me Tommie. It stuck."

"What a jerkwater thing to say. You're good at all that and he acts like you should feel bad about it."

"When did you become so cynical?"

"The day I learned I couldn't have what boys got."

She squinted at me. "Well, Frank never once made me feel bad about being a tomboy. Are you kidding? I would win and he would cheer. I felt sorry for Frank, that my being so good might make him feel he was less than he ought to be. But, even so, he helped me make the life I wanted, the excitement, the ups and downs, this, all this. I'm a kid in a candy factory. Frank never wanted me to be bored. He knew that would be the worst for me. But sure, he wanted me to be safe too. He's very loyal. He'll go down with my ship."

I wanted to ask why Frank thought being a tomboy was unsafe, and why Tommie was all right with that thinking, but I didn't want to waste my question.

Then, as if I'd asked it, she said, "He's not entirely wrong. The girly things you drop to play? You'll probably need them again after you win."

Tommie had a practical boldness. It braced me to be near it. I wanted to take notes, though I wasn't sure she was right.

"Question number two," she said. "Why the menswear?"

No one but Momma had asked so directly. But she didn't ask in a mean way.

"When I came to The City two years ago, I dressed like a boy, Ben," my voice clogging up a little on his name, "to find a job. I was an Okie and being a girl on top of that? Hard to get hired. That's how I got on at the *Prospect*. I wouldn't have been hired for the copy boy gig as a girl. So, at first I faked it for money and food. Then, for more."

I didn't mention Ben egging me on in my head.

"What was the *more*?"

"I mean, it's funny that the two outfits you've loaned me have pockets, because the pockets were really something to me. Those and the pant legs. I like having a place to put money. Not that I ever have any money. But if I ever do, I want to carry it myself."

"I have them add pockets to whatever I buy or have made."

Luxury.

I said, "I like the feel of men's shoes, too, flat and wide enough that I can go where I want, fast as I want. Everything seems more doable when I dress like a boy."

Tommie stretched her bare arms up to the sky. "None of the girls on tour can believe I wear shorts instead of a dress on court. Then, after they play me, they go out and buy themselves shorts."

"When I was pretending to be Ben and asked a question, people answered with 'maybe' instead of 'no.'"

"So, you kept it up for the maybes?"

"Maybe was a starting point. So, I lied about it for about four months. Finally, I gave in and told them I was a girl. There was hell to pay but things are all right now. I just have to work a lot harder for maybe."

"You don't actually want to *be* a boy?"

My face felt hot, though she didn't look to be judging.

"Because there's places in The City, Mona's in North Beach, where you can—"

"That's your third question."

"Then, it's my third."

I took my time. I wasn't in the habit of putting this in words.

"I don't want to be a boy. I like who I am. I want to be who I am. But I want to be it the *way* I want to be it."

"A tomboy."

"I guess. I don't have a word for it." I didn't have Frank to back me up. The brother in my head wanted me to go full on boy, wanted to be that boy himself, using my body to do it. Out of guilt at my living, his dying, I'd tried to give him a little of that, letting him travel through the world in me. But he'd been quiet for days now. Without him and his needs, what would I want for myself? I wasn't sure. "Tomboy works for you. I don't want just one word for me. Unless it's *best*."

Tommie laughed, approving.

"Question two," I asked. "How did you feel about Coach? I mean, I can't tell if you're all torn up or if you kind of don't care." I believe the wine and the fact I'd been so honest myself made me ask that question that way, the absolutely wrong way, which I immediately regretted.

Tommie sat upright and wrapped her arms around herself. "That's mean," she said, frowning. "I'm twenty-six. I've lived with her since I was eighteen. She made me what I am. I wouldn't be Wimbledon champion without Coach. I was devoted to her, and she to me. I can't imagine what I'll do or be now she's gone. But I'm not going to curl up and die."

An orchestra started up behind us, playing Tommy Dorsey's *Our Love*. Red and purple lights flashed inside the grill, which had converted into the Starlight Club.

"But you'll play tennis. You're the champion."

"You're excused, ingrate," Tommie said, getting up. "Go back to the warmth and comfort of my suite."

———•———

CHAPTER TWENTY-FIVE

MONDAY, JULY 10, 1939

Tommie's Suite, Main Deck 117–119
RMS Queen Mary

"This is wrong . . . something's wrong . . ."

A tiny lady, maybe forty, all in brownish gray, looked left and right down the hall, and again at the number on our door, and then again at me. "No. This is the right room. Who are you?"

"Jane," I said, raspy from a fitful sleep. "Who are you?"

"That is not your concern."

"Well," I said, and started to close the door.

Before I could complete the act, she said, "Stop, all right."

Opening the door again, I took in the frayed trim on her blouse cuffs and pictured her chewing on them with those sharp little teeth.

"I'm Helen Carlson. This is supposed to be my aunt's room. This *is* her room."

"*Was* her room," I said, not as polite as I might have been. "Come in." I cinched the belt of the ship bathrobe a little tighter and pulled up the lapels. "Looks like they dropped off coffee while I slept," I said, nodding at a silver tray loaded with fixings. "Would you like—"

"No, I wouldn't." But she grabbed a scone, popping bits of it in her mouth, chewing fast, shedding crumbs onto the front of her blouse.

"Have another, why don't you. Sit?"

Helen perched on the edge of the sofa, chewing her scone. Was she counting her bites? With her pallid skin and hair, she had the look of a thousand others, the very opposite of Coach's unique appearance of physical vigor. There was something about her that made my spine stiffen. This lady wasn't right. I knew it the way you can instantly tell about somebody at the bus stop or in the elevator.

"Where's Tommie?"

"She came in after I was asleep last night. Looks like she isn't up yet." I wasn't aware if she'd come in at all, but I wasn't going to say that.

"You're staying in my aunt's room?"

"Tommie offered it."

"Tommie doesn't like to be alone. Some people can't stand to be alone, even for a few nights," she said, upper lip curled.

Helen probably had lots of chances to prove her superiority by staying home alone. The fourth place setting for dinner last night was hers but I couldn't imagine the conversation at a table shared by Helen and Tommie.

"Did you spend a lot of time with your aunt?"

"Ha!" Helen laughed like a gag. Both eyebrows came down in a sharp V. "My aunt was not *present* in my youth, when her presence would have been *helpful*."

I couldn't tell whether she said "presence" or "presents" the second time and wondered if it would change the meaning. "What should she have done to help you?"

"Oh, so we're going to do the *talking cure* now. Are we going to examine my *neuroses*?"

"Listen, lady, I'm just making conversation."

"Ho, yes. Just a friendly tête-à-tête. No ulterior motives, I'm sure."

I didn't have a credential to tell me what was wrong with Helen Carlson but my gut did its calculation. She was nutty. Still, I wanted information about Coach, no matter the source.

"You grew up near her? In San Francisco?"

"Near enough that she might have chosen to come around. Might have. Given the circumstances."

"Which were . . ."

"Hmmm. Have you got your notepad? Your pencil?"

"Go on. I'll use my ears."

"Well then, true to prototype, my father left us when I was young. My mother worked. She wasn't exactly *available*, trying to keep a roof over our heads. Good thing I had so few needs. I asked almost nothing of her and she found little of interest in me. We maintained a workable arrangement, if not sustaining. She died when I was eighteen of Spanish flu."

I was seventeen when I made myself an orphan, not literally, of course.

"So, as any competent girl would do, I came to my aunt and asked if she might share some of her inherited money. She got everything from my grandparents. My mother said my aunt was always the *favorite*. But my aunt thought it would be best for me to *work* for it."

So, I guess she did mean "presents" before.

"I understand a little—"

"Will you let me *finish*?" Helen's eyebrows were raised very high. My job was to listen, not talk. "So. I continued to work, without family help, at a bookstore, becoming excellent at that, for *twenty years*, until I was laid *off,* due to the *Depression*."

She emphasized so many words. Did she think I should understand why her voice double-underlined them? I wanted to make a list and break the code.

Something clicked. This was the woman sitting next to Coach in the stands. The one who'd grabbed Coach's arm and whispered in her ear after her fall. Coach had shrugged her off, moments before she collapsed.

"So, I came to her *again*, to ask for work." Helen squinted her eyes, examining the room, the art and the fabric and the luxury. "Tommie recommended I ask Adam Lowe for a job. So, *Tommie* is why I work with Adam Lowe."

"The way you *say* that, it seems like *Tommie* has a significant meaning right there in the middle of your story."

"Oh, Tommie *does* have meaning to everyone and everything. Don't you think?"

Now I had no patience. "So, why are you here on this boat?"

"Haven't they told you? It's a ship."

Boat was like *ain't*. It kept slipping out.

"You must have some friendship with the two of them, or you wouldn't be here. You wouldn't have been sitting next to Coach in the stands at Wimbledon."

Helen flinched. "I saw them on occasion. This was . . . an occasion."

"Did Coach pay for you to come?"

"You're rude!" She stood.

"Would you like me to give Tommie a message?"

Helen pulled a notebook out of her bag and thumbed past pages crammed front and back with heavy scribbling until she found a fresh sheet. She retrieved a pencil from the bottom of her purse and pressed so hard on the word, *Tommie*, that the tip broke.

"No! This is supposed to be the most reliable brand. Do you have one?"

I pretended to look around. "Tell me. I'll remember."

"You'll tell her?"

I nodded.

"Tell her Coach is ready for burial. She's embalmed. I okayed it, as her next of kin, which is my legal right." She met my gaze for this. "I researched it, to make sure, to confirm, so we could be confident her body's all right until burial."

What a batty little speech. That defensive legal talk. Not the way somebody talks when they mourn the dead person. "You didn't want an autopsy?"

She sniffed and raised her chin. "The doctor said that would be unnecessary. She died of a heart attack. He said it would have been a shame to do something like that to her body unnecessarily."

"Wouldn't want to harm her body."

"Tell Tommie she doesn't have to worry about anything. I've taken care of it."

Were they in cahoots?

"There's no reason she needs to linger unnecessarily over what's done. She can go on and do what she needs to do, what she wants to do, now. Just get on with it."

This got weirder and weirder. "Are you sure . . . do you want me to wake her?"

"No. I just wanted to let her know. That's all." Then she scuttered out.

Chewing on this bizarre, unplanned interview, I dressed in Tommie's blouse and jacket and skirt from yesterday. I'd lost a button on the blouse, but you couldn't see that when I tucked it in. I put on her Oxfords too and immediately felt the blisters, making it even harder to think. Nothing fit as well as I thought.

I closed my eyes and tried to picture Helen with either Coach or Tommie, what they did together, what they talked about. But that picture didn't come.

All I saw for sure was that Helen reminded me of Vee.

———◦———

CHAPTER TWENTY-SIX

November 1937
Auto Ferry, San Francisco Bay

Vee was slim and pale, with an oversized coat cinched around her waist, ending just above bare ankles and thick-heeled black leather shoes that seemed too big. She had almost-colorless hair and a thin neck. Her bare, ridged collarbones were exposed where the coat stood open, which didn't seem right. She gave the impression of being dangerously breakable.

I was dressed as Ben, riding the auto ferry from Berkeley back to The City.

"Can I bum a cigarette?" She had a trace of West Texas in her voice.

Handing her a lit Lucky, I asked, "Where y'all headed?"

She didn't answer for a second. "Y'all?"

It was hard to be perfect all the time with the grammar.

She shrugged. "I do that too."

I'd been feeling a little above her. *Y'all* messed that up. I wanted to let her know I was better than an Okie now, so I lied. "I'm a reporter."

"Really?" She flicked her ashes over the rail.

"Rookie, but, yeah," I said, feigning self-deprecation.

Vee blew smoke into the wind, thinking. "I've got a story for you, rookie." Again, she dropped her ashes, this time on the deck. "It's a conspiracy."

I wasn't prepared to receive such a thing. I wasn't a reporter. I was a copy boy. I had another assignment. What would a reporter say to this?

"I've got something else brewing right now. How about we meet at Breen's tonight at eight? We can talk about your story there."

I gave her the address and we agreed to the time and place. I thought the skin around her eyes looked strained. The whites were red.

After she left I began to consider her *offness*. Something about her too-bare neck, like she had no clothes under her coat, like that was her only outer layer. Either way, whether because she didn't have anything to put below the coat or because she just didn't choose to, that wasn't normal. Her hair was so colorless, like she'd over-bleached it in the sink. Was she disguising herself? What was she hiding? And what kind of person approached a stranger with a conspiracy?

I'd always been on the outs, a tomato picker, living on the side of the road, despised by all the townsfolk who hated the dirty people, thought we were lazy, stupid. Now I was the weirdest, least normal girl I knew of, pretending to be a boy. Faking everything because I wanted to be normal almost as much as I wanted to succeed.

I was done being off. I didn't need to hang around publicly with somebody that might drag me down that way.

I was seventeen.

I didn't keep my eight o'clock meeting at the bar with Vee.

I couldn't risk losing the identity I'd worked so hard to gain. Joining up in public with a girl like that, no matter how interesting she might be, no matter how potentially useful her story, that would put eyes on the two of us, maybe make people realize there was something off about me too. I had to protect myself. I had almost no choice.

Waiting for me outside the bar, Vee was attacked, hit in the head with a crowbar, brain matter splattered on the threshold I crossed every day after work.

She never woke from her coma. This day of the ferry was our only two-way conversation. The rest of our talks were monologues, just me at her hospital bedside, reading her the paper, whispering apologies as she slept, looking less vulnerable unconscious than she had awake, when she was asking me for help.

———o———

Verandah Grill, Sun Deck
RMS Queen Mary

The Verandah maître d' pointed at Sandy and Zimmer having breakfast across the room. I waved at Sandy in a subtle way, which didn't work, so I waved more dramatically, arms overhead, like a traffic cop, and that caught her eye.

She patted her mouth with a napkin and gave this submissive little smile to Zimmer, making some excuse, picked up her purse and headed my way. She deployed a sweet docility to manage him. That wasn't a tool in my box.

Sandy walked past me, mouthing, *Come on,* and headed out to the Sun Deck.

The sea air hadn't fully hit me in the face before she grabbed my arm. "Okay, okay, okay, got my update?" Even looking so delicate in a pale floral dress, she got down to business.

"What happened with your head?"

"Thanks for that, by the way, for getting me there. I've got a broken nose and a concussion."

"Holy moly." That was enough comforting. She rushed on. "What have you learned about Tommie, Coach? Oh wait, I also forgot. That dress last night? Snazzy! So, what'd you find out? Like is he a boyfriend?"

"No, he's her brother, Frank. Edgy sort."

"I know who *he* is. I'm asking about Lowe. Do they have a thing?"

"I'm not sure. Tommie says she and Coach were close, really close. Says she feels lost without her. But she also stayed out late dancing at the Starlight Club. She asked Lowe to join her, but he said no. I mean, she's a flirt."

"So, who'd she dance with?"

"No idea. I collapsed into bed."

"You left her at the club and went to bed?"

"I have a concussion."

"Okay, okay, okay. Just not such great reporting. God knows what you missed."

True enough. I wouldn't miss anything else.

"So, I found out Coach's niece had her embalmed on board."

"What niece? Embalmed? What?"

"Helen Carlson. Mousy type. She sat next to Coach at Wimbledon."

Sandy tipped her face to the sky, trying to pull the picture from memory, but shook her head. "Do they even do embalming on the ship?"

"They've got an *operating theater*. They're saying there was no autopsy, just the embalming. There were all these tubes . . ." I thought of the vitality drained from Coach's body.

"How'd you see that?"

"When you dropped me off at the hospital, I sneaked into the next room, that theater, and she was there. Helen requested the embalming, as next of kin, and left this message about it with me, for Tommie. That she should go ahead and do whatever, everything's fine. Like that. So, why?"

"Were the two of them conniving or something?"

"I know. And also, Helen's completely, legitimately strange, county hospital strange. She really doesn't like Coach, says she didn't give her any kind of help when she needed it, when her mother was dying. And that Tommie got her a job with Lowe. I mean, she's completely off, and kind of sad. And Lowe? He's creepy. Handsome, but creepy."

"He's not a creep. Edward says he's a captain of industry."

"Don't mean he ain't a creep. Maybe those things go together."

"*Ain't?* I hope you're not doing that in front of them."

"Just you. You bring it out in me. Anyhow, did Coach die of natural causes, really, like they say? And if not, what?"

"The doctor must have the answer."

"Not according to the nurse."

"You asked her straight out?"

"Over beer and whiskey. In the Pig 'n' Whistle."

"Pig in what?"

"It's a pub for the crew down in the hull. Nurse was there. She said there was no autopsy and she seemed uncomfortable about it. I think she doesn't agree with keeping whatever they have a secret, but she insisted the doctor's the boss."

Sandy said, "Ugh." Neither of us was terribly interested in following the boss's orders, though Sandy *was* aiming to marry him, which I guess didn't mean she'd follow his directions.

"But," I continued, "she did say they detected this spot on the back of Coach's arm, like from an injection. Also, lots of them in her belly, because of her diabetes, so she did these shots every day. But she said Coach and Tommie both had the shots in their arms for competition, some kind of vitamin. The doctor didn't go into that, or they're not sharing what they found."

"Geeminy, great doctor. He must be on the take."

"He smelled like whiskey, so keep that in mind. We need to find out more about the shots, and Helen, and Lowe, and Frank. And Tommie's love life, I think."

"That's why God made the telegraph."

———◦———

CHAPTER TWENTY-EIGHT

Receiving Room, Sun Deck
RMS Queen Mary

"The most perfect wireless telegraphy equipment installed in any ship, ever, anywhere." Senior Radio Officer Michael Fox was proud of his workplace.

"We're in constant contact with Europe and America, right here in the Atlantic Ocean, by telegraph, radio telephone, and broadcast. Our transmitters and receivers weigh eleven tons, if that gives you some idea of the heft of the *Queen Mary's* technological status."

Fox pointed at two walls of equipment and four junior officers, busy at work. "We've got a high-power, medium-wave transmitter to talk to ships and shore stations, and for signals on the distress-wave length, and two short-wave long-range transmitters for telephone calls and telegraph messages anywhere, on the continuous-wave and modulated continuous-wave systems."

I had no idea what this meant but figured any information is useful because it's hard to guess what you'll need before you need it.

The four junior officers sat at two wall-long desks, each with a telegraph keyboard and Morse key, on which they entered dots and dashes—they called them dits and dahs—in patterns representing words.

"It's a kind of music, like speech. Every operator has his own voice. Working here long enough, you learn to hear the code just by listening to the clicks."

Fox beamed at the crew, with their magical, musical skills, those dits and dahs a dialect between them, the way members of a family can sound alike to outsiders but different to themselves.

The first operator handled general telegraph traffic to ship and shore stations on the medium wave, Fox explained. The second handled press messages on long wave, the third handled long-range telephone calls using short wave and the fourth handled short-range telephone calls using short wave. My options expanded as he talked. I might be able to do some communicating for items beyond the list Sandy and I had agreed on.

I pictured Rivka holding the telephone to Elsie's ear, wondering whether she'd be capable of hearing me, knowing me, without seeing me and touching me, too. Though I'd felt so incapable lately of giving her what she needed, I knew there was something between us, that she came to me in a way she didn't go to Rivka or any of the housekeepers, or even Momma. Was I imagining that? Was that true when we were physically apart? Could an invisible telephone line connect us when we couldn't see or touch each other? I thought of my connection to Ben. Was he gone now, or just more subtly connected than before?

Sandy said, "Officer Fox, we need to send five telegrams to the *San Francisco Prospect*." She shared the location information and said, "The first will go to Wally Nelson: ZIMMER SAYS FIND INFO ON COACH'S NIECE HELEN CARLSON STOP KEEP QUIET STOP SEND BACK STAT VIA PRESS TELEGRAPH TO SANDY ABBOTT STOP."

She had the information coming back to her, not me. I thought about making a different suggestion but decided not to fiddle with her arrangements.

"This next one goes to Quentin Reynolds: ZIMMER SAYS FIND INFO ON ADAM LOWE." Using the same kind of instructions, she arranged for the others. "For Shawn Kingsley: ZIMMER SAYS FIND INFO ON FRANK O'ROURKE. For Louis Ainsley: ZIMMER SAYS FIND OUT ABOUT SPORTS SHOTS ATHLETES GET." She inhaled. "And the last one goes to Barry Devers: ZIMMER SAYS FIND INFO ON TOMMIE'S LOVE LIFE."

"Uh, Miss?" Fox took off his cap to scratch his head at the cowlick. "Maybe you don't need to send that last one." The closest junior officer chortled, his hand to his mouth.

"What are you saying?" Sandy asked.

"I think that information is pretty widely available, without a telegram."

"Excuse me?"

"It's in the papers."

"I read the *Ocean Times* this morning. I didn't see anything about Tommie's love life," said Sandy.

"What's the *Ocean Times*?" I asked.

"It's right outside your door in the morning. Summarizes all the news on land," Sandy said, staring straight at Fox, not looking at me, a little critical I hadn't read it.

"Not in every case," Fox said.

"I didn't have a paper!" That familiar sense that I didn't have the same tools as everybody else.

"I believe you're in M117–119? We don't put a paper outside that suite. At the request of Miss O'Rourke's brother. He'd rather she not see it."

Frank was very controlling.

"That's also why you have no telephone in your suite."

"You don't have a telephone?" Sandy asked.

"We're supposed to have one?"

"Everyone in cabin class does, ship to shore calls for all of you. Just not your suite, or tourist or third class. Per Mr. O'Rourke's requested arrangement."

"Does Tommie *never* have a paper or telephone on ship?"

"Just on this particular passage."

Frank limited her contact with others, limited her access to information. I'd known men who did that, even in the government camp, men who dominated girls or women, controlling their ideas. I had a bad feeling about Frank.

"But what's that have to do with Tommie being in the news?" Sandy said. "I have the paper. Nothing was in there, except about the match."

"We go through what comes into the teleprinter from land press all night. We *choose* what to include in our passengers' news and print it up by morning. Understanding how Mr. O'Rourke wished to shield his sister, we didn't reference crude things other papers put out."

I guessed I shouldn't act too shocked. I'd seen plenty of questionable editing at the *Prospect*.

"Can we see the original land news?" I asked.

"Since your publisher's already read it."

"Zimmer's read it?" I directed this at Sandy.

"I imagine so."

"It's a service we provide to passengers like Mr. Zimmer."

A prickle of confirmation shot up my spine. Class wasn't just about wealth, but access to information.

Fox handed me the *Examiner* printout. "Champ Tops in Tennis and in Love." Three captions described Tommie, with three different men.

"All right," Sandy said. "Just the four telegrams, then. We may have a fifth later. Thank you for everything, Officer Fox."

"You're very welcome, ladies."

Outside the receiving room I admitted, "You should be a reporter, Sandy. I mean, you're pretty good."

"I'm aiming higher." Sandy thought being Mrs. Zimmer was better than being a reporter. She'd have money, be on boards, host parties, mix and mingle, manage things. She had the skills for it. She'd throw elbows when needed. She wasn't wrong. But still, I wondered if she just didn't see she was a torrent, built for a river, not a pipe.

"I've got to get back to Edward. I'll whistle when I hear from the boys, so you can write your story." She kind of shimmered with fun as she sped away to our boss.

What kind of gossip could I write that hadn't already been written? I wasn't going to waste my time on Tommie being a typical hoochie coocher. That was no scoop.

I could maybe find out more about Tommie and Coach. I cringed at the cruelty of the thought, of poking around there, when I knew she cared for Coach, or I thought she did.

Could I even find the bottom of such a story anyway?

Would it be possible to figure out exactly what any person feels?

Did I have a right to try?

I caught myself grinding my teeth.

I returned to the receiving room and asked Fox how I could place a call, since there wasn't a ship to shore phone in our cabin.

"We've got public telephones in the passenger writing room. Pick up and an officer will connect you. We'll set you up, honey."

That was a new one for me.

———◦———

CHAPTER TWENTY-NINE

Cabin Class Writing Room, Promenade Deck
RMS Queen Mary

"Can you please connect me with San Francisco, California, Chinatown-8-4203?" I whispered into the telephone handset.

A middle-aged couple sat in the writing room corner farthest from me. Luckily the wall-to-wall rug was thick, so at least the room didn't echo like a library.

"One minute please."

I'd been in the receiving room with this radio operator. All of them saw me, heard my questions, knew I was from M117–119. And I knew from working at the *Prospect* what switchboard operators do. This guy was *going* to listen in on my call.

It was tiring to always have to think of everything from below, above, all sides. I knew, to a certain extent, everybody worked this hard. But when you don't fit in, when you've got something to hide, that vulnerability adds so much extra work to your every day, in minutes and hours spent worrying about ways to fail.

As I waited to connect, the couple in the corner scrapped.

"Would you ever just *stop?*"

"It would be a change if you would *start* doing what you ought!"

I curved my shoulders, leaning in over the phone, staring at items on the pale wood desk. Thick, deckle-edged stationery in heavy stock, embossed in gold, *Cunard Line, RMS, Queen Mary*, with matching envelopes, pens, even stamps.

I wanted to bag it all up, go home and make a scrapbook, like I used to when I'd dream about going places. This was the kind of place I'd dreamed of.

"Connecting you now, Miss Benjamin."

My stomach constricted.

"Shangai Low." The voice was abrupt, verging on rude.

"Mrs. Lee, hello. This is Jane, er Pat Shea. From the train? You gave me your business card."

"Pat? Oh yes, Pat. Are you coming in? Do you want a table?"

"No. I'm calling from the *Queen Mary*, on my way home from England."

"You're calling from the Atlantic Ocean?"

"How was your visit with your daughter and her baby?"

She hesitated, then returned in her own whisper. "Not good." I could hear plates and glasses and voices in the background.

"Are they all right?"

"She doesn't . . . I'm not needed there." I didn't know how to respond. "Why are you calling, Pat?"

"First, Mrs. Lee, my name isn't Pat. I'm Jane Benjamin and—"

"Are you tricking me? Why would you lie about your name?"

"I didn't exactly lie." She'd pried into my wallet, seen Pat's name, assumed it. I hadn't corrected her mistake. I let that hang a moment, then added, "And I'm not pregnant."

"Did you lose your baby?"

"I was never pregnant. I had a concussion."

"I don't understand what's happening."

"I need to ask you a favor," I said, steeling myself. "To go on this trip, I left my baby sister with my roommate. She's furious with me. I'm worried about both of them."

"What does this have to do with me?"

"I need your help. I need you to go to my house and knock on the door to see how they are. I need you to tell my roommate Rivka and my sister Elsie I'll be back in a week and tell them I'm sorry and I'm worried. But mostly I need you to see how they are. And I need you to tell me about it, because I trust you and I need to know."

"Why did you leave them like that? You said on the train this was all about a man. I thought you were pregnant, that you had no choice. Why would you do this?"

"For a job. To make things more stable for my sister."

Mrs. Lee fell quiet again. Somebody hollered in the background, the sound of glass breaking, then "I got it!" then laughter.

"What are their names and their address? And your name again?"

I told her.

"Who is Pat Shea? Do I want to know?"

"He's just a guy who missed the boat. Will you help? Please. Please."

"If I can, I will."

"Thank you. You can send me the information by telegram, to this number," I told her. "When I'm home in San Francisco, I'll pay you back."

"You've probably got a bridge to sell me, too."

"Mrs. Lee, you're the only one I can ask."

"All right already, Pat." She clicked off. I heard another click, the switchboard.

"I told you this would happen!" said the woman on the other side of the room.

"Can I experience even ten minutes without your constant carping?"

They were together in the same room and didn't seem to hear each other.

She whooshed through and slammed the door. Behind me, the man made paper-shuffling sounds and a thud landed before he left the room.

Their waste basket was overturned, papers scattered all over the plush carpet. A thick business envelope lay on the floor. I picked up all the papers and set them in a pile on the desk.

I checked the waste baskets next to every pale wood desk, collecting all the papers that had been discarded by cabin-class passengers with something to write, putting them in the same pile.

Maybe Lowe had thrown a fit in this room, tossed out important papers that might reveal something relevant. I read legal paperwork, a crumpled love note, pages of a stage play. Nothing that might be written by or to Lowe.

I threw the irrelevant papers back in the waste basket. Then I pulled them out again to keep. *You never know what might be useful later.*

———o———

Tommie's Suite, Main Deck 117–119
RMS Queen Mary

"Tommie?" I said it quietly at first, then louder. "You here?" The suite was silent, the door to her room closed. I picked up the silver coffee urn, still heavy with coffee, cool to the touch. I pressed my ear against her bedroom door and couldn't detect movement. I turned the handle and pushed it open.

Atop the peach satin covers of the bed on the right, she lay sprawled on her stomach, wearing last night's slinky gold gown, she and the bed together projecting a rose gold glow to the room. Her ribs rose up and dropped. I breathed along with her.

I took in the elegant furniture, a puffy chaise lounge, an ornately framed, full length, lighted mirror, gold brocade-padded walls, a dressing table strewn with bottles and papers.

Tommie groaned and pulled a pillow over her head, blocking the sunlight streaming through an un-curtained porthole. Her movement floated a smell to me. Toast, almonds, mushrooms—expensive champagne—mixed with the onion odor of sweat. Under the pillow, she snored softly, like a purr.

I took a step, wondering if I could cross the room without waking her, glad of the pillow over her head. I got to the dressing table and found an open memory box filled with little things, invitations, ticket stubs, news clippings.

"Out of my way," she mumbled under her pillow.

I froze.

She started purring again.

My hands and the soles of my feet prickled with nerves.

I shouldn't do this. A friend wouldn't do this. *Ingrate.* I felt the truth of Tommie's accusation. I liked Tommie. But I was a reporter.

This was about family survival, period. I needed the column to make enough money to take care of Elsie. I didn't want to hurt Tommie, but that box of mementos was a package I had to open.

I sifted through cards and folded notes. I opened one and read its dark, slanted cursive. "I'm sorry. I'll loosen. I understand. oxoxo, Me." I unfolded a square of sketch paper with a hand-drawn butterfly, sitting on somebody's open palm. I refolded it, put it back, and kept snooping.

At the bottom of the box, I found a photo booth strip, four pictures of Tommie and Coach, with writing on top, "Playland-at-the-Beach." In the bottom snapshot, they were kissing.

I turned to check Tommie on the bed, still snoring, head still under pillow.

In the picture, Coach rose a few inches taller than Tommie. Coach's wavy silvered hair was parted on the side, glimmering over a black shiny blouse and sweater, the blouse tied up high with a string at her neck. Her eyelids were closed, lips closed too, smiling in their kiss.

Tommie's torso half turned to Coach, her head tilted up, shoulders raised. Her draped white short-sleeved blouse left her collar and neck bare except for a thin chain, exposed, as if Coach was in shadow, while a spotlight shone on Tommie's pale throat.

Holding that strip in my right hand, I realized my left was touching my mouth. I dropped my hand, hitting the edge of the box on the desk, knocking her mementos to the floor.

Tommie rustled again, rolled over, grumbled, purred.

I knelt to pick up the jumble. My own breath, my own heart beats, were loud in my ears, my thoughts thumping. I didn't hear anything behind me until Frank growled in the doorway. "What are you doing?"

My heart bashed against my chest.

I picked up the box, carrying it to the door. Inches away from him, I held my finger to my lips, *shhh,* and squeezed by, back into the drawing room. He closed the bedroom door and we faced off.

"I hadn't seen her all morning. I was checking on her."

"That's not what you were doing."

"I was cleaning up. This box and her things were on the floor. I thought she might be upset when she woke up to the mess."

"You're such a helper," he snarled.

"I'm sorry. I guess maybe I should have left the mess as is."

"Why are you spying on her?"

"I'm not."

"I see you worming your way in."

"That's ridiculous."

"Get out! Go on!"

"Maybe you ought to let her run her own life."

"Get out."

"I'll talk to her when she's up." I headed for the door.

"Give me that." He wrenched the box from me.

"You upset me. I forgot I had it."

"You act like other people are idiots."

Then he slammed the door.

I escaped down the hall, photo strip in my pocket.

———◦———

CHAPTER THIRTY-ONE

Promenade Deck
RMS Queen Mary

Cabin-class swells gossiped with Sazeracs or Pimm's Cups balanced on their arm rests, judging strollers in the glassed-in promenade's social parade. Not a one of them had a single idea of the bombshell in my pocket as I passed their tattling chats.

Coach and Tommie were "odd girls," "lavenders," "twilight lovers."

"Friendly sisters," Momma used to say when she was being nice, or just "funny" when she wasn't.

Why had I been surprised? Was I? I hadn't been looking at things directly.

I thought of Rivka and our now long-gone roommate Sweetie. The two of them shared a room. There were great emotions between them. But Sweetie left Rivka for Mac, my editor. That didn't last long.

People thought I was funny too, because of the way I dressed, maybe because I was a tomboy. Tommie herself implied I might be.

But I wasn't exactly like Tommie or like Rivka.

Then again, I wasn't in the habit of analyzing myself. Everything in my life so far had been about surviving. I hadn't given much thought to love. I couldn't. There wasn't room for it yet. But this picture overturned things.

I crossed the promenade foot traffic over to the glassed-in rail, pretending to admire the view. I got out the picture, held it low, where I could put it back into my pocket in a hurry.

What anybody would see in this photograph was romance. Maybe Tommie and Coach were in love, maybe not. But, in this picture, they were happy, flirty. They worked together on tennis, lived together, for eight years. And yet they also had this romance. A picture like this could sell a lot of perfume. Or cause a brand of perfume to be banned.

God, why'd I take it? This was theft, illegal. When Tommie found it missing, Frank would tell her I did it. I had to return it to the box. I knew it was special. I'd taken something meaningful to Tommie. I was the thief of her memory.

But even that idea threw me. I wasn't sure I owed her loyalty. Because she'd lashed out at me, and Frank had booted me from the suite, I didn't know where I was going to sleep tonight, where I'd be allowed to eat. Obviously not at Tommie's table at the Lady Jane dinner. I didn't even know where I'd go to the toilet or wash myself up.

Pat's original ticket would put me in a men's four-bed berth. I couldn't go there.

Maybe Tommie would override her awful brother, but maybe not. She didn't seem the type to bother. She'd climbed the ranks, moving up over her childhood poverty. She'd gotten hers so now she probably didn't care what anybody else got.

I'd met so many people like this since moving to The City. Back in the Hooverville camps, folks chipped in. Well, some folks. Remembering Momma, I had to admit that wasn't so accurate either, just cheap sentiment. Poor folk and rich were alike in their flaws and gifts.

"Hello Pat."

I slipped the picture into my pocket and turned to see Sandy and Zimmer standing there right behind me, fitting so neatly into each other, two jigsaw pieces.

Sandy's hair was styled just right, but not fussy, in spite of the pale green feather tucked into its waves. The feather matched the same sage dress she'd worn earlier, its structured collar making her look trim and official, tidy. Its open neck conveying vulnerability, the way a woman was supposed to look.

Zimmer wore his usual black suit that matched his dark hair and mustache, but he had a handkerchief tucked into his top jacket pocket, black with pale green dots, the same color as Sandy's dress.

She didn't have a ring, but she'd marked her territory. *She's gonna nab him, yes, the love but also the career of being his wife.*

"Sandy says you're working on a story I'm going to want." This was my moment.

Sandy nodded me on.

"I am." I fingered the picture in my pocket.

"Pitch me while we walk." He headed back onto the promenade, Sandy connected, and I hurried to get in the lineup.

"I don't have it all worked out yet."

"Give me the general picture. Don't need the details."

Things are so unstable. I haven't figured it out. I'm not ready.

There were canyons between me and a plan, but I was the leaping sort.

"I'm working on a story about Tommie's love life."

Sandy's nostrils flared. We knew that was already done.

Zimmer said, "You're behind the eight ball there."

I didn't want to be behind the eight ball. Couldn't let that happen. Couldn't lose everything I'd worked for, my independence from Momma, Elsie's safety, my own survival, and yes, the work I wanted. I took a breath, pulled the picture out of my pocket and handed it to him.

Zimmer stopped walking. Others behind us parted and flowed around us, like together we were a big rock in the river the current surges to accommodate, changing everything, even the shoreline, the landmass. Things eroding all around me. Zimmer's eyes bugged. Sandy's face fell. He put the picture in his own jacket pocket.

"I have to think about this," he said, turning the other way, against the flow. Sandy glared, then followed Zimmer storming off. Even he knew this was wrong.

What have I done? A tsunami struck the top of my head and tore down my spine to my toes. I'd ruined myself, who I might become. I would ruin people I cared about. *What's wrong with me? Why am I a person who could do this?*

But I knew the answer.

I was Momma's girl, raised to survive, not to be squeamish about what that would require. Momma let my brother die in a sack on the side of a potato field so I might have the resources to survive! I was here with this opportunity because Momma taught me to do the things that had to be done. Even the awful things.

But maybe it wasn't the way I was raised. Maybe it was in my biological design, my genes, to leap gaps, no matter how widely awful. Maybe I didn't hear the same moral alarms that other people did. Maybe I wasn't sensitive enough to hear them.

But I don't want to be like that!

I gave him that picture. I could take it back. My choice.

———o———

Cabin Class Main Lounge, Promenade Deck
RMS Queen Mary

"I don't care to hear your stupid excuses. I don't even want to talk about it. Edward will probably say no anyway, what with the likely lawsuits." Sandy sat across from me in the golden cabin-class lounge. "I just need to share the reports the boys sent and get back to our room. I told him I wanted to check on a hair appointment."

I struggled to swallow the lump in my throat. The lounge buzzed with social noise, somebody playing piano, someone else singing, foursomes gathered for tea, all kinds of chitchat giving us the sort of privacy you only find in a crowd. Sandy pulled papers out of her purse, shuffling them in a brisk, official way. She read through the first bunch herself and then summarized.

"Wally says Helen is Coach's only living relative, so she'd have reason to hope Coach would leave everything to her in her will. But there isn't much to leave. Helen's mother Kara and Coach were left an equal amount when their parents died."

I interrupted. "Helen made it sound like her mother got nothing."

"Well, Helen's father absconded with Kara's share."

Again, my feelings rose up for Helen. She was *made* the way she turned out.

Sandy continued. "Coach burned through her inheritance

pretty quickly with tennis expenses. Coach and Tommie have a great place in the Marina, but it's rented. Coach pays all her bills on time, nothing left over. Let's see . . . yes, Kara died twenty years ago. That's about it. Coach had a car. No insurance. Ummm, and this: Helen did work for twenty years at a bookstore, A. Roman and Company on Montgomery. Ever been there?"

I shook my head.

"Me neither. It's antiquarian."

"Perfect place for Helen. Probably no customers."

"Anyway, owner says he let Helen go a month ago. Said in the Depression nobody's buying old books, just using the library."

"That's what she said."

"She specializes in religious texts. He said she's brilliant and fantastically odd."

"I gathered that."

"So, no paycheck and no inheritance. She's recently been working at Lowe Construction. Secretary."

I nodded. All confirmed. "Now Shawn Kingsley's. Can't I read it myself?" I took it from her, frustrated to be the one listening, not the one talking. She sighed.

"Frank . . . baseball . . . Tommie's manager. Coach fired him from that. Then hired by Lowe." I paused reading. "He wouldn't like Coach much for cutting him out of his sister's business." I remembered the note in the memory box, Coach promising to loosen her grip. "He doesn't care for Coach and he doesn't like Lowe much, either."

"Any particulars about that relationship?"

"It appears the feeling is mutual."

"Now Quentin," Sandy said.

She thumbed through that report, and then read it again. "He says Lowe's richer than God. His construction company started with paving, then expanded when he got an eighteen-million-dollar contract. Eighteen million! To build roads in Cuba. Whooeee, listen to this. He built the Hoover Dam and the Bonneville Dam and the Grand Coulee Dam! Looks like Frank's got himself well hooked."

"Is that what it looks like?" A line from one of Daddy's songs flowed by my eyes, *big fellas posh, little guys squashed.*

"And this, Quentin found a picture of Lowe and Tommie in public, her on his arm, a symphony concert at the War Memorial last fall. Quentin points out, Mr. Lowe is very married." Sandy's eyebrows made three trips up and down. She was on her way back to my project. If Zimmer said no to the piece on Tommie and Coach's kiss, we'd be back in business. Sandy might be willing to help me find a story that didn't make either of us want to throw ourselves overboard. Hope surged. I liked Sandy.

"What about the sports shot?"

She riffled through the papers. "Says the European bikers are kind of famous for taking shots to make them go faster, last longer. Some tennis players do it too. It's all under the table, no official pill or something. A lot of them have homemade mixtures, like moonshine. They inject it, apparently. Not exactly by the book."

"Jeez."

"Let's look again, make sure not to miss anything." She spread the papers between us, less concerned for the moment about rushing back to Zimmer.

———o———

Wheel House, Top of Ship
RMS Queen Mary

Tommie slapped me on the back of the head. "Hey Houdini, where'd you disappear to?"

I couldn't find anything to say due to the cymbals clashing in my ears.

She tucked her arm into mine. "Jane Benjamin, meet Captain Peter A. Murchie."

I could see his importance, with that cap and uniform and handheld telescope.

"Seasick, Miss Benjamin?"

When I didn't answer, Tommie said, "Sometimes Jane goes mute."

She acted like I was still in her circle.

"Captain Murchie's offered to show us the bridge."

She looked fresh and healthy, especially considering the state I'd found her in a few hours earlier. Her clothes were on the plain side, solid navy with a narrow white trim. Her wavy hair blew around her head on the unprotected deck and her face was bare. Few women looked so bare in makeup as Tommie.

"Follow on," Murchie said. He didn't seem to mind our lagging. Maybe he didn't relish making small talk with passengers. Maybe that's why Tommie wanted me along, someone to receive her conversation.

"So, I'm still your suitemate?"

"I didn't know you were the sensitive type. Can't a girl lash out ever?"

"Your brother kicked me out of your suite."

"Really?" She giggled. "Ooooo, Frank!"

"I was picking things up off the floor of your room, putting them back on your dressing table. Kicked me out for snooping."

"He's protective."

"No kidding. Why?"

"Long story."

"I've got two days."

Captain Murchie led us up a flight of outdoor stairs, a distance ahead of us, out of earshot. I held onto the rail, aware that falling due to dizziness was a possibility.

"Just my stupid sob story, my father didn't like me."

I couldn't figure that. "How could he not . . ."

"He didn't. I could always tell. Anybody could. My big brother stepped in there, always, trying to make things right." We walked a little farther and swung around to another flight of stairs. "He didn't try to fix things up between my father and me. More like, he tried to protect me from getting my feelings hurt. Frank wasn't going to change my father. We all let him drink himself to death, didn't interfere with it, including my mother. Then things took a surprising turn and he died faster than you might have expected. But everything got better after that. Frank kept on working to make things nicer for me, to shield me from what wasn't pleasant." She smiled and nodded, having summed it up, her brow so open, unwrinkled.

"What do you mean, 'what wasn't pleasant'?"

"Like I said, anything that would hurt my feelings, or my chances."

Almost anything could hurt most girls' feelings. But what would hurt Tommie's chances? Her love relationship with Coach could. Tommie said she made her. But if people found out about the two of them, that could ruin her, too.

"Here we go, ladies," said Captain Murchie, holding the door open. "The wheelhouse."

We stepped out of the wind and onto the bridge, the most beautiful room I'd seen on board, with a vast view of striated blue and gray ocean and sky. Varnished teak paneling and floor, darkly groomed officers in uniform. The place exuded significance.

"Welcome to the navigation control center." So many gleaming brass wheels and gadgets, waist high, polished to an unblemished shine. The gorgeousness of some machines always got me, ever since I first witnessed a new green tractor.

"That's the magnetic compass," Murchie said of the device I stood over, gaping. This was high technology, and yet the points on the compass were hand wrought in brilliantly colored thread. "Silk, stitched by needlewomen in Glasgow. A touch of home, I think." I wondered if this combination of art and technology was because the ship was English, or because Cunard had piles of money to spend.

"We've got two wheels, a Sperry gyro pilot connected to the servo gear, providing both hand and automatic steering for a predetermined course. Electronic telegraphs connect to docking, steering, and the engine room. Our telegraphs send independent signals to each of four propeller shafts. Over there, mechanical sounding equipment and echo sounding equipment, a fathometer. Oh, and here's the loudaphone, so we can ensure pure transmission of voice commands undamaged by extraneous noises."

I asked, "You said hand steering and automatic steering?"

"We have options."

"What do you use? I mean, is it best to let things go according to what you decided before, or to grab it and change directions?"

"Depends on the circumstances," said Captain Murchie. "I've captained ships for a long time, ships with more complex missions than this. It requires a lot of planning, making decisions in advance. But then we adapt, based on experience and the changes we see ahead."

I surveyed the endless ocean and sky.

Tommie said, "Clear sailing, far as the eye can see."

"Ah, but how far ahead can your eye see?" he asked. "What lies beyond the horizon, what you perhaps can't yet see, and how well you predict it, that's what matters."

An inexperienced person like me found it hard to predict what's coming. When you're like Captain Murchie, and you've done it all hundreds of times before, understanding must come to you like memory, without your even working at it. But for me, with so little of this, to see ahead required imagination, because I didn't have those memories. I had to invent solutions rather than envision the ones already out there.

Tommie said, "Well, I can foresee a very deluxe dinner that requires two very deluxe dresses." Her smile lit the wheelhouse.

She wasn't deep, but maybe her shallowness was a skill too. Maybe that's why she competed so well. There wasn't all this extra stuff cluttering her mind when she played. She was a simple machine. That was a gift.

Maybe Coach hadn't understood that all the other stuff Tommie liked to do didn't bollix her up and distract her because when she played tennis, that was all she saw. Daddy used to say, "No head, no headache."

Tommie was smart, but not deep. I liked being around somebody like that, who looked no farther than the distance of a tennis court baseline. I wished my head worked that way so it wouldn't ache so much.

———◦———

CHAPTER THIRTY-FOUR

Cabin Class Dining Room, C Deck
RMS Queen Mary

We entered the dining room through giant, silver-glazed screens.

Even before I registered its luxury, I was struck by its size, as wide as the ship's full body, seemingly stretching forever, and topped by a two-story dome. The room seated the entire cabin class at once, maybe 800 people, so we could see for ourselves where we fit in the scheme. In cabin class, I was on bottom, the size of an anchovy.

Once again, Tommie had dressed us for the room.

She put me in a clinging, bronze gown that showed too many of my bumps and points. But the dress did match the room's autumn-colored paint and the paneling in three shades of wood.

The diamond-patterned floor of russet and buff matched the colors of Tommie's own gown, low cut, ivory chiffon, with bronze and silver inserts.

I wondered if she'd arranged to have the gowns made for this trip, or if designers created and advertised clothes to go with a ship, expecting there were enough rich passengers to buy them. Anyhow, I was grateful. If I backed up against a wall, my gown would be camouflage.

I stopped to look at the painting, *Map of the North Atlantic,* as large as M117–119's drawing room.

At one end was a small, rocky island off the coast of Britain, with London's buildings looming, at the other, Nantucket light-ships docked in front of New York City skyscrapers.

In between, under an Art Deco moon and stars, a lighted, crystal version of the *Queen Mary* moved across ocean waves, displaying our exact, current location. I only had to look at the painting to see how far I'd come, how far I had left to go. I was smack dab in the middle of the Atlantic.

While I gawked at our surroundings, Tommie scrutinized people. She found someone she knew, some decorative fellow, and squealed, waving both arms in the air. Before she deserted me, she plucked a card out of her purse, read it, her face lighting up. She pointed in the direction of the portside private dining room. "I'll meet you there," she said. "Private room!"

I wobbled in Tommie's too-high shoes, on blistered feet, toward our table. The route took me through bronze grill doors, a service lobby loaded with bottles and condiments and what-not, and a matching second set of doors. I found myself in a room paneled in champagne-colored wood, as if made for Tommie O'Rourke and her ivory chiffon gown.

Three people stood in front of a mural at the end of a long, formal table.

First there was a familiar-looking, tall, thin man in white tie and tails. Every man there was dressed that way, but he wore it best, like white tie and tails were invented for him, like he was the *purpose* of white tie and tails.

His brown hair was pomaded back, his face clean shaven, with a cleft in his chin. I may have sighed a little, thinking, *How is he so very very perfect?*

He spoke to a round old woman in a navy lace gown and a pale, skinny young man. It took me a minute to recognize them,

Pearly Grandma and Lawrence the Grandson, the two I'd met in line to make reservations, the ones I'd asked not to be seated with.

"Well, hello, dahling!" the old lady said. "I'm so glad they were able to seat us together after all! I don't believe we were ever formally introduced. I'm Vivian Yardley and this is my American grandson, Lawrence. And, of course, you must recognize George Underhill, my all-time favorite male Wimbledon champion, now a professional!" I'd seen him in the stands on the day Coach died, though not in this glamorous getup. "George, this is Jane Benjamin, traveling companion of Tommie O'Rourke."

We shook hands all the way around, my own a little shaky because of Gorgeous George. He smiled and regarded me, from my neckline to the hem of my dress, with curiosity. I wondered if I'd already ruined the gown or if my bumps or points weren't measuring up. He turned back to the painting.

"At any rate," he said, "this is my favorite onboard work. Something deliciously bizarre about it." He pointed at a large canvas of five circus performers and two horses standing on stage, peeking at an audience through red curtain panels. "Dame Knight does a lot of circus scenes, but this one's tantalizing. These minstrel costumes, and, though the figure in the center looks like a child, on further examination, one wonders if he's a circus dwarf." I could see that. He *was* a dwarf.

Mrs. Yardley's grandson Lawrence said, "Well, circuses must object to this portrayal. The plain old outlandishness of it must drive people away. Surprised they haven't sued her."

"Have you *been* to a circus?" George laughed. "When the curtain rises, outlandish converts to magic. No weird? No magic. The audience doesn't want to know what happens backstage. They prefer the illusion."

I disagreed. "People get bored with illusion. They want to

see the hidden bits. They don't mind if the characters turn out ugly. They like it. Makes 'em feel better than the performers they used to admire."

"Hmmm. I see what you mean. People are awful." George pointed at the painting's circus performers gathered at the red panels. "To peek through a curtain is everything."

I agreed with that.

"Well, the curtain's about to rise on tennis," said Mrs. Yardley.

Lawrence sniggered. "About time they applied their morality clauses. It's outrageous to pay pros sponsor dollars when they behave so abominably. There ought to be a law."

Morality clauses?

"Litigious at birth or did you learn it?" George gave Lawrence a withering look.

"Why, I'm in my third year at Harvard Law."

"Ugh, how dreary!" Tommie entered with the insult, handing an empty champagne glass off to a waiter. A bell dinged over the address system, signaling it was time for passengers to move to their tables.

"Well, it's not Oxford or Cambridge, but a Harvard law degree must mean something in America," said Mrs. Yardley. "They're still holding the line at the admissions gate, I believe. At least until the rabble has its way."

I was one hundred percent rabble, though I didn't think I was the variety of rabble she referred to. I wasn't colored or Jewish or any kind of immigrant, except from Texas. So, on second thought maybe she'd want to bar me from getting in Harvard too. I could see that her giving other people the rabble treatment was the same as giving it to me. It got my back up.

"What do *you* think of athlete morality clauses, Tommie?" asked Mrs. Yardley.

Tommie said, "It's unnecessary, don't you agree? I haven't met a single athlete who behaves worse than the executive who wants to put her face on a box of kiddie cereal, or the lawyer who wants to lock her up for being naughty."

"Oh, you are refreshing," Mrs. Yardley said. "So irreverent."

Refreshing and irreverent but not rabble.

"We'd best take our relegated positions, don't you think? The rest of the group is arriving," said George. I turned to see Zimmer and Sandy approaching the table, along with Helen. "We mustn't let the maître d' catch us disrupting the itinerary."

"YOU DON'T MIND if I order for the table, do you? Anyone?"

Zimmer's tone made it clear he expected no objections, though Lowe's nostrils flared and his jaw muscles twitched.

"We'll start with the Terrine de Foie Gras Truffee, Clear Turtle with Sherry Soup . . ."

I tried to follow along, reading the menu as he chose, relieved to see some recognizable English food.

He continued, "Supreme of Halibut with Lobster Sauce, Poularde braisée Demidoff, Fresh Green Peas, Chateau Potatoes, Salade de Saison and the Fresh Peaches Cardinal." He said this all with a complicated accent, but I wasn't sure he got that right, judging from Sandy's pursed lips. She may have studied French in high school.

"Well done sir, ideal order. Wine for the table?"

"God yes!" said Tommie. "And don't forget the champagne."

Zimmer and the waiter conspired for a few minutes to chart our drinking plan. I tried to follow along on the wine list, looking for the prices, which weren't included.

Charles Heidsieck, Sec Gout American,
Chambolle Musigny, Cote de Nuits, 1920,
White Hermitage, Corton Charlemagne,
Chateau Latour 1917, 1921 Chateau d'Yquem

"We'll discuss cigars later." Zimmer performed it all with that accent again. Sandy's face twisted in disapproval. Maybe this was the start of mutiny.

Captain Murchie entered the room, white hair glowing in candlelight. The lowliest guests at the table—me, Helen, Frank, Sandy, and Lawrence—perked up with the captain's arrival. But Tommie, Zimmer, Lowe, George, and Mrs. Yardley all sat at attention too, arranging their superior faces into respectful masks. It wasn't Captain Murchie's command of *this* ship that got me, but knowing *all* the ships he'd commanded, all the ships that weren't floating parties. There was something reassuring about an expert. In this private room, Captain Murchie was the one who seemed most like an expert to me.

The captain said, "I expect you'll dine well this evening, celebrating Lady Jane's nine days in the Tower of London, though her unpleasant end does lend our occasion a whiff of disaster."

That was close to the bone, but the rest of them laughed.

The waiters distributed champagne flutes.

"To Captain Murchie's excellent command," Zimmer said, raising his glass. Everybody toasted, mumbling agreement.

"I should share," Captain Murchie continued, "that we'll be coming into weather tomorrow morning, through tomorrow night, and our Queen's a ship that can roll milk out of a cup of tea. But we've got our eyes on it, much more than our eyes. We're in communication with weather ships throughout the Atlantic." I thought of those machines in the bridge, and of the confidence of the men at the wheels. "The *RMS Queen Mary* does not let events sneak up on us, as some unfortunate ships have done. Let's hope our world leaders are taking that same level of care. Good evening!" And he sailed off to another table.

Zimmer made a fake horrified face. "He tamps down a mood. I always like to start a party with talk of beheadings and autocrats." My tablemates laughed like this was funny.

"And the Titanic!" George made the hand motion of a sinking ship.

More laughter. I faked good cheer. Helen tensed, the tendons in her neck tight as bungee cords.

"But in all seriousness, you understand that we in America have no worries about the ridiculous pretensions of this Hitler. We're absolutely, geographically safe," Zimmer consoled.

Some of the articles that had appeared in our own paper made a different argument. Now I wondered about our actual, physical remoteness from it. I'd had an uncle who fought in World War I, an experience that defined him, the blank eyes, the touchiness. That, together with the Depression. No one at this table had his haunted look, outside of Helen.

"I don't believe we are *all* geographically safe," Mrs. Yardley huffed. "But our Neville Chamberlain understands what must be done in such a dangerous time."

Chamberlain's name was always in the paper, but I got the feeling this appeasement thing he aligned with wasn't great. I wasn't sure. There was so much to study. I'd focused on the stories directly connected to what I was trying to do, about the important people of San Francisco. Now I regretted not looking more closely into events in the larger world, as the people around me seemed to have done.

"And neither are American politicians about to be sucked in. We've got our neutrality acts," Zimmer said.

Frank's arms were crossed over his chest, his head vibrating with annoyance.

"I know this for sure," Zimmer continued, "as someone who talks to politicians regularly. Our interests are better served by staying out of foreign fights, focusing instead on our problems at home. We're still pulling out of the Depression, for God's sake."

Who were the politicians he talked to and what were they doing to help my people out of their lean-tos and soup lines? I didn't usually care about politics. But this conversation was pressing on old fractures.

Frank released his crossed arms and exploded. "You're not saying you want us to be part of the *me first* crowd, are you? What Europe did to Czechoslovakia, giving it away to the Germans out of fear and cowardice? That was betrayal! Sometimes you've got to do the hard thing. You can't always cave to a bully!" Frank's hand slapped the table, rattling place settings.

Silence.

Was he going to get away with insulting the man sitting at the head spot?

And then I thought, *Rivka's from Czechoslovakia.* Had she said anything about it to me? Had she been worried without my being aware? Did she still have family there? Had I failed to see this whole mess might be happening to her, to her people?

I reconsidered Frank. Maybe I'd misjudged him.

Tommie laid her hand on her brother's, but he pulled it away.

She said, "That stupid little man is horrible. The European players are all saying Wimbledon may be cancelled next year because of him. I'll be devastated if I can't go back next year to win the whole thing, women's singles plus the doubles, like I should have done this year, if only—"

Helen started coughing hard, covering her mouth with her napkin, her face turning red. As soon as she stopped coughing, she picked up a dinner roll and began to chew, increasing the likelihood of a second fit.

Tommie continued. "We can't let the tiny tyrant change the way we live. He'll win that way. We've got to live our lives the way we choose, not let him control us." I thought she lived very much the way she wanted to. I heard more than a little selfishness in her speech.

"Time for you to go pro, love," George said, winking. "We'd have loads of fun on a pro tour together. We've both got our Wimbledon notches. Let's make some proper money. Your fire's got all that oxygen now, but winning isn't forever. Fire dies out. An athlete's got to live beyond that."

This room was proof that they were both living pretty well. I rubbed my hands on my napkin. Tommie glanced at Lowe, whose own eyes remained on George. Lowe was Tommie's private sponsor.

"Ugh, money," said Mrs. Yardley, lifting her chin.

Helen's face reddened shockingly. Did no one else notice?

Lowe stood and lit a cigar, walking around the table, stopping just behind and above Zimmer, who made a face, like Lowe had cheated at chess.

"Money's always part of the equation," Lowe said. "A person *has* to think about money."

Helen downed a glass of water and blew her nose, which did not interrupt Lowe. Then she picked up a second dinner roll, gnawed on it, and put it down again, right on the table. I saw the way her hair was clumped on her forehead, the sheen on her nose. She hadn't showered. I thought of Vee, of my deserting her for being *off*, abandoning her because of her vulnerability. A guilty anxiety rose in me.

Lowe said, "Unless they don't think about money because they're freed by someone else doing that thinking for them."

For how many people at the table was this true? It had been for me, receiving gifts that worked like money, which I'd relied on without always admitting the difference they'd made.

Mrs. Yardley frowned.

Lowe continued. "Far as I'm concerned, whatever the politicos decide about war is fine. It isn't for me to make that call. But I keep my ear to the ground because the coming *whatever* is going to shape this economy for decades. I'm not so stupid as to ignore clues that tell me what I ought to do next."

This whole conversation lit kindling in me, reigniting memories related to money, made worse by Helen's obviously growing anxiety.

Frank answered Lowe, "A man like you, an *industrialist*," saying that like a dirty word, "is in a position to shape what happens next, not react to it."

Even in my agitated state, I thought that seemed too aggressive if Frank aimed to keep his job.

Tommie's eyes cut over to Lowe, who smiled with his mouth but frowned with his eyebrows, the way someone does when they think you're an idiot. "I don't just react, Frank," he said. "I act. I *take* action."

That stilled the table, even Frank. What action was Lowe referring to?

I thought of Redhead and Yellowhead and the rest of the crew, down in the Pig 'n' Whistle, thought about what they'd said about poor blokes versus lords and masters.

Three glasses of champagne combined in my gut with the resentment that had been churning in me ever since I got on this ship, to make me blow open my trap.

"Ain't nobody at this table gonna bear the weight of a decision to fight. That'll be a fella without any cash or power, somebody not eating turtle soup or halibut supreme. That's who'll carry the weight, the fella who's used to dragging bags of wet cotton for the farmer and the banker. If you want to know who'll kill or die, follow the money. Follow the debt!"

I felt the heat from my face to my chest.

"Where's my purse? Where's my purse!" Helen screamed. A waiter handed it to her and she ran out of our private dining room.

Tommie said, "Medicine time. All that bread I guess." My tablemates signaled confusion with their raised eyebrows, slightly open mouths. "She's got diabetes, inherited. It messes up her head."

Frank stared at me, shocked.

Ten waiters swooped in, setting plates of what might have been ground liver in front of each of us.

I picked up my fork to move the meat around.

"Did you say 'bags of wet cotton'?" Lowe asked, amused.

Zimmer's eyes shifted left and right, checking reactions. Sandy gave me the *don't do this* face.

"It's a metaphor," I said. "I'm a writer."

I thought I heard Zimmer mutter, "For the time being."

I dropped my first bite of liver down the front of my dress.

———o———

Observation Lounge and Cocktail Room,
Promenade Deck
RMS Queen Mary

"Sing, Jane, sing!"

Tommie entertained a group at a little table at the edge of the Observation Lounge and Cocktail Room at midnight, somebody else's guitar on her knee, the slit of her gown showing off those gams everybody always jabbered about. A semicircle of fans gathered around her.

The bar was crowded and buzzy, but a good number of people were focused on Tommie, even with Fred Astaire, Marlena Dietrich, and Johnny Weissmuller schmoozing nearby.

I'd learned that Tommie was famous for this, singing impromptu at bars and nightclubs, when she ought to be asleep in her room, acting like a healthy person. This night club stuff was on the list of things Coach hadn't wanted her doing any more.

I stood at a distance, against the curved bar, waiting for my drink, thinking maybe I could keep hiding here in the dark and noise.

"Let's be a duet, Jane!" Tommie called across the room.

"Do it, Jane!" George was drunk and eager to see me make an idiot of myself.

The bartender handed me a glass of bourbon. I signed to bill it to M117–119. I shouldn't take the drink. All that wine already.

And my head. But I sipped out of habit and resentment. Not the best combination.

"Come on! Really! I want you!"

She wouldn't accept no. People didn't say no to Tommie.

I decided to play along, sing silently, make some joke to show I was above her routine. She'd forget about my singing once we started. She'd start bursting out as lead voice and I could disappear, let everybody stare at Tommie.

I wasn't going to do something I'd fail at. *This is how I'll prevent that.*

I joined her circle, glad my bourbon matched my dress so when I spilled it wouldn't leave a mismatched stain like the liver.

"I've got just the song for my suitemate Jane."

How would she know what songs I liked? She hadn't exactly focused on me and my preferences. Yet the first few guitar notes sounded familiar, something I recognized but couldn't place.

Tommie spoke as she strummed. "It's a showtune, yes, but you'll see it's different. Hear how it starts in a minor key? Because the song's serious." She said *serious* in a comical way. Then she started singing, in her lilting voice, *"You said I was your muscle, I got it done, And yeah, I bore all the weight. Other guys were out having fun. But I tied my boots, jumped the gate."* She waved me over, "Join in Jane, this is your song!"

She was mocking me in front of this cabin-class crowd, showing them, *She's not one of us! She's got the stink of work on her!* Or had I done this to myself, saying *ain't* and *wet bag of cotton* at dinner? Or maybe it was the drinking.

Zimmer stood at the edge of this crowd, staring at me. Returning his gaze, I felt something rise in my throat.

I finished the bourbon, trying to wash it down, but instead it insisted on coming. It was my damn voice again.

I sang along with Tommie, angry, in my crackly, rough, Valley Fever-ruined way, like a girl version of my own daddy, who would never sing this song, who'd never honor a New York City pretender's Broadway version of his own Okie hard luck story.

"I dammed all of the canyons, lit you up. Helped you sell the big dream."

My voice built, got louder, more angry, even more like Daddy. Tommie wasn't singing with me now or even playing the guitar. I was belting it alone.

"Once I dammed a canyon, now it's done."

Mrs. Yardley stood in the background, arms crossed over her prodigious bosom.

"Buddy, now I get your scheme."

I dropped my eyes to my feet, shoved into those borrowed, too-high heels, then up at the faces. And people began to applaud. Gorgeous George whistled. Across the room Fred Astaire stood and clapped.

Did they understand how I felt about them? My resentment? Their applause was absurd. But I wanted it. I liked it. I felt like Daddy was right there with me, not somewhere on the road, searching for gigs.

In the background, Zimmer stood with Lowe, cigar smoke circling their heads like consensus.

"Well done, sister," Tommie said, pinching my hip.

I ought to have despised her for putting me in this position. But I'd always wanted applause, always expected it to be like a great wave of love lifting me higher than I could climb alone. At the same time, there was my resentment, really my contempt, for what I wanted.

I left her and her circle. *I need another one, after that stupid display.* I elbowed my way to the edge and waved to my bartender, who nodded.

"Well, well," said the man to my left.

"Frank."

"I guess that went better than you expected."

"I knew I'd wow 'em. I'm Jane Dang Benjamin, star of cabin class and all the high seas."

He saluted me. "You're a regular jack-in-the-box."

"So I've heard. You brought that up the minute you met me."

"I'm not talking about the cross-dressing thing."

"Then what?"

"At first I thought you were what Stein says, there's no there there."

"I've got too *much* there! A spoon more dust in my gullet and I'd choke."

"Listen, just let me pay you a compliment. I don't do that often."

"Go on."

"Surrounded by people who could do you good, you still said what you ought to say, because it was right to say it. I respect that. You've got character. And backbone."

"I wouldn't take that too far. I'm as ambitious as the next guy."

"But you draw a line. Very important to draw a line."

Frank was so handsome, with those sharp cheekbones, those dark eyebrows, that bottom lip, those lean muscles, those compliments.

What an awful, scheming liar I was.

But Zimmer wasn't going to give me that column, so I wouldn't have to gossip about Tommie and Coach and unravel the protective veil Frank had been weaving for his sister for so long. He'd never find out who I really was.

"Jane, got a minute?"

I turned to see Zimmer standing behind me.

"Called to the office," I said to Frank, before following Zimmer a few steps away from the bar, ready for a snide remark about my singing or what I'd said at dinner.

"We're running your column."

My column.

"We need to beat the rest of them. The way gossip's flying about Tommie onshore, somebody else will write this soon. We've got to get there first. Coach and Tommie are going to make a solid first gossip column for the *Prospect*."

"But how about, instead—"

"You're going to twist it a little. It's not about them *having* an affair. It's about Coach trying to *influence* Tommie into having an affair. A Svengali thing. Find more on Coach and on Tommie's being manipulated by her. So we don't spoil our Tommie connection." He meant *my* Tommie connection. The twist sounded like a Sandy thing, seeing my friendship with Tommie as an advantage, and wanting to protect Tommie from the headline. She wasn't protecting Coach, but then again, Coach was gone.

"You have until Wednesday to pull it together, two days. We're not going to send it until we hit New York. I don't trust the fellas in the telegraph room. Got it?"

"I just—"

"I wasn't going to give you this, Jane, but Sandy convinced me you're interesting enough to play this kind of role at the *Prospect*. Just don't get *too* interesting. Too interesting's a pain in the ass."

He wheeled around, leaving me stunned.

I knew what Ben would say. *Don't whiff this! Hit it out of the park!* But what would this do to Tommie, and the memory of Coach? How many people did I always have to think about? Elsie was already enough for me, too much! She'd take everything I had if I let her. I didn't fathom what she wanted from me. I was never going to be allowed to be myself unless I grabbed this moment now. I might never see who I could be. No one would.

I *needed* to be seen.

I rejoined Frank at the bar.

"You got something to drink in your room?"

CHAPTER THIRTY-SIX

————○————

JUNE 1936

Rotten Egg Hooverville
Sacramento, California

I did algebra homework under the dome light in the Studebaker's ripped driver seat, windows down in hopes a dusty breeze would relieve the unrelenting nighttime heat.

Momma and Daddy were at it in the tent, far enough from the car that you'd think I wouldn't hear their calling out of names, thumping of tent walls, moans, and laughter, all of which floated through the Studebaker window while I filled in mathematical blanks, wondering why x or y mattered to anybody.

I was used to hearing it. They did it all the time. How else were they supposed to do it? Where else was I supposed to go?

They'd kick me out for as long as it took. Minutes, hours. One time, a whole day.

Then, when the air around the tent got still and quiet again, I'd go back in, settle into my pallet on a pile of quilts, roll to my side, my back to the two of them, and try to fall asleep.

I wasn't the only kid growing up with a permeable canvas barrier separating me from my parents' private life. That was reality, part of what made government housing camps so appealing to Hooverville tent dwellers. Actual walls, actual doors, actual privacy. Maybe an actual childhood.

You might think I'd have learned all about the carnal side of things as a teenager, but I didn't. You don't learn about love and sex by listening to other people do it.

I didn't choose to investigate it on my own behalf, not because I disliked the promise of love but because my parents' coupling seemed too wrapped up with anger and manipulation to appeal.

That night, they made the trip from joy to cruelty quicker than usual.

"You're a castrater, Kate. May as well hold the knife yourself!"

"Don't blame me! You're light in the pocket. You find a way to make and keep money and maybe you'll make and keep me!"

Everybody in the camp could hear. I rolled up the Studebaker windows and climbed into the back seat, lying down. I'd rather sweat out there with no breeze than listen to it and watch everybody else listening.

I heard the thump of something being thrown, hitting the dirt without breaking. An impotent gesture, like so many of them were. I tried to drown out the noise by singing a Carter Family song to myself, "Would have been better for us both had we never, in this wide and wicked world never met."

Above my own singing, I heard the voices of camp men. A subcommittee of them came tramping around to our tent.

"Abraham! Come on out and let's walk into town, brother." Sent by their wives to quiet Daddy up so the rest of the tent kids could sleep. Daddy didn't require much persuading to leave his screaming wife and head to a bar.

I didn't want to hear what Momma had to say after he left, so I stayed in the Studebaker and slept for a few hours before Daddy returned alone, whiskeyed-up and repentant.

Outside the tent, he cried, "Katie, baby. She don't mean nothing," his usual refrain. It was hard to know which woman. So many of them in the bars.

You could see flaps lifting, eyes peeping, all around the levee campsite. Even among the poorest people, my parents were the most embarrassing. Not because they had limited talent or taste or attractiveness, none of that, but because of how they behaved, like they didn't care how they were *supposed* to act. They thought they were above all the boring regulars. They just didn't care about fitting in. But I cared. I cared.

They got something out of fighting this way, piercing a skin that allowed them to tap into some essential charge. They needed that. It was almost the most important thing to them.

Momma stepped out of the tent in her nightgown, taking three or four steps closer to Daddy before stopping, stiff as a fence post. She put her hands on her hips, turned her head aside, her feet planted inches into the dirt. This was her *ain't having* it stance, Daddy's invitation to beg his way back in.

So he did beg, and he cried.

"I didn't mean it. You ain't castrating. The opposite, baby."

"You're a fool, Abraham. A tragic fool."

I knew he hated her calling him fool. But I don't think he minded the tragic part.

I watched him drop to his knees before her, wrapping his arms around her legs, sobbing into her belly, "It's just, I'm so, so hungry for things."

"Don't eat your baby," is what Momma said.

———————o———————

TUESDAY, JULY 11, 1939
Frank's Cabin, Main Deck 38
RMS Queen Mary

I can't say the night I spent in Frank's cabin was all butterflies and candy. It wasn't. But Frank was nice, more than another guy might have been.

We were both drunk or we wouldn't have wound up there together.

I'd felt a huge door opening, Zimmer saying yes to the column.

The picture of Tommie and Coach kissing had made me think about love, how I'd never had it, not in the fields, not in The City, a whole county in my mind and body I'd never explored, as much as *Queen Mary's* cabin class had been before I'd boarded it.

Other nineteen-and-a-half-year-old girls had done plenty of this exploring. In my world, even thirteen-year-olds had. If I didn't have to just work to survive all the time maybe I would have by now too.

But that night Frank was so handsome and willing, and he'd been complimenting me, and I was wearing that dang dress, drinking those dang drinks, and I had questions for him. So, he wound up the first person I ever fell into bed with, my initial experiment in which parts fit where.

We fumbled. I had no idea what to do. He ripped Tommie's already-stained gown. The actual sex felt a little painful and mainly embarrassing, what with the blood and other fluids. I vomited after, Frank passed out, my head swirled and swirled and I harangued myself until I finally passed out too, exhausted from humiliation, finally deciding, *Well I checked that off the list.*

But I didn't sneak back to Tommie's suite while Frank was passed out, though that's the kind of thing I might have done. I was trying new behaviors.

I stayed until morning. And when we both woke up, I lay there on my side, right next to him, naked, and I looked into his eyes and he looked into mine and we talked in a friendly, companionable way, while an Atlantic storm raged outside the porthole.

Not perfect. But there was no tragedy in it at all.

"Sorry," he said. "Not my finest hour."

"Are there usually cartwheels?"

"I was soused."

"I think I was too. I can't remember."

He propped himself up on his hand. "Where do you live?"

"Clay Street." I gave him the address.

"Posh," he said.

"What about you?"

"I live in my mother's place in the Sunset, now she's gone."

Momma's neighborhood too.

"I could find my way from the toilet to the kitchen grate in any house in that neighborhood, blindfolded. Every one's the same, exactly, except for ours. Ours is *special.*" He made quotation marks with one hand.

"In the Sunset?"

"Ours was the first one there. Fourteen twenty-seven 39th

Avenue. We were the pioneers of Doelger City, the most unique of the average, star of the sandy suburbs."

I could see what he meant. Those Easter egg-colored, cookie cutter houses, built two inches apart with no trees to break up the flatscape, like cans on a shelf.

"But with the wind blowing so much sand off the dunes and up the street, sometimes it looks like you're walking on the moon. So, we've got a little funky in the mix. Ordinary *and* funky."

"You two turned out special." *More than me.* But I'd come from dirt, not sand.

"Are you all right?" he asked, thumbing a freckle on my arm.

"Like I said, hung over."

"It's not just the booze, is it?"

"What are you asking?"

"You look like something's . . . are you sick?"

"Thanks. I was feeling so pretty."

"Even when you haven't been drinking, you're off balance. You've got that darkness under your eyes. And the irritability. Maybe that's your personality."

"You should write greeting cards."

"It's not serious, is it?"

When I consider how much I normally lied, it was surprising that I stepped right into it but, again, we were naked so anything was possible. "I have a concussion and a broken nose, though that doesn't hurt much now."

He didn't push, so I told him more.

"I have a little sister, a toddler. I take care of her." I thought of Mrs. Lee and how she hadn't sent a telegram yet, reporting on Elsie and Rivka. "I was holding her and she threw this tantrum and her head hit mine a couple of times, and then my head hit the wall." What did I want him to say to that?

His eyes rounded. "Jesus. Should you be doing something for it?"

"I talked to the ship's doctor, but he's a lush. He said to sleep, stop drinking, stop smoking, stop thinking."

"So, you've got a D-plus in following doctor's orders. Where's your sister now?"

"I left her with my roommate so I could come here."

"Lovely roommate."

In for a penny, in for a buck.

"She didn't choose to babysit Elsie. I just left her."

He didn't answer quickly. But then, "That's not good, Jane."

There. I'd probably been waiting for it, wanting it, the judgment that made me resist some people, but then again also made me respect them resentfully.

"Not something Frank, the A-plus brother, would do?"

"I try to do the right thing. Sometimes I can't. I botch it up."

"Your sister's a grownup, unlike mine, who's not even two."

"I don't think of Tommie as a grownup. Childishness is part of her charm. But I wonder if I hover over her to avoid doing other things I should be doing."

"Things like?"

"Last night, you said nobody at our table would pay the price for the decision to fight. I know what's right to do, but here I am, drafting on my sister's wake. I took a job from that ass, who I hate, to keep here in this little circle, where I can protect her."

"I don't get . . ."

"I was talking about fighting the bully but would I enlist to do it? Maybe I'd just stay here, fighting battles Tommie doesn't even want me involved in."

"Fights against who?"

He sighed and rolled onto his back. "For a while, Coach. She controlled everything in Tommie's life, and it put Tommie at risk, the morality clauses."

I felt the blood rush to my face, thinking of my column, how its interest to Zimmer was based on Tommie's being tempted to violate moral codes.

"And having these shots to improve her performance. Who knows what goes on with that stuff? But now, that's over. Coach's heart attack isn't the worst thing. But Tommie always surrounds herself with users. The work never stops."

Users like me, I thought. Maybe like Frank himself.

"Do you mean Lowe?"

"Hey, news flash: men like Lowe, they win what they want because they've got the dough. Bet you never knew that. Forget it. I'm saying I respect the way you tell the truth. You insulted me and you were right to do it."

I felt bad to hear him say this. He didn't have all the facts.

"Still," he said, before kissing my nose. "You better call your roommate, and your sister. You owe them. Make it right." He got up and walked to the bathroom without slipping on anything to cover his hindquarters. "When you're changed, we'll eat breakfast in the big room," he called over his shoulder before he closed the door and turned on the shower.

Bile rose in my throat.

He walked around naked, like he had nothing to hide. He didn't even know me.

Was I going to dress up nice and go to breakfast now with him, in public, admitting to everybody that something had started here, *letting* something start here?

Was I going to jump track for somebody else who wanted to judge me, tell me what I ought to do?

I moved so quickly from comfortable to irritated, from sweet to mean. I wasn't sure about Frank. Was I right to be bothered?

I got up and pulled on last night's ripped, stained, designer gown and examined myself in the mirror over the dresser. I tucked my hair behind my ears and checked my face. I did look sick, a fright, my eyes kind of crazy. I wasn't myself. *Who am I?*

On the dresser were Frank's two room keys. I picked one up and put it in the pocket of the gown because I might need back in here later. He wouldn't mind.

Then, since I'd already put his key in my pocket, I checked his drawers and his closet and his pants pockets, too. I only found a few dollars. I took them, because I'd already taken the key and his story and his time.

And then I left for his sister's suite to get rid of this gown, her gown, before Frank was out of the shower.

Because that's how I did things. I ruined what I already had on my way to something I thought might be better.

CHAPTER THIRTY-EIGHT

Movie Theater, Cabin Class Main Lounge,
Promenade Deck
RMS Queen Mary

I parked myself in the back row of the movie theater set up in the converted lounge.

When the captain delivered a bridge report over the public address system announcing rough seas, cabin-class passengers who'd planned to hunker down inside had requested all-day movies.

Though the purser had new reels to choose from, the social director decided to replay *Love Affair* over and over. They'd screened it on the first night, with the stars, Irene Dunne and Charles Boyer, on board to schmooze and celebrate and sign programs. Everybody loved it. *But over and over?*

Posters in the hall outside our suite announced today's twelve hour, back-to-back showing, but the "Coffee, pink champagne, and croissants served in the dark," drew me. It seemed like a better idea to eat breakfast there than to risk seeing Frank or Tommie in the Verandah Grill.

The room was full of couples and friend pairs, everybody acting much freer than usual. Maybe because they'd been on the ship for a while, and were feeling more at home, or because last night's dinner and cocktails and dancing had broken down some walls. Or maybe their comfort came from the movie itself.

From the behavior of the crowd, the chitchatting and drinking, it didn't seem like they felt the usual pre-movie tension, wondering whether the story will deliver you somewhere else, answering questions you weren't aware you had. Maybe they'd all seen it already on opening night, so this was a last-minute lark.

I could have done with a different movie.

Irene and Charles have this steamy affair on an unnamed ship crossing the Atlantic. They're so charming and gorgeous and, though they're star crossed and all that, they find a way back together because they're both so perfect and because, you know, they're in love.

I consumed at least three croissants and two glasses of pink bubbly to get through it. I hesitated an instant before accepting the first glass, and two before taking the second. But I didn't stop. Maybe I had no brakes.

Some parts I did relate to, the jokes, the longing, the barriers.

But the grace of both characters, their kindness and loyalty, that felt like a cruel fiction. I didn't sniffle at the sappy end like everybody else. I just asked a waiter wandering through the rows to bring me some coffee before I left.

The *British Movietone Newsreel* started before the next showing of the feature.

First came the title, in block letters: *A Model of Devotion: Edith Coach Carlson, April 8, 1895–July 7, 1939.* An orchestra played "Stairway to the Stars." A collage of photographs and videos of Coach's life floated across the screen, as the narrator told the story.

Edith (Coach) Carlson, who taught some of the top names in tennis, including number one ranked player, Tommie O'Rourke, died of an apparent heart attack during Miss O'Rourke's Wimbledon championship match against British star, Beryl Davis. Miss Carlson was 44 years old.

The film showed Tommie hugging Beryl, curtsying to the Queen, then switched to the crowd, whirlpooling down to where Coach had collapsed. The scene was so familiar to me, burned in memory, but from a new angle, changing it.

She was noted for training such luminaries as George Underhill, guiding him to multiple Wimbledon championships, and then to his career on the professional circuit.

The film showed young George on the court, impossibly tall and handsome.

Miss Carlson learned tennis as a girl in Golden Gate Park in her native San Francisco.

Like Tommie, I thought.

She developed the knack of teaching and in 1915 moved into the Beverly Hills Hotel, where she taught girls the game.

She came East in 1920 and caused a sensation the first time she played on a grass court, defeating national indoor runner up Nancy Sigourney in straight sets, losing only one in five games in a match at the Greenwich, Connecticut Field Club.

The film showed a young Coach, fit and intense on the court, with a worried look, not loose and confident, like Tommie.

But her greatest career was as a teacher. As pro at the Beverly Hills Hotel in the nineteen twenties, Miss Carlson coached such film stars as Groucho Marx, Bing Crosby, Charlie Chaplin, Joan Crawford, Marlene Dietrich, Clark Gable and Carole Lombard, who gave her the nickname Coach.

Then came the parade of celebrities with shiny rackets and enviable smiles.

Miss Carlson helped Miss O'Rourke develop an all-court game, unlike the more typical baseline slugging characteristic of other winning women players. Miss Carlson famously suggested Miss O'Rourke sharpen her serve by practicing throwing a baseball.

Here were scenes of Coach at the sidelines, Tommie on the court, stopping drills to listen and enact Coach's instructions. No pictures of Tommie pitching for the boys' baseball team at her high school or catching for pro Lefty O'Doul. How'd they miss that?

Miss Carlson was a devoted coach, particularly to Miss O'Rourke, not only focusing for the last eight years of her coaching career on this player only, but taking her into her home, living and traveling with her fulltime. "I'm like a mother to her," Miss Carlson said.

Was that a snide tone in the narrator's voice?

Now there was a photograph of the two of them smiling in fur coats, standing near a train platform. Behind them stood Frank, holding suitcases, frowning.

What would have happened if the *Movietone* producer had seen the photograph I'd stolen, or if he knew about their kissing and chose to hint but not reveal it in the newsreel, and whose decision would that have been?

Then the music volume dropped, and a video of Tommie came up, in white shorts, holding a racket over her shoulder, younger, even more hopeful and open looking than now, a girl who would make anyone watching smile without thinking. She spoke straight into the camera.

Coach cuts through the chaos of tennis, and life, really. She sees the path ahead. And that's very comforting, very calming, for a girl like me, who's not built that way. Sure, sometimes she pushes me harder than I want, but she's fair, and she tolerates my havoc.

Tommie gazed up through her eyelashes at the camera, bashful to admit the chaos she caused.

She sees it all as part of who I am. She says it's part of my creativity. I'm just grateful she never gives up on me. Never.

And then the screen went black before the cartoon came on.

I didn't see her whole life with the newsreel. You can't do that in six minutes. But it gave me the gist.

The waiter delivered my coffee with a concerned expression. I touched my cheek to find it wet. The ending had been so romantic.

———o———

Sun Deck
RMS Queen Mary

I reclined on the least stormy section of the Sun Deck on a chaise, in the reserved spot of a Miss Beatrice Olson, who didn't seem to need its use on a late morning when the ship was rolling. All the spots on the covered Promenade Deck were taken, of course.

I sipped my movie coffee and contemplated the dark gray sky, thinking about Coach in the newsreel. Tommie honestly seemed to love her, and could she have loved her if Coach had been as controlling as Frank said? Could I write the column Zimmer wanted, calling Coach a Svengali, when I didn't believe that was true? Waves slammed against the ship's side, jostling my cup, spilling my coffee. I dumped the rest on the deck.

Even with the dark clouds, the glare seemed bad, causing yellow spots in front of my eyes. I wrapped a lap blanket around my head, leaving a slit for my eyes. I covered the rest of my body with two more blankets. I must have looked like some kind of flannel plaid mummy, but still that was better than going back to Tommie's suite and having to answer her questions.

I burrowed in as chatty passengers rushed by—"Quite a wild ride!" "Beats the carnival!"—exhilarated by the camaraderie of risk.

I heard a scuffle at the rail in front of me, a man bellowing,

"Go on! Give a person some privacy, will you?" I lowered my blanket, widening my eye slit. There was Gorgeous George, yelling at two shipboard photographers snapping photos of him and Helen, of all people, standing at the edge of the storm. "Go on! I'll report you to the purser!" The photographers ran off like hyenas with bloody chunks of meat in their mouths.

George urged Helen. "You can find a new position, you must be . . ."

Now a noisy trio rushed by, interrupting my listening.

I leaned farther forward, trying to gain a couple of inches more hearing space.

"Some things are worth it, some things . . ."

Again, noisy strollers.

Were they talking about money? What about it? I heard him say, "Trust," before he turned his shoulder, facing the ocean full on, so the waves stole most of the sound. Helen shook her head and I heard a scrap of her answer, "Promises!"

Helen rotated to walk away, and so did George, but first they both paused there, staring at me, mostly hidden in plaid.

———◦———

CHAPTER FORTY

Tommie's Suite, Main Deck 117–119
RMS Queen Mary

T ommie wasn't in our suite. Probably at breakfast.

I sneaked again into her room to find the ship's welcome materials. Everything was moving. Waves hit the porthole
glass, open a crack, leaving water on the sill. Her clothes swayed
in and out of the closet. A toiletry bag slid across a table to the
fiddle rail keeping it from going over the edge. I found what I
was looking for on her desk, on a pile pushed near the back. I
picked up the welcome packet, searched for the guest list and
found Helen Carlson, cabin class, M162.

Next in the pile were loose sheets in Tommie's loopy scrawl.
Many pages had one word and doodles, adding up to nothing. I
flipped to a page that was all phrases, each underlined: contest
winnings, teaching/coaching, corporate sponsorships, magazine
writing, radio, singing, Adam L. All the ways she could make
more money. Or maybe these were the things she already did to
make money. It might mean anything or nothing. I thought of
what Lowe said at dinner, "A person has to think about money."

Tommie enjoyed so many opportunities, experiences, luxu-
ries. Obviously Lowe sponsored her. But what did she owe him
for that? And how was Helen able to afford cabin class? Did she
buy her own train fare across country and then cabin-class passage to see Tommie play at Wimbledon? I had a column to write
about love and sport, but I couldn't stop thinking about money.

———o———

Helen's Cabin, Main Deck 162
RMS Queen Mary

"Oh, thank goodness. Please let me in. I forgot the key!" I laughed, so very light and easy, to two maids headed down the hall toward me with a cart of canvas trash bags, spray bottles, mops, feather dusters. One of them held a pile of towels.

They glanced at each other, sharing silent information.

"Miss Carlson said I could wait here for a little while. My suitemate needs privacy." I raised my eyebrows up and down, lascivious. *What am I doing?*

One cringed at my joke. The other shook her head, no, very slightly.

"It's kind of important I stay out of my roommate's way, and I have to make a telephone call, and Miss Carlson said it would be all right."

They both remained silent, keys dangling from loops on their uniforms.

I reached into my pocket and handed Frank's dollars to the tallest of the two of them. "I appreciate your help." She counted the bills in her hand and checked the shorter girl before stepping over to unlock the door. The shorter one handed me the pile of towels, which I took with a smile.

"She'll want these too." She set an ice pack on top of the pile and handed me an urn. I was overloaded.

"Thanks so much," I said, slipping the key I'd pulled from her uniform loop into my own pocket.

I closed the cabin door. A master key would be useful. I wouldn't need Frank's key anymore. I put the towels and ice and urn on a table just next to the door.

Helen's room may have been cabin class but it was nothing like Tommie's, not even as good as Frank's, much smaller, one room, without the special artwork and everything. But that wasn't it.

It seemed like she'd delivered some dingy San Francisco studio directly into this cabin-class room. Though her closet was almost empty, just the one forgettable gown I'd seen her wearing last night, and dark-heeled shoes, a couple of skirts, a coat and a blouse, every flat surface was covered with books and papers.

She must have packed a trunkful of them to bring on this trip. She had a medical encyclopedia, a history of Wimbledon, an engineering textbook, a picture book about the ship, all sorts of newspapers, with articles about Tommie, Coach, Lowe Construction projects, a huge dictionary.

She had a map of the *Queen Mary* spread out on the dressing table, with little pencil marks noting her room, the dining room, the promenade deck, the stairwells and hallways between them. She had piles of notebooks, like she was a detective of everything. I needed supplies like Helen brought. I saw an empty moleskin and put it in my pocket.

I flipped through the marked-up notebook on top, growing more annoyed by the cramped, dark pencil scrawl. I found an entry, dated three weeks before:

Great Depression has turned on floodlight, shown dangers of corporatists and financiers. Before, people depended not on assets, but earth, weather, disease. These created own tragedies, but GD is new kind of plague. Began with greed and pride of rich. Now they see, and know others do too, they're villains and not heroes of story, capitalists have turned to religion for solution, following charlatan preachers, who assure them money equals virtue, not vice. So, they lobby to end Christian support for generous government, calling it welfare state. They've rented out Christianity to rationalize lies about good of continued dominance!

What should I think about this? The writing was so dense. I'd need to study it to understand, but I didn't have time, and it made me angry.

Helen sounded crazy, but maybe also right about some of it. It reminded me how the bankers had driven us off our Texas farm. But then, too, in California, how Momma told the troublemakers trying to talk her into joining a union, "Right, sure, so I can share the poverty evenly, with everybody." I didn't have time for this sorting out of facts and analysis and experience.

I kept flipping and read from a page labeled, "Ships."

Lowe/Maritime commission (MARCOM)/Merchant Marine Act (1936) = contract for construction of 50 merchant ships/tankers convertible to wartime use by US Navy. One hundred more maybe in 1939. Likely contracts for Brit ships, depending on war engagement. Plus, possible US engagement.

A different kind of gibberish. Helen had pressed down hard on her pencil, underlining "possible US engagement," talking about the potential war with Germany. I couldn't let myself be sidetracked. I wasn't investigating war.

Now here was something about Coach and Tommie. "They parade their illicit behavior in front of scores of people who accept it because they're famous! No consequences, ever!"

I kept flipping. Near the end of the journal, she'd written, "... drain blood, gases, fluids ... replace w/ preserving chemicals ... artery and vein ... small incisions." Details about embalming, which made me queasy to read. I skimmed for the basics. Several pages later, I found an entry, "*Pot Belge*: cocaine, heroin, caffeine, amphetamines. 1–2 subcutaneous ... bolleketten, rocket ball ... time release."

Holy hell. This was worse than I thought, much worse. She pushed the dope shot. She put herself up to Coach and Tommie as the one to give them the shots.

I left the desk and rushed to the bathroom, looking for supplies. I found a hard-sided toiletry kit and opened it. Inside were a small, empty brown bottle marked "PB" in cursive. I opened it and held it under my nose. Nothing recognizable. I put it back.

I found a half-full pint bottle of Nor-Co-Hol Rubbing Alcohol and an ice pack, melted. I pulled that out and untied the ribbon that bound it around some vials of liquid, "Iletin Insulin/ Lilly," with little rubber lids.

I opened a metal case like a tiny coffin and found a glass syringe and a thick metal needle. A sharpening stone lay loose in the toiletry case. I touched the end of the needle, tried to picture it piercing my skin, healing me, ruining me.

I'd never once in my life had a shot. Did Helen do this every day to herself, in her stomach? Would doing that affect the way she considered putting a needle in Coach? Had she injected her with *Pot Belge*? Was that what killed her?

Keys rattled at the door. I flipped the needle case closed, and the toiletry box. I scrambled into the bedroom, onto the floor, and rolled under the bed. The door opened and, from under the bedspread, I watched Helen's scuffed brown shoes move toward me. She came straight to the side of the bed and sat, pushing coils down almost to my nose.

She picked up the telephone and mentioned a room's number. I started to chant it in my head, wanting to remember the number. But my head throbbed and I forgot it at once.

"You were wrong," she screeched, after a moment. "I should have found out myself. You didn't investigate this properly!" She bounced her foot on the floor, jiggling those coils above my face. "What am I supposed to do? I don't have enough." She listened. "I can't. She's watching me. I think she knows."

Was *she* me, sitting there right below her?

"All right, all right. Why not now?"

My heart thumped so hard I feared she'd hear it.

"Promise me. You said I would be all right. Okay, I'll see you then."

She hung up the telephone and stood, the bed coils bouncing up, away from my face. I breathed through my nose. A door opened and closed and then came the sound of sobbing over water running in the sink. I almost felt ashamed of the way I'd been thinking about her. Almost.

I rolled out from under the bed, stood and stepped quietly across the room and out the door, into the hall, and rushed to Sandy and Zimmer's room.

—————◦—————

CHAPTER FORTY-TWO

Cabin Class Pool, C Deck
RMS Queen Mary

"Everything's an emergency with you," Sandy hissed at me through a crack in her door.

"We have to talk now," I insisted.

"Hold on." She closed the door to M110 and I paced in the hallway until it opened again and she joined me.

"Not here," I said, leading her to the exit to the deck.

Outside, the wind blew straight to my bones. Sandy pulled her coat tighter and said, "It's terrible out here."

"Gee, no kidding," I said, eyeing her heavy coat. I wasn't prepared for this, in Tommie's thin jacket, skirt and blister-making shoes, my ankles bare.

"Let's go to the pool. I can't stand this wind."

I followed her to the ship's bizarrely ornate cabin-class pool. The gold and the pearl ceiling made it look like we were inside a jewelry box.

"Ever seen anything like it?" she asked.

"Never."

"You ought to see the Fleishhacker."

"Fly swatter?"

"In the Sunset District. Biggest pool in the world, a thousand feet long, pumped full of ocean water. Once, the pipe sucked in a shark. Think of it, ten thousand kiddies and their mommies playing Marco Polo with a shark!"

"Jeez."

"One time the gardener found a hand floating in the pool," she added.

I shivered, looking at this pool. I didn't need further disturbing ideas.

"How's your *story* coming?" She put a mean voice on the word story.

"I know that wasn't right."

"You don't say? You have a friend who's doing all this stuff for you, helping you up, and you're trying to promote yourself by doing the worst possible thing to her? A career-*ending* thing for her? I'm ambitious, but this is something else entirely. Besides, how imbecilic to poison the well! Who's ever going to talk to you after this?"

"I understand!" A couple of women in swimsuits passed us, tittering. "That was wrong. I was wrong. I'm trying to fix it."

"What do you propose, Einstein? Edward's all over this now. He thinks it has legs! He's going to run with it!"

"I'll give him something better."

"Right, you've got two days to find something to top a gossip column about the world champion being bullied into an illegal love affair with her domineering coach, in violation of the morality clauses? That's a pretty tough story to beat. And if you don't turn it in, believe me, you're back to the soup line."

"So, I'll shift to what happened to Coach instead."

"She died!"

"Simmer down. I can't think when you scream."

"All right," she said. "Come here."

We backed against the wall, farther from the noise of adventurous bathers.

"She didn't die of natural causes," I said.

"You said the doctor said heart attack."

"The doctor's a quack. Well, I don't know if he's a quack, but he's a drunk. At least I wouldn't say he's reliable, or that he cares that much what he's doing, and maybe she did have a heart attack, but what brought it on?"

"That's a lot of *maybe* and *what if.*"

"Listen, I was in Helen's room—"

"What'd she say?"

"She didn't know I was there. I was under the bed."

"Jehoshaphat!"

"So, I heard her make this telephone call, arranging to meet someone, in a panic about something going wrong, crying."

"Well, who'd she say it to?"

"I couldn't tell."

"When and where are they meeting?"

"I don't know. She headed into the bathroom and I got out of there fast."

"And you couldn't tell who she was on the phone with?"

"I heard her ask for the extension. But I don't remember the number."

"Oh, for crying out—"

"Concussion, remember? But also, she said something like, *I think she knows.* I think she's talking about us, or me."

"Maybe. Or she could be talking about Tommie."

"So, let me say the rest. The nurse said Coach had injection marks in her belly, because she has diabetes and she injects herself with medicine."

"Right."

"But she also had this injection mark in the back of her arm, supposedly because she and Tommie got a competition shot before the match. And the nurse acted like the doctor didn't put it in the report because he didn't want to cause a fuss about that."

"So . . ."

"Well, Helen's a diabetic too and she has all these medicines in a toiletry kit in her room and she has a needle right there."

"For herself."

"But also I found a journal in her room with notes all about some homemade kind of injection with cocaine, heroin, caffeine, and speed."

"That's the shot that Tommie got? Is that against the rules?"

"It sure sounds like cheating, don't it?"

She glared at my grammar.

"So Helen pushed that shot on Tommie? Why would Coach have it?"

"It's confusing. Helen seems depressed about Coach, or probably depressed generally. Maybe she didn't approve of Tommie and Coach? Maybe she thought Coach had an insurance policy or something? So, she wanted to kill her for that?"

"If Helen did this, that would explain her arranging to have Coach embalmed as soon as possible, so nobody would see anything."

"That's what I'm saying. She'd shot Coach up with amphetamines and all that, so that's why she'd ask for an onboard embalming."

"I don't know, some parts don't add up," she said.

I felt so hemmed in and trapped by the things I didn't understand. I moved away from Sandy and toward the pool.

The deck was wet and I stepped onto a slick spot. Tommie's stupid shoes had no grip, but did have heels. One foot slipped out from under me and then the other one did, in another direction. And that's the part I remember.

———————o———————

Hospital, D Deck
RMS Queen Mary

"Can't you give me medicine to fix it?"

Nurse Fleming wasn't even faking a bedside manner. She was sick of me.

"Details." She made me think of the telegraph officer in Utah, when I only had enough money for one or two words per message.

"I must be sensitive in the back of my head."

"You've got a concussion, as we told you."

"Right."

"You blacked out?"

"That's what they say."

"How do you feel?"

"Bad," I said. That covered it.

"There's no pill for what you've got. The advice is the same. The question is whether you'll follow it. Do we need to keep you in the isolation area? Or can you be trusted to go back to your cabin and stay in bed?"

That's all I wanted to do. But I couldn't. "Could I see Coach's body in there?"

"No."

"Is there a reason I can't?"

"There are so many reasons. One is that she's no longer in

SHELLEY BLANTON-STROUD

here. We've got her in the proper place for the remainder of the
cruise. But there are plenty other reasons."

"Can I ask you some questions?"

"Can I stop you?"

"What about the shot she and her player got, the shot in the
back of the arm? Do you think it caused her death?"

"There's no evidence at all . . ."

"In the autopsy?"

"I told you, we didn't do an autopsy. Her next of kin requested
the embalming and that's what we did."

"Doctor definitely didn't do any kind of tests?"

She groaned.

"Who gave her the shot in her arm?"

"That's not our area of responsibility. You could ask the
player, since she got it too. But I don't think you'll find anything
newsworthy." She said that with a special level of snottiness.

"Is there some problem?"

"You're wasting my time. I have a full day ahead of treating
retching passengers, and I'll double that later when the pills lose
their psychological magic. I'll give you a compress, and I'm
telling you to climb in bed and stay there, only rise to eat, for the
rest of the cruise. I doubt you'll follow that advice, but if you
don't, something more significant could happen. I'm betting this
isn't the last I'll be seeing you in the next day and a half, and next
time it will be worse and I'll be blamed. That's what."

"But nothing else about the shot?"

"No, but there *is* something else about your being a dangerous busybody, trying to muck up people's lives." She sighed. "I'll
fetch you another compress. Go to bed. I'll arrange for them to
bring lunch to your room."

I had to figure this out.

It could have been Tommie who'd killed Coach.

If she was really tired of being controlled, like Frank said, and wanted out from under Coach's thumb, to live her life more freely, Tommie could have arranged for Helen to give Coach a shot that would kill her but not look suspicious afterwards.

But I couldn't believe that. Tommie loved Coach. I'd seen that kiss. Tommie was for *living*, not dying. And I thought she enjoyed the drama. It didn't trail her as some tragic side effect of her life. She lived that way. I think it made life interesting for her. She wouldn't kill that off with Coach.

It could have been Frank.

He'd obsessively protected Tommie, believing Coach dangerous for her, and that she put her at risk of being caught violating the morality clauses. Tommie's life got better when their father died early, a drunk. Tommie'd said Frank would be willing to go down with her ship. He'd do whatever he needed to do for his sister. He had good reason to get rid of Coach, and he'd felt relief at her death.

But Frank was *moral*, I thought, annoyingly so. He wouldn't cross that line, even to protect Tommie.

It was Helen, close enough to Coach to know her ins and outs, sitting next to her in the stands at Wimbledon when she died. She had all those notes, those tools, the medicine, acted so odd, erratic, conspiring. She'd lost her job, started up with Lowe, and taken this trip, as if money would be coming in, like she'd benefit from Coach's will. And she'd pushed for the ship quack to do a quick embalming. Helen did it, I knew it. I needed proof.

And of course Lowe was awful.

Everybody was guilty until I proved them innocent.

Nurse Fleming came back with my compress and handed it

to me with a sullen look. "I couldn't order you lunch. Tray ser-vice is cancelled because of rough water."

"Well, thank you for trying," I said.

She sighed. "If you want to know about what was in her blood, you ought to ask them at Wimbledon, the doctors who processed her onsite."

I went cold. "Processed?"

Nurse Fleming sat on the edge of my bed.

"They tested her blood, and the player's, before the body boarded ship. Wimbledon was concerned about the shots, from a tennis perspective."

"You don't have the results?"

"They weren't ready when we set sail. That's all I've got. Don't tell anybody what I've said. And *please* don't come back."

———○———

CHAPTER FORTY-FOUR

Tommie's Suite, Main Deck 117–119
RMS Queen Mary

"Give it back!" Tommie dropped her burning cigarette on our drawing room carpet.

I stepped on the ember to put it out. I'd thought she wouldn't be here, thought I could make my notes, gather my thoughts, in privacy.

"What are you talking about?" That was stupid, pointless. She knew I knew.

"You stole it. That's why Frank was mad yesterday. You're a rat."

The ocean sprayed against our windows.

"Just wait. Let me—"

"You're worse than a rat. You're a thief and a liar. You don't earn what you want by working for it, you steal it and fake it, Pat Shea! What are you going to do with my picture? Publish it in the *Prospect*? Blackmail me?"

"No, I'm not, neither of those things." God, I hoped Zimmer wouldn't put it in the paper. More than anything I had to stop that from happening.

"Give it back. Now."

"I will."

"Now."

"I've got it in a hiding place."

She burst out in a sardonic laugh. "Get it."

"I will," I said. "I won't let it go in the paper."

"What are you trying to do?"

"I shouldn't have stolen it. I was so . . . taken . . . with how in love you were."

"Oh, how sweet!"

The ship rocked and a glass of champagne slid off the coffee table onto the rug.

"I made a mistake. And . . . I did show it to someone who wants it in the paper."

"God, Frank was right! The publisher?" She grabbed her head with both hands.

"I'm not going to let it happen. But you've got to help me. I can turn this around. I'm on your side. But I need your help." I knew as I said it how it must sound, like a criminal begging for another chance.

"My side? My help? Why would I trust one thing you say? This will ruin me."

"What about the shots you and Coach took?"

"What?"

"I need to know if Helen injected the Pot Belge, and if she thought of the idea."

She rushed across the room, pushing me up against the wall. "You want to be me so badly, that you want to steal what I've earned? Do you think you're the first one who's applauded me, gotten close to me, then torn me down, tried to destroy me and take what I have? No! That happens two, three times a year. You are a dime a dozen!"

She lanced me clear through. I was no better than the rest of the media pack. I couldn't even deny that maybe I did want to be her, in many ways.

Her head hovered so close to mine, her fist gathering my shirt, her shirt, up under my chin. The blood vessels in her eyes stood out, the saliva glistened on her lips. I hadn't seen anything like this in her before, except from a distance, on the court. The radio reporter called her "a perfect American monster," and I remembered how angry it made me. She was trying to survive the best way she knew how.

"I'm not trying to ruin you. I'm trying to protect you."

"Oh yeah, sure, that's what they say." She let go of my shirt. "You're so selfish, you can't imagine what it means to love someone else, to stick with them, like I stuck with Coach, through everything! You tricked my brother into sleeping with you, just to sample it, didn't you? You couldn't even stay for breakfast. But that's not what you want, is it? If you can't be me, you want to have me, is that it? You were trying Frank because you can't have me! I see the way you study me, like I'm some kind of installation manual. You want to either have me or be me!"

"You're crazy," I said.

Her eyes blazed. She moved in fast and stepped hard on my instep.

I cried out in pain.

She hissed, ". . . like a fox, you jackal. Bring me my picture!"

---o---

Receiving Room, Sun Deck
RMS Queen Mary

"I have to send a telegram to London," I whispered, looking around the receiving room. "With no one else in here, please."

Fox turned to his junior officers and then back to me, appearing offended at the idea they couldn't be trusted. But Zimmer had said they couldn't, and one of them had already listened in on my call with Mrs. Lee. I couldn't let this information out.

"It's important." My voice cracked with urgency.

"Is this for the *Prospect*?" He said it with disapproval.

"It's about a crime," I said.

"We're on international waters. Under the British flag."

"It happened on land, in England. The British officials will be in charge."

"Does this involve one of our passengers?"

"Two or three or four of your very important passengers."

"It is our policy to treat our passengers with utmost respect." His posture stiffened when he said that.

"Then you'll want to respect the passenger victim."

"My men can work in here without eavesdropping on you."

"Do they recognize the sounds of those dits and dahs you told us about before? Do they know the sound of your transmissions? Do they snoop at all, ever?"

"This is a busy time for our office. Maybe you've noticed the storm?" Then Fox groaned and then said, "Take fifteen, gentlemen."

When they'd gone, he said, "Who is the recipient?"

"The Wimbledon Medical Office."

"The All England Club?

"That."

He found the number in a big book. "Go on," he said.

"Send blood test results for Edith Carlson and Tommie O'Rourke STAT STOP. Police matter STOP. Tell him it's Doctor Simpson asking."

"Do you have any idea at all how many rules—"

"A woman's been killed. We have almost no time to find out how."

Calculation registered on his face. He was required to follow ship rules, but Fox answered to guidelines higher than rules.

"Repeat what you said before."

"Send blood test results for Edith Carlson and Tommie O'Rourke STAT STOP Police matter STOP."

He typed in the message and sent it, and then got up and crossed the room, checking charts and other busywork with his back to me. He'd do what I asked him, sensing its rightness, but I knew he found it painful to betray procedures.

I paced the room for ten minutes until we heard the coded pulses of electric current, the clicking of short and long keypresses. Fox fed the paper strip into another machine that translated those marks into characters representing the answer to my question. He showed me the piece of paper.

"But, that's not clear, is it?"

"Looks like they've used their social security numbers, not their names."

"Can I call them?"

I waited as he placed the call.

When the Wimbledon medical office secretary answered and Fox identified the ship, he handed the telephone to me.

"I need to clarify these results. Is the first test you sent, with the amphetamines, is that for Miss Carlson's blood, or Miss O'Rourke's?"

I closed my eyes. Fox scraped a chair behind me just as I needed it and I dropped. He cleared his throat.

The junior officers returned, and dits and dahs began singing all around.

"Miss Benjamin?" one of them said. "I have this for you, from a Mrs. Lee."

I read: R SAYS E HAS MOVED IN WITH YOUR MOTHER STOP.

CHAPTER FORTY-SIX

Cabin Class Writing Room,
Promenade Deck
RMS Queen Mary

The bankrupt couple sat on a couch in the back of the writing room, reading documents together, looking resigned. They were making the best of things.

I picked up the telephone and a junior officer asked, "How can I help you?"

"San Francisco, California, Tuxedo-5-9267, please."

"Just a moment, Miss." There were some background noises and Fox came on: "Connecting you now." He patched through the call, protecting me from eavesdropping.

"Hello? Jane?"

"Hi Rivka."

I heard the click as Fox left the call.

Rivka was silent for a few seconds. "Are you all right?"

"I am. How about you?"

"I'm all right."

"And Elsie?" My voice cracked.

"She's fine now."

"I'm sorry for leaving you both like I did."

"I didn't understand what was happening. Neither did she."

"I didn't either. I thought I had a chance at this job, and that would mean more money, that we could move out, hire a babysitter, take the pressure off of you . . ."

"That wasn't the right way to do it. Not the adult way."

"It wasn't." My eyes filled.

"Elsie needs a stable situation, you know that too."

"Momma isn't someone you can trust."

"She is not who she was before."

Rivka didn't understand. "Her money can't solve everything."

"No, but it can buy a certain degree of reliability. That is important to children. I am sure it is important to Elsie."

"How would you even know what Elsie—"

"I was a child once. I remember wishing I had been surrounded by reliable adults. Wishing I hadn't been asked to be responsible for myself. I know how being made an adult too early changed me."

I choked back a sob. I knew that too.

———◦———

CHAPTER FORTY-SEVEN

Aft Engine Room, G Deck
RMS Queen Mary

I needed Sandy but I wasn't doing the logical things I ought to do to find her.

My head was getting in the way of logic, everything turned kind of sideways, not up and down, back and forth, like reading a book. More like looking up at a sky full of stars when you didn't know their patterns. Plus the rocking of the ship in the storm.

I was desperate. I needed a normal person to listen for me, see for me, someone I could trust, and I thought I could trust Sandy.

I found her with the help of a slight bellboy whose name badge read Raymond Peterson. Wandering the blustery deck, I'd seen him at his deck department shift's start of duty inspection, all lined up in uniform, getting checked cap to fingernails, and released to assignment. I'd heard his boss tell him to lay down mats and put up signs about taking caution while walking on deck. Raymond had a sweet, unimposing face, so I felt confident interrupting his work.

"I need your help."

"Are you seasick? May I get you a chair? Take you to your cabin?"

"Please, I'm trying to find my friend, Sandy Abbott." I think my voice cracked when I said *friend*. "I can't find her."

"I'll check. My boss has these lists." Raymond ran over to a short, crimson-faced fellow, whose rank I couldn't decode by uniform. He had a clipboard of papers, which he flipped through when Raymond asked.

Raymond came back and offered, "She's on a private VIP Captain's Talk in the engine room. I'll take you to her, Miss."

He got me to G deck without my paying much attention to anything but the back of his cap, the steps right in front of me, and all available handrails. We climbed down into the clanging steel space as Captain Murchie was talking. The rocking was less pronounced there, at the center of things. I should have slipped Raymond a tip, but I didn't have any money. I mouthed *Sorry* and he sagged but mouthed *That's all right, Miss* before scurrying away.

I nudged my way up to Sandy, who brightened to see me. With my uninvited arrival, there were ten in the talk. We two were the only women. Zimmer stood on the other side of the group next to Lowe, who seemed to be ignoring him, his shoulder angled so it blocked Zimmer.

In this dark place of steel and grease, Lowe glowed in a dove gray jacket, his vest buttons all done up. I didn't recognize the rest of the VIPs.

Captain Murchie spoke into a microphone that amplified his voice over the thunder of revolving engines. "This is the engine room's nerve center. Power is controlled right here. Men working the engine room stay in constant communication with the men at the bridge, who steer the ship. But the men down here provide the power. I believe you understand that dynamic."

The very important men laughed and nodded. Sandy smiled, supporting the mood. I frowned, thinking about the relationship between power and steering.

He explained that the bridge sent orders by telegraph, which made a loud clanging to alert the crew, and caused a green arrow to point at the desired instruction. "The engine room makes our speed goal possible, but the bridge makes what's possible happen."

More confident nodding. They understood. Captain descended into further detail. My mind wandered to the difference between deciding to do a thing, and actually doing it. Every idea was so complicated with my head this way.

"The men in the boiler rooms cannot bring a response on their end. They simply receive instructions and follow them as fast as possible."

This made me think of Raymond. He brought me down here, but not before I asked him and not before his boss gave him the information and permission that allowed him to do it. I thought of myself, when I was a girl, running secret messages, sometimes for Momma, sometimes for Daddy, helping them make things happen, things that would hurt the other one. And I thought of Sandy and wondered if she was a messenger for Zimmer. If our secrets were really secrets. I thought of this ship as a network of messengers, doing good, doing harm, with a handful of people steering the rest of us.

"This room can be run by five men, each one of them knowing what every gauge and dial are for. They work four-hour shifts, because of the heat. See their shoes?" He pointed to two guys working near each other in front of dials. "These are specially designed boots with a wooden, half-inch sole. Anything else would melt in the heat." Captain beamed at the guys working this room, at their toughness.

Lowe said, "I think some of us could stand that heat."

The captain stopped talking and fixed a stare on Lowe.

Lowe grimaced, like he'd caught himself out, doing something naughty. His momma may have told him his arrogance was a problem. "Go on, go on," he said.

One of the two guys in those boots turned to look at him with contempt. His yellow hair glowed like Lowe's suit. I almost bit my tongue.

I flicked my eyes over to his crewmate. A redhead. The two fellows from the Pig 'n' Whistle.

Information crashed in my head.

Lowe and Zimmer and the other suits on the tour were pigs, like the yellow-haired guy said that night. Lords and masters who can't look up, in charge of all the things that had been happening this week, this year, the coming years, yet without essential knowledge due to their pompous inability to see what others below them saw.

I thought about Helen's notebooks and our Lady Jane dinner conversation, about the coming war. I thought about the grease-smeared guys in tough shoes, expecting to hear the poor blokes' whistle, like he'd said, signal of mutiny.

A clanging sounded and the green arrow on the dial swung around to point at "Loudaphone." Captain Murchie picked it up. Then he hung up and said, "I'm afraid that's all we have time for. Back to your cabins. Safety in a storm, you know."

VIPs grumbled.

"Get me out of here now," I said to Sandy.

Her face shifted fast from annoyed to worried. She headed up stairs and I followed her, ahead of the others. Sandy remembered where to go. When we got to the final doors leading to one of the decks, she put her coat on.

A bellboy was putting up new signs, PLEASE STAY INDOORS.

"Don't do anything stupid out here, like slipping and hitting your head again. That's getting old. How are you even up and out of bed?"

"I found out only Tommie had the Pot Belge in her. None in Coach. I heard it from the doctor's office at Wimbledon."

"That messes us up."

"But I know Helen's feeling guilty and panicked, even if she didn't inject her up with benzedrine and the rest of it."

"You've got to talk to Helen. Time to stop sneaking and talk. Do you want me to go with you? I could do the talking." Her face took the shape of concern, her eyes widening.

A great flame of irritation rose in me, burning my brain.

I didn't want Sandy to look at me that way.

I didn't want her talking for me, didn't like her fake-helpful attitude, like I was a child. I wasn't a child.

I was sorry I'd come to her.

I liked it better when she tried to be bossy and I could discount it, than when she pitied me or acted like I needed her to do the important parts on my behalf.

The fire in my head hissed, *I don't trust her.*

"I believe I can handle it," I said. "But . . . can I have a couple of dollars?" I was so hungry I thought I'd faint.

CHAPTER FORTY-EIGHT

Observation Lounge and Cocktail Room,
Promenade Deck
RMS Queen Mary

I stood at the Observation Bar, trying to get the bartender's attention. Out of the corner of my eye, I saw Lowe at one of the tête-à-tête tables at the edge of the room, receiving one after another of the good-suited men.

He smiled, as if glad to see me, beckoning me over.

The ship heaved sharply.

"Best fetch your lifejacket," said the bartender.

When I approached his table, Lowe said, "Sit."

Like a hungry beagle, I did as he said. My fingers grazed the tabletop, the fiddle rails, through the linens. "They think of everything," I said.

"Almost everything. You look starved, Miss Benjamin." He waved at the waiter.

"No thanks," I said, fingering Sandy's dollars.

He smiled, tolerant.

The waiter arrived, handing Lowe his bill.

"I'd like a menu please," I said.

"So sorry, Miss, the kitchen is closed. Captain Murchie's instructed us to shut down early."

I reflexively glanced at Lowe, worrying the panic would show on my face.

Lowe said, "Norm, please tell Chef that Miss Benjamin would like an odd hours breakfast. Bring coffee with cream and sugar, the omelet, ham steaks with deviled sauce, and the potatoes. Orange juice, too, please."

"Of course, sir," Norm said.

Was he a mind reader? He'd ordered perfectly, everything I wanted right now. "I can't be had for the price of potatoes," I said, trying to unclench my teeth.

"Ha!" His eyes twinkled, like he enjoyed that. "Well then, what price? Should I have offered waffles?"

"Waffles might have done it," I said. "I do have money, you know." Those two soft borrowed dollars in my pocket.

"Money's necessary but not enough," he said, so at ease.

"I guess being a man helps too."

He reflected on that for a beat. "Not just any man. Plenty of men go hungry."

I pictured Daddy, dirty overalls, sunburned wrinkles, collecting nickels in a can as he sang and played banjo at so many Hoovervilles.

The bar rolled side to side, creaking and groaning. The waiters around the room danced a ballet of balance, clearing away platters of other diners' breakfast leavings. One of them headed our way, laying down a wooden grid in front of me, setting plates, flatware, mug, and orange juice each into its own protected little square.

"Thank you, Norm. As I said, they think of almost everything."

I took my first bite of egg, and cut a piece of ham to follow, and potato, and thought it the best food I'd ever eaten. I ate ravenously.

Lowe said, "Glad to see you like it. Careful, though. You'll be retching soon."

I laid down my fork and swigged the orange juice, setting my half-empty glass on the table between us. "So, you've been giving Helen money."

He sighed. "Poor Helen. She came to me for a job in The City, weeks ago, begging for help. Tommie had sent her my way. Desperate straits. She'd been laid off from the bookstore where she worked since eighteen. The Depression."

"I've heard of it. Did you make some kind of deal?"

"I created a research task for her. She's good at that."

"What kind of research?"

"That's none of your business, Miss Benjamin. Especially as you aim to become a gossip columnist. Work hard, aim low, I always say."

I'd touched something sore. He was showing his mean.

The waiter returned with a new bill and Lowe signed it.

I said, "Thank you," managing not to grit my teeth.

The ship rolled again. The liquids within me shifted as white-capped waves struck the window on the port side of the third highest deck.

Then the ship squealed, turning, turning, turning onto its starboard side, until we were horizontal, it seemed. The crash of tumbling and breaking all around the room. My juice glass tipped, staining the table orange.

Lowe grabbed me with one hand and, with the other, gripped the table. "Steady, it's bolted. You're all right."

We held the horizontal position for what seemed like forever, his grip on my arm, eyes locked, before things rightened.

Over the public address system, the captain announced: "All public areas will close now. Passengers return to your cabins."

Norm swooped to our table. "So sorry for the mess. Please do as the captain says and return to your cabins."

Lowe nodded in agreement, and Norm left again.

But I needed more. "You make deals with the people you give money. The money's a gift, but it isn't free."

He took on a patient expression. "Miss Benjamin, maybe you're too young to understand, but when a person gives, it's never altruism that makes them do it."

He made me think of Momma, her constant distrust of everyone she dealt with, her expectation that everybody was dirty, and that this was a natural state. It made her cruel in small ways, discounting the offered pie, the silly compliment—"What a pretty girl you've got there"—but it also protected us. We were never victims of some flimflam man, never expected herbal tincture to cure the Valley Fever. But it was exhausting to live with constant distrust.

"What deals did you make with Helen and Tommie and Frank?"

He set his napkin on the table.

"I never attach to one version of a deal. Most of them fall out, no matter how solid they seem at first. Deals evolve. They're hard to pin down. Sometimes they disintegrate."

"How are they supposed to pay you back?"

"You might be surprised to hear that money itself rarely motivates me. It's just a simple way to keep tabs on progress. Much better than applause." He stood now.

"Did you make a deal with Coach?"

"Jane, some of my best investments are those I never make. This is something your mother and Mr. Jones understand. Or if not yet, then they will soon."

The ship lurched again, sending me and my chair to the floor. Lowe didn't move to help me this time.

"What are you saying about my mother?"

"Get up off the floor and go back to Tommie's cabin, where you'll feel safe."

Looking up at him, I thought of Helen, what I suspected her of doing, and remembered what my daddy taught me, that it isn't the fiddler who writes the tune. Momma was in Lowe's sights now. And so was I.

———◇———

CHAPTER FORTY-NINE

Turkish Baths, C Deck
RMS Queen Mary

I used my stolen key to enter Helen's room.

An abnormal silence marked not only her absence but that of all her notebooks.

I snatched the phone and barked, "Connect me to the head of stewards!"

A few seconds later someone picked up the line.

"Miss Carlson's not in her room. We're supposed to be in our rooms!"

"I'm sure she's fine, ma'am. Where did you see her last?"

"She's *not* fine. Her name's Helen Carlson, a tiny lady, she's not . . . right. And . . . she's not someone . . . you might not notice her."

"One moment." Then he came back.

"No word, ma'am. Just wait a few minutes and I'm sure she'll turn up."

I slammed down the receiver and paced. Minutes later the telephone rang.

"Miss? This is Raymond Peterson. Bell boy?"

"Have they found her, Raymond?"

"It's possible, she . . ." His voice dropped to barely audible. "She interrupted me locking up the cabin-class pool area and asked for a couple of minutes so she could find something. I meant to go back to finish locking it up, but then everything—"

"So she's at the pool?"

"Maybe."

I hung up and headed downstairs toward the entrance to the pool and baths. The ship listed and I grabbed handrails in the deserted halls to keep from pitching to the floor.

I pushed through the pool room's brass double doors. Water surged, big as salt waves. White sheets of paper fluttered down from the Turkish Baths level above, where Helen straddled the balcony ledge, her notebooks under one arm, dropping ripped pages one by one into the pool.

"Helen! Get down!"

Her face glowed furious. "I don't want anyone."

"I came to make you, get you . . . safe."

She laughed. "Safe?"

"Please, don't. You don't have to do this!"

"Stupid! You're too late."

"Somebody hurt you, I know. Please let me help!"

"Everyone's hurt me. No one helps me. Everyone's guilty." She keened.

Everyone. *Me.* I hurt people. I used them. I saw myself through her eyes, through the eyes of everyone I'd used. So much selfishness, so many scenes of it, so many acts. Always making other people bear my burdens, everybody. Stealing Pat Shea's job. Lying to Mrs. Lee and taking her money, food, asking her to run interference for me. From Sandy to the maid in the hallway whose key I stole, who might lose her job because of that stolen key. Invading Helen's room, and her very thoughts. My heinous abuse of Tommie's generosity, the unforgivable theft of the photo that could end the life she'd worked so hard to build.

And Frank too, stealing and disrespecting the kind of tenderness I'd never known before. All of this was on me.

And oh my God, abandoning my *sister*, my baby sister. Forcing her on Rivka, without giving her the *choice* whether to do this for us. I stole Rivka's choice and endangered her job, her livelihood and home, so I could pursue work. I gave Elsie one more memory of abandonment.

Like a slow-motion flip-book, then I saw myself swinging a crowbar at Daddy's knees two years ago because Momma told me to do it, her eternal messenger. I swung, and he disappeared. I'd lost my father by swinging that crowbar, to please my mother, of course I had.

But at least he lived.

Because right there, ragged under the rubble of my terrible history, beat the most awful heart of it, Vee. A girl my own age, an Okie like me, working so hard to climb her way up, to provide for her family. She took the risk of talking to *me* to try to stop a bad man, and I'd walked away, let her take that crowbar to the head. I should have been the one in a coma, dying at eighteen, but I *just kept surviving*. This history was in my cells. It's what I was made of.

I hated the selfishness of my survival so much I didn't know if I could stand it. But I had to. Helen clung to the ledge, more vulnerable than Vee had been.

Ben, how do I fix this? Vee, how?

"It doesn't matter." Helen dropped another notebook into the water.

"Tell me, anything you want." My voice tore my throat, unrecognizable to my own ears. "Ask me to do anything you want," I said, sobbing. "I'll listen. We'll sit down and you can tell me." *Please let me get her off that ledge.*

"Too late."

"It's not. We have time, so much time, all the time we need. We can fix this." *Don't jump! Don't!* I had to get up there, pull her off the ledge. I had to save her, save me, save Vee. I ran to the stairs.

"Do *not* come close to me!"

"I won't. I won't." I stood at the bottom, looking up. "I'm staying here. Now you climb off the ledge. I'll do anything you need."

I looked left, right, before me, behind, searching for a telephone, not seeing one down here, but remembering a check-in desk upstairs. Maybe it had a telephone.

"What are you looking for? Is he coming?"

"No one's coming. Everyone's been ordered to their rooms. This is just us."

"Oh, no, we're never alone. We do not control our own lives. We are manipulated."

"Is it Lowe you're talking about? We can take him down together."

Helen laughed, bitterly. "You're a baby. You think this can be fixed. It's sad, to see you believing. You make me sick."

"You're right. Just tell me—"

"I'm tired." She moaned. "I can't sleep, everything's horrible, what they've already done, what they're going to do. I've tried to work it out. I'm exhausted."

"I'll take you to your room, get a doctor. He can give you medicine to sleep."

"Too late. No matter all my work, it's too late. I have no money, no job, no home. Nothing. And I'll be blamed. I shouldn't be blamed." She sobbed and dropped the remaining pile of notebooks into the pool.

"I won't let them blame you, no way, I will not let anybody blame you, I won't!" I begged, as notebooks splashed and sunk.

She twisted her body toward the baths, making my stomach clinch. "They *call* this a Turkish Bath." Her brow wrinkled with condescension. "*Supposed* to be cleansing. Victorians made it relaxation, *entertainment*, like this ship. But that's not what it *is*. No one here understands what anything really *is* or *should be*."

"I want to understand." *Tell me what to do!*

"Ablution. Purification. I need it. You need it."

"I do, I know!"

"Everyone who touches money needs cleansing," she continued. "We all touch it. But the baths are *not open today*. Too too bad." She swiveled again toward the pool.

"Helen, please. I've felt hopeless. I've felt blamed. I understand, I do. But this is not the last of it. Tomorrow's going to be better."

"You're a tourist. I live here. For a long, long time."

The pool water sloshed in surreal waves, attuned to the ocean. Helen brought her second leg over the ledge, sitting on it like a chair, a spectre of Vee, a horrifying vision of a vulnerable person, wounded beyond help. I saw myself up there too.

"I won't let them blame you! You can't jump."

"Too late. Same as Coach."

"What?"

"Just insulin. Too much of a good thing. Like everything else on this ship. Too much of a good thing is a bad thing."

"Why, Helen, why?" Why would she do this to herself?

Helen screamed, answering a different question, why she did it to Coach. "She didn't help me, didn't *help* me! Then she didn't *believe* me. I told her, and she didn't believe me. She called me crazy. She was so selfish. I needed *money*, to live, just to live.

And I needed her to believe me. So, I've done what I've done. Money."

I screamed, "Help!" over and over, knowing no one would hear me or come.

Helen grew tall in her torso, raising her arms in supplication, like the ship's figurehead.

I ran for all I was worth, taking stairs two at a time.

I got there in enough time to grab the sleeve of her sweater. But Helen said, "Gone, gone, already gone." And she dove, ripping the sweater out of my hands, taking brief flight. I felt like I flew with her, and with Vee, so real, the three of us gliding before hitting the pool's edge, toppling into water, together.

The sickening sound of the collision knocked the breath from my lungs. I wheezed and gulped for oxygen and then stumbled to the telephone and begged the receiving room officer, "Emergency! Turkish baths! Suicide!" I dropped the telephone and ran downstairs to red in the water around her body in the sloshing pool.

I didn't know how to swim. I didn't know how to move. I didn't know anything.

I jumped in anyway, only to be thrown by an indifferent wave against the lip of the pool.

Casting about, I didn't come close to reaching her, didn't come close to grabbing her sweater, her hand, her arm, anything. Now a wave smacked me sightless. *I'm worthless.*

I couldn't will myself to swim when I didn't know how. Some things aren't fixed with effort. A ghost of relief rose above me, pale, just visible through my panic. *The hard part's over.* We would die together, Helen and I, joining Vee. Everything telescoped into narrowness.

Then I saw a blur of blue pull Helen out, heard yelling over the turbulence. Then the blur rushed back to me, hauling me out, turning me on my side, thumping my back, making me vomit a torrent of pool water, as Lowe had foretold.

"Save her," I rasped.

His voice and hands tried to still me. "I'm saving you," he said.

Not again, not me again.

I heard the blaring alarm, more help on its way, too late, too late, too late.

Sputtering, unintelligible, I gripped Raymond the bellboy's sleeve, struggling and failing to do something, anything.

PART THREE

CHAPTER FIFTY

WEDNESDAY, JULY 12, 1939
Women's Isolation, B Deck
RMS Queen Mary

I lay on a bottom bunk in the women's isolation ward, at the aft end of B deck, back behind the emergency generators and the capstan machinery rooms. Nobody would get close enough to catch what I had, major concussion and related case of despair.

Nurse Fleming put me there to recover because I wasn't welcome in Tommie's suite and the regular hospital's beds were packed with seasick passengers. She evicted a teenage stowaway from women's isolation and moved her to men's isolation, which Nurse Fleming said gave the girl a better story to tell back home in Southampton.

Nurse Fleming took a stool at my side and verified my symptoms. "Confusion, drowsiness, dizziness, blurred vision, headache, vomiting, light sensitivity, balance problems, and slowed reaction to stimuli. Every last one of 'em." She shook her head.

I wanted to add to her list, *loss of brother's voice in head.*

"How's your frame of mind?"

I didn't answer.

"People with concussion sometimes say they feel like ending it all. And considering what you've been through . . ." She screwed her mouth up to the side. "That's true of many people with head injuries. But it's worse for you."

"Why's that?"

"You're a drinker." She said it plain, no accusation. "I expect it's making everything harder for you. It's something you're going to want to think about."

"*You're* a drinker," I said, defensive.

"That's how I know," she answered. She patted my knee. "You're very young. Do you want to talk about it, any of it?"

"No." I already had everything in the world to think about.

"I'll give you quiet, then. I'll be at the desk outside your door until somebody else arrives to watch over you. We're taking shifts."

"I don't want . . ."

"Regardless," she said.

"I'm fine."

"Keep saying that, and you'll find somebody to agree. It's after midnight. Sleep."

Finally she left, clicking off the light.

Everything in that room was white: sheets, bunkbed, sinks, walls, the view of gray-white sky out the porthole window. I thought about Helen saying she'd gone to the baths for purification but hadn't found it. I wondered if white isolation would have helped.

It's hard to know which of my thoughts that night were caused by concussion, and which by Helen's suicide. Or by her ideas and accusations. Or her murder of Coach. Or by my failure to save her. What was the point of trying to figure any of this out? That was Helen's conclusion—what's the use?

She killed herself because I wasn't good enough at helping her, at trying to stop her body from crashing into pavement, because she felt a hound on her trail, and I was the hound, because I asked questions when she needed quiet, like I needed now.

The things I'd done and not done sent Helen over the edge, an edge I could go over, too, as Helen's shadow, Vee's shadow.

I felt so distant from myself. I didn't know what I'd been trying to do, or why. I'd blundered into Helen's life at its crisis, when she most needed something other than a densely clueless foil. I'd been worse than incompetent. I'd pushed her to suicide with my selfish ambition. This knowledge laid me flat, limbs heavy, sinking into that mattress, part of the mattress. I couldn't move.

All my life, I'd adjusted myself to what would work with the people around me, what would save me from trouble. Now, there was no one on this ship for me to use like that, to find my real boundaries. Down here, in isolation, I was surrounded by no one. I didn't sense the edges of anything. I was unmoored.

"MISS, ARE YOU all right?"

I heard the voice but ignored it.

"Miss?"

I rolled to my side, facing the room, and my next shift babysitter, Raymond, flipped on the light. I blinked. His eyebrows were high and open, helpful.

"Let me sleep."

"I brought you something. That's why I volunteered to sit down here. But I have to give it to you in private, before Nurse Fleming returns."

God, I thought.

"Just let me . . ." He left, made some rustling sounds and returned with a bag. "May I?" He gestured at the stool.

I thought *no* but was too tired to say it.

He dragged a little table over, in front of the stool, sat, and pulled wet notebooks and loose paper out of the bag, laying them out. A soggy, unrecognizable mess. I realized. "Are these . . ."

"I fetched them out of the pool before the rest of the crew got there. In case you wanted them. I knew she must have meant something to you."

His kindness. "Raymond . . ."

"They're so wet. Tell me what you'd like me to do."

"Get me some pillows, please?"

Raymond harvested them off the other bunk beds and built up a soft backrest for me to lean into. I rose up, dizzy, and blinked a few more times to rid myself of the blur.

"Pull the table right here? And, I'm sorry, would you wait out by the desk?"

"Of course."

"But I have to say, I'm so so . . ."

"No miss. I'm sorry I let her stay in the pool area alone. I'll never . . . ."

"I know, I feel the same."

I picked up the first notebook. How to go about this? I tried to peel the first page off the next but they were glued to one another. Could I dry them? Should I try to read them wet without tearing them apart completely? Some pages were closer to liquid than solid. Those I glopped onto the floor. Some were like delicate fibers, ripping when I touched them, irreparably. Some of the unripped pages were impossible to decipher, markings faded, ideas forgotten.

On other pages, I could see a whole paragraph's worth. Much of it led nowhere, telling me nothing but that Helen was troubled, that she had an extremely suspicious mind, suspicious of everything. The pharmacy, the grocery clerk, the landlord.

Ideas she tried to connect didn't make sense, as if attached by invisible threads, so frustrating to read. It broke my heart for her, the fear and anger and distrust on these pages, mostly the fear.

Sometimes I read a paragraph that was utterly lucid.

Helen was not only against corporatists doing bad things for money, but against the way they were able to make it look like those tricks were virtues.

She wrote a lot about politicians, about President Theodore Roosevelt, and California's former Republican Governor, Frank Merriam, and its new one, Democrat Culbert Olson.

But most of the pages centered on Lowe and the government, and Lowe and money. I didn't know what to do with it. But Helen wasn't crazy to follow these threads.

Interspersed were entries about being alone as a young girl, taking care of her mother, dying of the Spanish flu. No help from doctors or from Coach. How abandoned she'd been.

There were so many pages about working in the bookstore, the right job for her, how devastating to lose that job because of the Depression. And how Tommie had connected her with Lowe for a secretarial job, how for a time she'd felt such gratitude to Tommie.

There were pages about Lowe hiring a private detective. It said he reported that Coach had received family money, and that she withheld it from Helen when her mother was dying, when Helen was suffering, alone.

This conflicted with the information we'd found.

This was it.

I couldn't write about the business and economic stuff Helen wrote about. I didn't understand it. Sure, I could learn, but that would take time, lots of time, and I didn't have that. But I didn't want to write about Helen killing Coach with an insulin injection and committing suicide because of her despair. That was true but removing the context made it a lie, made it wrong.

What I needed, what I wanted, was *proof* that, though Helen had given Coach the injection, Lowe had goaded her into it. He used money as a tool to manipulate her. But *why* had he done it? It had to do with Tommie, with their relationship, its particulars.

"They're coming."

Raymond rushed in and grabbed the notebooks, moving them from the table onto my bed, spreading blankets over it all, excess pillows around me. He picked the wet mess up off the floor, put it in the trash and hid the can in the corner, behind the farthest bunk bed. I lay down, rolling toward the wall, pretending to be asleep. He turned out the light, and resettled at his desk.

It grew quiet. From around the corner, I could hear Raymond breathing heavy from the rush. A few minutes later, his breathing quieted and footsteps clopped down the hall.

"Is she in here?"

"Yessir."

The light switched on, bright through my lids, like I was in the lightbulb itself.

"Miss Benjamin?"

I pushed up onto my elbows and blinked at a huge man in a uniform festooned with stripes and whatnot, and a puppyish freckle-faced officer behind him.

"I'm Master at Arms Owen Harris, and this is Second Officer Warren."

I blinked again.

"You've had us running. Quite a game of hide and seek you're playing."

"I'm not hiding. I'm sleeping, right where they told me to sleep."

"Well, yes, yes. No doubt this little goose chase represents Nurse Fleming having some fun, making us work a bit to find you."

Pig 'n' Whistle, I thought. "I'm awful tired."

"Yes, and so are we. Let's quickly clear some things up."

"I've got a concussion."

"They told us you're not right. Just stay where you are. Warren, take notes."

The puppy assistant nodded and stared at me.

"What happened, from your point of view?"

Who else's point of view were they consulting?

"You called, looking for Miss Carlson, from her cabin telephone. Why were you in there and why were you worried enough to call about her?"

Warren's pencil scratched on his notebook.

"We're friends. I had one of her keys. So, I wanted to check on her."

"May I see that key?"

"I don't know where it is. I must have left it in her room or dropped it."

He frowned at that. "And why were you so worried?"

"Anyone who'd seen her in the past couple of days would have been." *She'd uncovered corruption that wouldn't be fixed. Broke. No home. She'd killed her last living relative for money that wasn't coming. She was going to jail.*

"What did she tell you about that?"

"Not much of a talker. And we were new friends. She'd offered to let me stay in her cabin. Things in mine were a little upsetting."

"With Miss O'Rourke?"

"That's irrelevant. I'm sure you understand."

He exhaled mightily. "What happened when you found her in the pool area?"

"She sat on the ledge up there, by the Turkish Baths. I tried to go up but she yelled at me, told me to stay at the bottom of the stairs. Most of the time, I was standing right there, yelling up at her, trying to talk her down."

"What did she say in response?"

"A bunch of gibberish, something about the Turkish Baths, how they're purifying and religious and so upsetting they were closed down."

"For the weather!" Warren interrupted. "The pools and baths were dangerous."

Harris rolled his eyes at Warren. "So then what happened?"

"I had the feeling she was getting closer to jumping, kind of scooting nearer the edge, so I ran upstairs to her, to try to drag her down, but she stood and she said, 'It's too late,' and she jumped." My face flamed at the memory of this.

"And then?"

"I ran to the telephone and called for help and I ran downstairs and I jumped in the pool to try to save her."

"I understand you can't swim?"

"I can't."

"And our bellboy, Raymond, pulled you out."

"Helen too. Raymond's a hero."

"We'll put that in the notes." But Warren wasn't writing that down. "Are you sure there's nothing else we should know? The way you describe this, it sounds like the suicide of a disturbed young woman."

"Right," I managed to say.

He sighed and looked around at my bare white room. "I hope isolation is the tonic you need."

"Thanks for that," I said.

Their clopping shoes departed. Raymond returned. "That turned out okay."

"Peachy. Didn't seem like he tried too hard to uncover anything."

"I don't expect the Master at Arms wants a whole big rigamarole on the last night of an Atlantic crossing."

"Does he normally investigate onboard crimes more thoroughly?"

"Let's just say, if you ever marry and want to kill your husband? A ship in international waters might be a good place to do it."

I TRIED BUT failed to sleep, exhausted by questions.

I walked around the corner, where Raymond snoozed.

"Raymond? I need to use the telephone. Do you mind?"

"Privacy?"

"Yes, please."

He studied the room to confirm his power to make this decision, then rose and walked into my room, closing the door.

"San Francisco, California, Tuxedo-5-9267."

After a minute, the communications officer said, "Here's your connection."

Rivka's voice came over the line, scratchy. "It's three a.m."

"I'm sorry."

"I was sleeping badly anyway. Where are you?"

"Onboard. This is the last day."

"So, about four days on trains afterward."

"Things have gotten complicated. Like they did a couple of years ago."

"Tell me."

"This woman on the ship, she killed herself, in a couple of ways, really, like a double dose of suicide. Overdose and jumping off a balcony."

"This is awful," Rivka said, her tone soft, sympathetic. I pictured her at the kitchen table in her pajamas, then I heard the hiss of cigarette paper burning.

"I tried to stop her. I talked to her, reasoned, begged. And when she jumped into the pool, I jumped in after her."

"You can't swim."

"Somebody pulled me out, but they were too late for her."

"This is terrible. I'm so sorry. What's happening now?"

"I'm supposed to write a column. A gossip column."

"A gossip column, not a news report?"

"I'm going to do it right."

"Put your byline where your heart ought to be."

"Rivka."

"You're so judgmental of others, heartless about their failings. You see horrible things your mother did at fifteen. You hate her for lying to you. You don't grant her any mercy due to her youth, or her condition, or the difficulty of that time."

"Her lies hurt me, too."

"*You* lie, cut moral corners, hurt other people, to achieve what you want."

"I'm trying." I choked. "Not to do that now."

"What about Elsie?"

I couldn't answer yet.

"At a certain point, you have to choose. What are you trying to do? If *everything* is just to secure the next job, the next check, you're going to regret it."

"You care about work. That's all you do."

"It's all I have. It's not all you have."

I did have Elsie. It was so hard to have Elsie.

"When you're home, we can talk, in person, about what you've decided."

I tried not to cry.

She said, "You know you're capable of better?"

"Thank you for believing that."

The phone softly clicked.

CHAPTER FIFTY-ONE

THURSDAY, JULY 13, 1939

Women's Isolation, B Deck
RMS Queen Mary

I woke to find Sandy beside me on my bunk. "Scoot over and give me some blanket. It's freezing in here."

"Jeez, Sandy, how *are* you? Can I *help* you in any way?"

"Oh please. You're no hothouse flower." She examined me hard in the grayish dawn light. "Then again maybe you are a little orchidy."

I rolled away from her.

"Okay, okay, okay. I'm sorry. How are you though, really?"

"Terrible."

"I heard about it all through the grapevine."

"The *Ocean Times*? I'm sure that's a hundred percent accurate."

"No. The official version, through the policeman."

"Master at Arms."

"Master, yikes. So, what happened?"

I didn't know if I wanted to tell her. Trust was a muddled topic. I registered that the ship wasn't rocking. Light was coming through the porthole. The storm had passed.

"You're going to write her up for Edward, aren't you?"

I groaned. "Did you have to?"

"You don't like Edward, do you?"

"Sandy, come on."

"I don't want to fight. I just want to know if you like him."

I rolled to face her. "No, I don't like him."

"Why don't you like him?"

"So, now you want to fight."

"I don't, really."

I propped myself up on my elbow. "Actually, I don't *dislike* him. Just, he's not as great as he should be."

"What does that mean?"

"He's not good enough for you. I think *you* should be publisher."

"Come on. Seriously, how many chances will I have to marry up, the way I've got with Edward? Not many. I'm already 24. My marketable years are dwindling."

"Oh Sandy. That's not true."

"Follow the evidence."

"Besides, I've seen the way you look at him. It's never like, 'Oh my God, he's divine.' It's more like, 'Yay, I think I've almost trapped him.'"

"That's mean."

"Sometimes you look like you don't even want him."

"Whatever, whatever, whatever." She sighed. "I know."

"Why are you here so early?"

"They've buried Coach and Helen at sea."

"What!"

Raymond appeared in the doorway, sleepy faced.

"It's all right, Raymond. I'm all right."

He gave Sandy a *who are you* look and then slouched back to his couch.

"They did it in the night. Both of them sewed up in canvas

bags. The ship chaplain said a few words. I think only Frank and Tommie were there for it."

"Why'd they do that?"

"Makes sense. They were each other's last remaining family. Burial at sea is a thing people do, I guess. And they didn't want a hundred million news cameras descending on some funeral. I understand that."

I got what she meant. There *would* be all kinds of press and rabble at a funeral.

"They've avoided that, then. Wonder what else they've avoided. Do they know Helen killed Coach?"

Sandy didn't answer, just gazed out the porthole. Something was bothering her.

"What else?"

"Hmmm?"

"I can tell you've got something else."

"I don't have anything."

"It's a secret?"

Nothing.

"Zimmer's secret?"

She waited before saying, "It's not about him, but it belongs to him, he told me."

This time, I didn't push. I waited for her to make her choice.

"Pillow talk. So . . ."

I waited further.

"He said Lowe had a love affair with his former secretary, whose husband died young, no warning."

"And . . ."

"And the secretary quit."

"That's interesting."

"And disappeared."

"Disappeared?"

"Edward says she maybe wasn't the first."

"Are you saying he had a lot of affairs? Or that he got rid of a lot of husbands or a lot of their wives?"

"I'm saying Edward doesn't think Lowe's such a good guy. Maybe a bad guy."

"If he knows, other people must."

"That I can't say."

"I have to use this."

"Gee, no kidding."

"When Zimmer finds out, he's not gonna be happy."

"Thanks for the hypothesis, genius."

"So, what if you lose him over this?"

Sandy opened her handbag and handed me the picture of Tommie and Coach kissing. "I'm definitely going to lose him."

I didn't breathe. This could only cause trouble for Sandy but she did it anyway.

"You've been working hard on this *get a ring* plan."

"So, would you stop acting like I'm Mata Hari or something?"

"Thank you, Sandy, really."

"What are you going to do?"

"I have to write what you said. You're confirming he's dangerous."

"I'm not confirming it. I'm telling you what I heard. It's not like gossip holds up in court. And you can't put it in the paper as a news story. You need evidence. That'll take time. You won't have it by Wednesday."

"But as a gossip column? How about that?"

"I guess, maybe."

"Thing is, if he's really somebody who'll do anything, even kill, over a relationship. If he's done that before, I have to write it. It'd be wrong not to write it. He manipulated Helen into killing Coach. This wasn't Helen's fault at all."

"First of all, we don't know for sure if any of this is true. And second, it *is* Helen's fault too. Don't talk yourself into something here because you're feeling guilty about her."

"Ugh!" Yes, I was trying to bolster Helen's innocence in my head. But still. "Zimmer wants a story with legs. He's gonna say yes."

"Maybe. Maybe not."

Definitely, not maybe.

I thought of what Momma said, "You're not faint of heart."

I would use this story to fix the messes I'd made. I would keep everybody from pursuing Helen as the murderer. I'd play it so Tommie wouldn't lose tennis on account of the morality clauses. And I'd prove to Elsie that she could count on me, that I would take care of her no matter what. I'd prove to myself that I was capable of treating Elsie as the greatest love and obligation of my life.

Because that's what I wanted more than any of the rest of it.

CHAPTER FIFTY-TWO

Tommie's Suite, Main Deck 117–119
RMS Queen Mary

The *Ocean Times* lay on the floor in front of M118, with a front-page photo of Helen and Gorgeous George, the shot I'd witnessed taking place on deck yesterday, George's arm wrapped protectively around Helen's shoulder, her face puffy from crying.

In a terrifically rejected scoop, the paper omitted the part about what Helen had done. Nothing like a suicide to improve the ship's brand.

When I knocked on the door to M117, Frank opened up and immediately tried to shut it, but my foot blocked his way.

"I have something for Tommie." He took in the clothes and shoes in my arms.

His sister growled within, "Turncoat."

I pulled the photo of Tommie and Coach out of my pocket and held it up in Frank's face. He took it and opened the door.

"What are you—" Tommie shrieked at him, but before she could finish, he handed her the picture. She stared at it, and then pressed it against her cheek. She took it to her bedroom and stayed there for a few minutes before returning without the picture.

Chin up, chest out, she asked, "Have you made a copy? Is it going in the paper?"

"Sandy took it from Zimmer and gave it straight to me. I don't think he's done anything with it yet. He still wants my column, but he doesn't have the picture."

"What are you putting in the column?"

"I want to make it about Lowe."

She walked away, shaking her head, "No, no, no."

"Wait," Frank said. "Explain what you mean, Jane."

"Don't let her trick you again."

"I'm not. There are a hundred things I've messed up this week and I owe you both for all of them. I am sorry. I *am*. But we have very little time to do this right or Zimmer will have someone else write the column we don't want written."

"Talk," Frank said.

"Tommie, there's lots of gossip about you in the papers and you deal with it, or Frank hides it from you. But you can't have them put anything out there about you and Coach without it ruining your tennis career, sport or moneywise."

"Obviously, Jane. You think I don't get that?"

"And you don't want to drag Helen through the mud about injecting Coach with an overdose of insulin."

"Are you sure I don't want that?"

"Listen, Tommie," Frank said. "You don't want it out about Coach failing Helen when she asked for help, do you? That didn't exactly show her off at her best, did it? You need to protect Coach's legacy here." His voice skated along an urgent edge.

"I agreed to the burials at sea, didn't I?"

Cogs weren't circling properly in my head, parts failing to line up right. But I jumped in anyway. "Lowe pushed Helen into killing Coach. Helen was falling apart, kind of crazy, but not completely crazy. He used that to goad her, just right, like he's brilliant at, to push her into giving Coach an insulin overdose, and then he took away the money he'd promised her, so all the rest of it, her suicide, would happen."

Frank added, "Almost like he injected it himself."

Tommie nodded and sniffed.

"But *why*, Tommie. I don't have the why."

Frank interrupted. "Wait, first. What are you going to do with this? You won't have enough for the police or the lawyers. You don't have enough proof for an article, even."

"I think, with your information, I could have enough for a gossip column, implying things." I forced myself to slow my flow of words. "Other people, straight reporters, will pick it up and carry on about Lowe. That's possible with your information." It made me sick not to be the one who'd pick it up and carry on, write the real story. I could only start it for somebody else.

Frank said, "But even if they *don't* pick it up, it may be enough to stop him from doing more. Jane may stop him in his tracks, Tommie."

"I can't," she said, and moaned.

"I know you rely on Lowe's money; I know he sponsors all this, but there has to be another way."

"It's not just that," she said.

"Tell me. Please."

Tommie pushed her hair away from her forehead. "Adam and I have had a relationship for a long time, since I was nineteen and we met in Beverly Hills. His wife was getting lessons from Coach, with all the celebrities, doing it for social reasons, like most of them. But he fell for me, for my playing, when he watched me on the court with the others."

She took a glass of water from Frank, drinking half, set it down and continued. "Coach told me, 'He can help you. He's rich. But you have to be careful.' That was before Coach and I fell in love."

The profound simplicity of that stole my breath.

"I've had a romance with him for longer than I've had one with Coach. But when he found out about me and Coach, he said he'd ruin us if I didn't cut it off with her. Meantime, she pushed me to break it off with him, even though he paid for everything, our travel, clothes, even our rent. We spent what tennis earned me so quickly, in minutes. His money is . . ." She paused. "Essential. So, I never broke it off. I thought I could balance things. They both began to tolerate each other. But then Coach became more upset by his demands, because she had more of her own demands."

"What did he want you to do?" I asked.

"He wanted to say where I'd go, what tournaments I'd play in, what opportunities I'd take, especially if it meant he could be there with me. But Coach liked to be in charge, too. She thought he discouraged me from taking sponsorship opportunities because that would give him less power over me."

And Frank tried to move you away from them both.

Tommie dropped onto the sofa, putting her head in her hands. "They were pulling against each other, a tug of war. And I didn't help." She swallowed a sob. "Sometimes, I played them against each other. For no reason. I hate that I did that."

Frank's shoulders rose up toward his ears and down again with a sigh.

I understood what it meant to do things you shouldn't, things you don't intend, things that hurt people, and then regret it later.

Tommie blew her nose.

I turned to Frank. "There was somebody at your work who had a problem like this with Lowe, right?"

He stared. "What do you know?"

"Very little," I admitted. "Please tell me."

Frank set his finger on his lips. Did he trust me enough? But he talked. "His secretary, Imogen Jenkins, he had something going on with her. She started keeping different hours, dressing nicer, suddenly had a new car, long lunches, all that. I couldn't have been the only one who noticed. After a time, I could see things were changing. She acted distracted, unhappy. Then her husband got sick and then died. Thirty-three years old. And then she quit. I've tried to find her but haven't been able to. She's disappeared."

Tommie said, "Why didn't you tell me this?"

"What would you do with it?"

"Frank," I interrupted. "Do you think there are others?"

"I don't have evidence," he said.

"But what do you think?"

"I wouldn't be surprised."

I paced the room, considering.

"Okay. I have to do this now. Zimmer wants it today. I'll hint at Lowe's pushing Helen to kill Coach, causing her to jump."

Frank said, "She was so fragile, all that lingering pain over her mother's abandoning her, and Coach refusing to . . . well, help her, at all."

I paused, considering the way Frank was jumping into this plan so fully now. Ever since my injury, I'd become suspicious of everyone. But I pressed on. "Right. I'll suggest people are saying this may not be the first time he's pulled something like this."

"But you can't turn this into a big story about me and Coach being in love," Tommie said, panic pitching her voice shrill.

"Let me write. I'll call you with questions, so go over to Frank's room, for his telephone." I blushed, remembering the things I'd taken from his desk.

"Should we do this?" Tommie asked Frank.

He nodded.

"All right. But first, Jane, take some clothes. You look like a rose hedge."

I was wearing a very floral dress and sweater Nurse Fleming rustled up.

I picked up the folded blouse I'd just returned to Tommie. I did like that blouse.

"Choose a fresh one. Go on." She pointed to her room.

I found some clothes that worked, a pair of light slacks, another blouse just like the first, and a black velvet jacket. They fit loose and felt good. I didn't want any more blisters so I pulled on my old black and white Oxfords. I didn't need to look in the mirror. I felt like me.

———◦———

CHAPTER FIFTY-THREE

Cabin Class Writing Room, Promenade Deck
RMS Queen Mary

Sandy commandeered the writing room, putting up a sign, RESERVED FOR PRESS USE, on the wall outside. She added an extra layer of defense by setting a writing carrel near the door, where she could stop anybody who intruded. I couldn't imagine what she'd do if someone actually tried to break in, but I didn't doubt her ability to block them by superior wit. In any case, we were lucky that with the return to clear skies and calm sea, all of cabin class had apparently opted for the deck on their final day onboard, so Sandy didn't have to tackle anybody.

Of course, we found the tools we needed there, good paper, fountain pens, pencils, erasers, a dictionary and telephone. Plus, we were near the receiving room, so we could consult with Fox about telegraphing for whatever information we might need. This was more useful than expected because, as it turns out, I didn't know how to write a gossip column.

Though for months I'd pictured myself becoming a gossip columnist, gossipers were the kind of people I hated when I met them, like the girls who made fun of me in school, calling me Okie, white trash picker, beanpole.

But I was practical.

And I'd wanted so much to succeed, so much.

A gossip column was something they could give a girl. Hedda

Hopper and Louella Parsons were famous, syndicated, and paid much more than regular reporters. They'd won the golden trophy that got them what I wanted, a huge audience and all the money in the world.

But now, because of Tommie, I'd seen what it meant to be on the celebrity side of that transaction.

I'd seen her hounded, caught in private moments, living in fear that somebody's rent check would turn on exposing her most private relationship, damaging her ability to be the person her talent promised, as well as her ability to survive in the world, to eat and have a home.

I understood these things at bone level.

I knew the nauseating gnaw of hunger, the desperation of homelessness, the contempt of *proper* people. I'd been despised by all the proper townspeople when I was a dirty picker living on the side of the road and eating at government soup kitchens.

And now I was aiming to be a scandalmonger who could expose people like Tommie to harm.

But I didn't have a perfect choice. Did I?

What's more, I didn't know how to do the work. Did I?

I was past pretending. I had to do it.

"I'll outline. You ask Fox to deliver us sample columns from Parsons, Hopper, and Winchell. So we can do this right."

"Don't you already know how—"

"Just go get them."

Sandy didn't react to my irritability but for the smallest tic of one brow.

I laid out my tools and started an outline, pencil scratching paper. First, I'd have a graf describing Tommie winning her match at Wimbledon. Then a graf with Coach dying in the stands. Then one on the strangeness of Tommie being treated like a celebrity onboard while Coach lay dead in the operating theater. Then the unconfirmed cause of death, with no autopsy. Then Helen's suicide. Then Lowe's attraction to Tommie. Then the big one, about his having an affair with the missing Imogen Jenkins, whose husband was dead.

That was seven. No problem.

I'd penciled in and scratched out several other ideas, paragraphs that connected the others, which I decided were too dangerous, heading places we didn't want the story to go.

I read through my outline and liked the scope, was fine with the order, but the style was a problem.

How much should I insert myself into the story? Reporters weren't supposed to do that. But what about gossip?

I was a witness to Helen's suicide. Did that go in the story?

And how could I imply what I couldn't prove?

In a column like this, how important was accuracy, compared to truth, compared to justice?

I wasn't sure I had a right to do any of this, whether anybody did. Did it matter that I was trying to accomplish something good? Did it matter if it would put a bad man in trouble, protect the dignity of a troubled woman, save another from unfair losses?

"Samples you want, samples you've got!" Sandy handed me a pile of columns, and we took turns reading aloud:

Guests report she sat on more laps than a napkin.
She plays a high-class bad girl, which is only half correct.
Their separation was caused by illness. She got sick of him.

"This is nothing but insults," I said. "This isn't what I'm trying to do."

"I'm pretty sure insults are part of it," Sandy said. "You're home from a long day on the factory floor, reading the paper? It feels good to see the high and mighty insulted."

"What about the made-up parts?"

"Listen: 'Insiders suggest . . .' and 'A little birdie told me . . .' and 'behind closed doors' and 'hearing whispers' and 'the rumor mill reports.' This is how you do it. You say what *you* want to say but put it like this. This has to be the legal way, no trouble."

"You think so?" I was nervous, really nervous. "And do I put myself in the story? Do I say, 'I saw her jump,' like that?

"Let me look." Sandy thumbed through the pile.

"It seems like it's up to you. It can go either way."

"What do you think?"

"I think, say it with authority, like you've seen it and you know it's true. But don't ever say 'I.' Say, 'She fell like a rock to the concrete' or whatever."

"I hate that!"

"I don't mean that exact sentence, just don't write, '*I* was standing there screaming and *I* saw her fall like a rock to the concrete.' Take yourself out as a witness. Leave it quiet where the information comes from, a secret source. Try that," she said.

Sandy hadn't been a reporter or a columnist even one day in her life but she knew what to do in this situation.

"You read this stuff, don't you?"

She swatted me, not the least embarrassed. "Don't you? You should! Okay, okay, okay, get going. And when you need a quote, write it down and I'll call Frank and Tommie for something."

And this was how I wrote it. How *we* wrote it. Sandy at my side, pushing me through my doubts, propelled by the urgent drive to do what we thought had to be done, with Tommie and Frank adding details by telephone. Sandy's pushing was a good thing.

This was not an abstract act but an aggressive one. My words would be muscles, pushing something terrible on stage, forcing people to look at it, judge it, do something about it.

It felt as physically violent as a few other things I'd done in my life. Knocking down a photographer who'd ruined the lives of people she claimed to be helping. Shooting my mother's murderous common law husband in the thigh. Hitting my own father in the knees with a crowbar, leaving him for dead in an irrigation ditch to protect my mother.

This felt like that, in some ways. Hit and run.

Though I might be wrong, I wouldn't be neutral. I was no Neville Chamberlain.

———o———

Deck Tennis Courts, Sports Deck
RMS Queen Mary

I found Zimmer playing *deck tennis*. His opponent was Adam Lowe.

The sun blazed and the sea was still, like we'd never even had a storm.

Apparently Zimmer and Lowe had decided to liven the last day up by fighting things out, man to man, in a kids' game, pretty much a first cousin to regular tennis.

Zimmer and Lowe occupied the middle court of three on the sports deck. To one side of them, were two giggling ladies in white dresses, on the other, mixed doubles, a mother-son, father-daughter match.

Spectators chatted in lounge chairs around the edges.

The two side games were friendly.

Lowe's and Zimmer's game was not. They looked like players I'd seen in an exhibition game of cricket in Golden Gate Park, in their white slacks and sweaters. But their faces glowed angry.

I wasn't sure how the game worked but I'd been to Wimbledon so it seemed like it wouldn't be too hard to figure out, especially since all I cared to know was how long I'd have to wait before I could peel Zimmer away from Lowe and sell him my story.

The court was set up pretty much like a tennis court, with a net strung across the middle and painted lines, making a rectangle about three feet to either side of the net, a line down the middle of the court and lines marking the outside borders.

Instead of using rackets and balls, the players threw a rope ring back and forth like projectiles, one pitching it over the net, trying to make it land on his opponent's side without being caught.

While the two matches on either side of them featured gently lobbed rings and laughter, Lowe and Zimmer zinged the rope back and forth.

Lowe got it to the far corner of Zimmer's side, and Zimmer dove to the ground for it, ripping out the knee of his white pants. Blood seeped through it when he stood.

"All right there, Zimmer?" Lowe asked.

"Aces." He pulled off his sweater, threw it on a deckchair, and returned the ring to Lowe so he could pitch again.

I gripped my story so hard it ripped a little at the top, so I folded it in half and put it in my pocket.

Lowe threw the ring hard at Zimmer's face, near his eye.

"What the hell!" Zimmer threw his arm over his face.

"Zimmer, sorry!"

Zimmer dropped his arm, revealing a pinkened eye.

"Want some ice on that?"

Zimmer picked up the ring and pitched it without warning to Lowe, who caught it in the box near the net, a place where you weren't supposed to catch it.

"That's neutral!" Zimmer yelled. "You got it in neutral!"

"I don't think so. No, I wasn't in the box."

"You were! You were in neutral!"

Lowe ignored him, stepping back to the far corner of his

side of the court and pitching the ring low, just skimming over the net. Stopping short of the neutral box, Zimmer caught the ring, raised his arm over his head and threw the rope ring overboard.

"Oh wow. Now that one's my mistake, Lowe." And Zimmer plowed off the court to the chair, where he grabbed his sweater.

"That's just poor sportsmanship."

"Fuck you, Lowe."

The players of the other two matches gasped as Zimmer stomped down the deck toward a refreshment table. By the time I caught up, a bellboy had given him a cold compress for his eye and Zimmer was swigging his second glass of water.

"He's a jerk, sir," I said.

"Understatement."

This was the best possible moment to give him my article. He knew with his whole body that Lowe was a bad guy. He'd said it to Sandy before and now he must be doubly furious, after what Lowe did out there, humiliating him. This was perfect.

I pulled the handwritten draft out of my pocket, unfolded it and handed it to him.

"You didn't type it."

"I didn't have a machine yet. I wanted your approval before I type it."

He held the compress with one hand over his injured eye and read my story with the good eye.

I thought of Elsie breaking my nose and me giving myself a concussion. I'd kept on working, right through it, like Zimmer. In this, there wasn't so much difference between us. The top of the ladder was like the bottom but with a better view.

Zimmer got to the end, put the ice down, and read it again with both eyes.

Sandy had proofread it. I was pretty sure there weren't any mistakes but started having doubts when he took so long.

"You got the gossip lingo down. 'The whisper mill,' 'witnesses surmise.' But you made it different than the others, not like Winchell or the LA ladies. It sounds more like you." He read aloud, "She flew off the ledge like a mockingbird, jumping up, fluttering down, where she hit the deck and the pool, white body sinking in red water." He tapped a finger on his lip and nodded. His eye was swelling shut. "I can't use this."

"What do you mean?"

"It's good, Jane, sure. But I'm not putting it in the paper." He crumpled up my pages and threw them into the ocean, after the rope ring.

"I did it the gossip way, no legal trouble. And he's a bad guy. You know that!"

Zimmer sighed. "You're an okay writer. But I'm a publisher."

"You said you wanted a gossip column."

"I do. But I decide our markets."

"They want this kind of thing."

"Sure. Regular readers do. But powerful people read my papers too."

"You're afraid of Lowe."

"I'm not afraid of Lowe." He glared. "I'm afraid what'll happen if we smear Lowe and he has to go to court and the United States has to go to war without any ships. That's what I'm afraid of. I'm afraid our measly last war armada won't do the job, and we'll get creamed, the whole of Europe will get creamed, and that little psychopath will have us all speaking German and marching in formation down Pennsylvania Avenue to the Capital. That's what I'm afraid of."

"But you're for neutrality."

"I'm for doing what I can to make what I think needs to happen, happen. Okay, Jane? Do you mind letting me do my job?"

I wanted to cry or hit him, but I couldn't argue with him.

"You've got two hours to show me a gossip column I can *use*, which is really a *gossip* column and not a goddam grenade, and won't endanger every man, woman, or child in the world. Or you can look for another job."

———◦———

CHAPTER FIFTY-FIVE

Frank's Cabin, Main Deck 38
RMS Queen Mary

I locked myself in Frank's bathroom. I didn't want to talk to any of them, didn't want to see anybody. I'd taken my shot and lost. I was wounded. I hadn't just written that column for me. I was trying to protect people, Helen, Tommie, Coach.

The writing was good. Zimmer said so.

But I hadn't seen the bigger picture. I was too inexperienced to understand what motivated Zimmer, or what role Adam Lowe played in the larger world.

I only understood the private worlds of very particular people.

It was all too vast a system for someone who hadn't studied it, so vast it had swallowed Helen up. Same as the knotted up chain of bankers and government and weather and economics had been for Momma and Daddy when we were run off our land in Texas. There would always be secret boss men pulling the strings.

In a gust of rage, I yanked the toilet tissue roll from its holder and hurled it against the door. It bounced pitifully to the floor and began absorbing unidentified wet stuff I hadn't noticed. How fitting.

Tommie pounded on the bathroom door. "What did he say?"

I picked up the mess on the floor, threw it away, and unlocked the door to Sandy, Tommie and Frank.

"I failed."

I explained how Zimmer wouldn't let me take down Lowe because of his apparently crucial ability to build ships in the run-up to war.

"Are you kidding? Zimmer wants the US to fight?" Frank registered doubt.

Sandy gave me a sympathy speech. "It's impossible. You can't get your name in the paper for anything but gossip and he's said no to writing it your way. It's not your fault, Jane, you've done your best. You found the only way and he rejected it."

Tommie frowned. "*Is* that the only way?"

"What else is there?" Sandy asked, annoyed.

She didn't expect Tommie to have something useful to contribute.

"Well, sometimes I put a spin on the ball. Sometimes I play a power game. I switch it up, make them expect what I'm not going to do. Like at Wimbledon."

Tommie had shocked the crowd, switching it up, taking down beloved Beryl.

I sensed something floating like smoke between us. I stood still, closed my eyes, breathing it in, absorbing it, waiting. And then it began to take form. "My name."

"What?"

"Zimmer isn't going to give me anything but gossip. And he isn't going to let me gossip about Lowe, because of the ships. But I can still use gossip to protect Helen from murder talk, and you, Tommie, from the morality clauses. I can put my name on that. I can write the Lowe stuff separately, as straight reporting."

"You just said."

"I won't put my name on the reporting. I'll use a different name, a pen name."

As I said it, I felt what that would mean.

Yes, I wanted money. But I also wanted to be *seen* for what I could do. That's why I worked so hard.

But still, other things were more important than that.

I had to figure out what Lowe was doing, and how, who else was implicated, who he'd hurt. Because I also wanted to do the *right* thing, the *important* thing even if I'd never be credited. Even if it took me months, years to do it. I was signing up for those months and years.

Using a pen name was a necessary loss.

Tommie said, "But where can you publish it? Zimmer said no."

"I know somebody." At Frank's desk, I picked up the telephone handset.

"Can you please ring me San Francisco, California, Mission-7-2073?"

Sandy laughed. "Yes, I think I know somebody too."

I faced Tommie and Frank, waiting for the connection. "I've got a guy who might like to bother Zimmer."

My editor in chief picked up. "Hallo? For Chrissake, where are you?"

"Mac! What a wild story I've got for you here."

"When is anything *not* a wild story with you?"

"Really, you're right. Never. I mean, my whole life."

"Spit it out. I'm shorthanded, Jane."

I gave Mac a straight summary of what had happened, all the way to my failed plan to put the important bits into a gossip piece. I could hear his breath quickening over the line and that made my heart speed, too.

"Ignoramus! Does Zimmer even want to run a real paper? What a jerk."

"So, here's what I need."

"*Here's what you need*? You're the most presumptuous . . ."

"I need to write a gossip column that doesn't scare him off."

"Obviously."

"But I need to report the real story, too, the Lowe story, the *big* story, all the background. Find out about his history with women, his business shenanigans, his political money-making, turn it all up, discover all the evidence. And I don't think this will be a single article. It's a series."

Tommie and Sandy stood, rapt. Frank paced.

"Yeah, sure, fascinating, terrific! Are you completely incapable of engaging with reality? Zimmer said no. He's not going to allow you to do it."

"But see, what if somebody *else* submits the story, to *you*, when all the i's are dotted, t's crossed? And you put it in the paper? You're the editor. You don't ask for Zimmer's permission about everything. He's gonna take off on some train, around to the Midwest or whatever, to all his different papers, different staffs. He thinks he's controlled this at the *Prospect* because he's controlled me. He told *me* no. He didn't tell *you* no. You can do this, Mac. We can do it together. And we have to. This is a *story*."

Mac made a mouth-clicking sound.

"It's obvious, Mac. Even with all the reasons in the world for the US to help our pals in Europe fight Hitler, and to have good ships to do it with, that doesn't mean we shouldn't also report the news. This is our *job*, even if the facts are inconvenient."

I heard a faint beat. I could picture Mac, sitting in his chair, telephone receiver between his shoulder and chin, tapping his pencil on his desk, end over end.

"How does that philosophy about facts apply to your gossip column?"

He had me there.

"You think you can make a gossip column morally palatable, now you're aiming to be some vengeance seeking hero?"

I was going to have to think on that.

"I'm working it out."

"You'll do the reporting without the byline?"

"My name will go on the gossip, not the reporting. It's the only way. But I want the reporting pay, on top of the column. I *want* the pay."

"Zimmer will drop kick us to the dump if this goes wrong."

I slowed down to acknowledge the math of risk.

"I know you've got more to lose than me, Mac."

In my gut, though, I felt the poison of Lowe mentioning Momma, warning he had my family in his sights.

"You've messed me up before," he said.

"True."

"You burned down the darkroom."

"I recall."

"What's the pen name?"

I picked up a pencil and scratched out some options.

"Leo Madaw."

"So you're gonna be a boy again."

"I'll be a man—I want all the readers."

Mac laughed.

"I need one more thing."

"How'd you turn into such a person?"

"Guarantee me, no matter what, no firing Sandy."

CHAPTER FIFTY-SIX

———o———

Sun Deck
RMS Queen Mary

I wrote the column in half an hour, using one of Fox's receiving room typewriters. He kept a respectful distance, but I could see his curiosity, so I told him to keep his eye open for my name in the *San Francisco Prospect* in the week to come.

"I hope telling you doesn't jinx it."

"No worries about that, Little Scribbler."

I laughed. "I'm pretty tall for that."

"Never question a nickname."

I FOUND ZIMMER standing alone at the rail, staring at the Statue of Liberty.

"I know it needs work," I said, huffing from the rush, and he took my column.

```
BETWEEN TWO BRIDGES,
by Jane Benjamin


What if you put San Francisco on a boat?
(Sorry, a ship—seems there's a difference.)
This week, The City's highest and lowest
packed steamer trunks with beaded evening bags
to sail the grand Atlantic on RMS Queen Mary,
```

Nob Hill in cabin class, the Mission District
in third.

Highfalutin' and penny scrapin' sportaphiles
alike anticipated a five-day celebration of
talented hometown tennis heroine, Tommie
O'Rourke, 1939 Wimbledon Champion. What they
got instead was enough drama to dine out on
for months.

Though Tasty Tommie did win the Championship—
huzzah!—her stalwart star tennis teacher,
Edith "Coach" Carlson, dropped dead of the joy
that kills, a heart attack, in the players'
box above Centre Court, just as Tommie
blushingly accepted the Queen's
congratulations.

Struck by tragedy, the moveable city boarded
for home in a despondent state, Tommie
ensconced in her high-design suite with gold
and pink oil paintings of tennis goddesses,
and Coach on a slab in the shipboard hospital.

Then, amidst heartbreak, Tommie detected the
dulcet tones of Cupid's harp. Our tennis
princess fell hard for the sport world's
heartthrob, Gorgeous George Underhill, a six-
foot-three-inch Lothario in white tie and
tails. Several little birdies say they peeped
the lovers flapping their wings and rubbing
their bills under an inky Atlantic sky every
night of their Atlantic crossing.

But bliss was not for all. Poor Miss Helen
Carlson, destitute niece of Tommie's coach,
fell herself for Gorgeous George. Miss
Carlson, a recently laid-off seller of
antiquarian books at A. Roman and Company, had
spent her very last dollar traveling to

Wimbledon in support of Tommie and her aunt,
only to plunge deeply, unexpectedly, into
unrequited love with George. Tragic for her to
have to compete with Tommie.

On their last night aboard, Miss Carlson leapt
to her death from the balcony of the Turkish
Baths to the deck of the cabin-class swimming
pool, leaving Gorgeous George free to canoodle
with the champ.

Such were the highs and the lows of The City
at sea. Next week, the tennis travelers will
cross the Bay for home on the Southern Pacific
Ferry, which is definitely a boat and not a
ship. Tune your ears for ongoing reports.
Sometimes the horns blow low.

Zimmer snorted. "You've got a knack."

It shriveled me to possess a talent for something that so diminished me. But still. "So, do you want this, from now on?"

"Five days a week when we're back."

"What are the rules?"

"Center it on San Francisco. They don't have anything just like it yet. This on the ship was okay, sure, but from now on, it stays within seven square miles."

I thought, *I want to syndicate it*, but figured, first things first. "Anything else?"

"Keep doing the 'little birdie' and so on. Keep us out of lawyer trouble."

"What about my pay?"

"We'll raise it."

"Hedda Hopper started at $50 a week."

He smirked. "She's in Los Angeles. They've got movie stars and she's got experience."

"Like you said, San Francisco doesn't have anything like this. We'll be the first."

"I'll give you $35."

I was currently making $20 a week. Fifteen more would change everything. It wouldn't be long before I could afford a new place for me and Elsie and a good babysitter too.

"This is a deal. I'm a deal," I said. "We'll renegotiate in six months."

"You don't act like a girl."

"Well, I'm not some kewpie doll, if that's what you mean."

Zimmer took in my Oxfords, Tommie's loose slacks, the crisp white blouse, the black velvet jacket. "So, this is all fine. But put on lipstick and keep it on before everything gets real. Maybe some lady hat, too. And earrings. You're going to be out in public, rubbing elbows, and you don't want to put the women off. They're your readers. You're gonna be writing for the women."

"Absolutely. Lipstick, earrings, for the women, got it."

But Zimmer was wrong. Everybody was going to be my reader. Everybody.

CHAPTER FIFTY-SEVEN

Tommie clutched me tight in a perfumed goodbye. I'd never been hugged so hard, so sweetly, before. *I've become a new person on this trip.* I was now a girl with a good job, good relations, good future, and a couple of good outfits, too.

"Frank says we're all set, right?" Tommie whispered.

Cars honked and swerved all around us, other passengers hugging and kissing their own goodbyes, waving at the friends and family arriving to welcome them back and ferry them home. A loud, loving assertion of connectedness.

I pulled back to see her face. "What do you mean *all set*?"

"Obviously," she said. "You're done with us, in the newspaper way. We're . . . friends, right?" She smiled, her face so open and flawless, so close to my own.

"Well, yes, we're friends, of course." Something prickled the back of my neck.

"All this business with Helen and Adam, that's behind us now. We'll have drinks in The City when we're back."

"Drinks, sure. But I'm still working on the Lowe stuff, too. Like I said?"

"Yes, just . . ." She gripped each of my shoulders with her strong hands. "It isn't going to involve Frank and me. He said that's all set."

I didn't know how to answer that. I leaned in to hug her again to hide my eyes.

Frank called, "Tommie!" from a little way up the street, where he'd hailed a cab. "Dinner when we're back, Jane, La Buvette. We'll celebrate, just you and me!" He smiled, ear to ear. I saw he had a new hat, one he hadn't worn on the ship.

Tommie gave me one last peck on the cheek and ran off to her brother.

Though the evening sun beat down on the Cunard Pier, I shivered head to heel. I stood on the sidewalk next to a small suitcase of clothes she'd given me. All around, people rushed and cried out to one another, climbing in and out of cars, chaos, communion. But I was still.

Why'd she say, *We're all set?*

Why'd he act like the two of us would go on a date?

Why did any of this bother me?

Irritation thrummed through my body. More than irritation.

They were acting like I belonged to them, like I was part of their intimate circle, when I knew it was really the two of them belonging only to each other, sister and brother, eternally protecting their unit. *Are they making a tool of me? A replaceable third?*

Frank took me to bed after the Lady Jane dinner, when he'd clearly hated me before. Now he was acting like we had some kind of romantic relationship, even though Tommie had accused me of wanting her, not him.

I moved pieces around in my head. Lowe and Coach wanted to control Tommie. Tommie and Frank wanted that to stop. Frank took a job at Lowe Construction, where he could see Helen, who'd also gotten a job there through Tommie. They were all there together.

Maybe, maybe, maybe . . . Lowe got the idea he could manipulate Helen into killing Coach. But how would he have known her susceptible state? Frank knew, through Tommie. Lowe promised Helen money and then retracted that promise. Why would he do that? Why wouldn't he keep her on his private payroll? And how could he know Helen might commit suicide as a result? Frank would know. Frank and Tommie knew as much about Helen as anyone could.

On Helen's eavesdropped call, I'd heard, "You said I would be all right!"

I tried to picture her trusting Lowe, after the things I'd read in her journal. She didn't trust Lowe, never had.

She was talking on the telephone to Frank, who was working at Lowe Construction to gather information to protect Tommie.

Frank manipulated Helen into giving Coach the insulin shot.

He convinced Helen that Lowe was hunting her, that I was hunting her, that she would be accused, that she had no safe place. He led her to suicide, with my help.

Maybe. Or maybe not. I had no proof of any of it.

I buckled, hands to my knees, head too close to the piss-smelling gutter.

CHAPTER FIFTY-EIGHT

JULY 18, 1939

Rivka's Flat, 3528 Clay Street
San Francisco, California

The comforting, toasty scent of cigarettes drew me up the
stairs. Rivka was home.

I heard her pause at the piano as I set my suitcase down
amidst a collection of stacked boxes. Behind them was my hope
chest.

"Glad you made it safely," Rivka said.

"What's all this?"

"My cousin is here from Prague. She got out safely. She'll
need to stay in the sun porch while she gets situated. Like you
did when you first arrived. Transition."

My sun porch. My room.

"That's so kind of you. It's just, I don't have anywhere to go
yet. I haven't gotten my new paycheck. Like I told you, I'll be
getting more—"

"I *am* sorry for the abruptness of it. I didn't know Margrit
would be arriving so soon. She sailed a few weeks ago and made
her way across country faster than expected. I would have talked
to you about this if . . ."

"If I hadn't left without warning."

"Yes."

"Maybe we could both—"

"It's time, Jane."

"But right now?"

"Margrit's situation is very difficult."

"Of course it is. I'm not comparing myself to her. I know she must have been through hell, I do. I'm just asking if there's any way to slow this down. For one month. Just until my paycheck? Then I can get a place for me and Elsie."

Rivka sighed, sympathetically. "No bargaining."

All the oxygen left my body. I dropped to the hope chest.

Rivka said, "You have more resources than you imagine. I don't know why you don't see your options."

I pictured Tommie and Frank and Sandy. "You're it."

"I'm not all you have."

"You want me to move in with my mother."

"No. I want you to talk to your mother. It's time to talk."

Why did that seem like the hardest thing of all? But I understood. I did have to talk to her about Elsie in order to move ahead. I needed to move ahead.

"May I use your telephone?"

Rivka wrapped her arms around me, rubbing my back.

We had so little experience at this sort of kindness. We were both awkward at affection, but I squeezed her because I knew things like this took practice.

"After you call her, you can tell me the story of these three weeks. And we can talk about what comes next. Would you like a drink, before you call?"

"Coffee would be good. I'll make a pot."

———◦———

CHAPTER FIFTY-NINE

FRIDAY, SEPTEMBER 1, 1939
Railcar
Ocean Beach, San Francisco

I sat on the sand outside my new railcar home, bundled in Daddy's left-behind field coat, looking at the gray horizon, the rough Pacific, the black sand of San Francisco's Ocean Beach.

An amateur geologist once told me, igneous rock erodes in the Sierra Nevadas, expelling the grit of magnetic iron ore into tributaries of the San Joaquin and Sacramento, rivers that converge in the Delta, where my family once lived in a cardboard and canvas lean-to alongside a walnut orchard.

The grit flows through San Francisco Bay, he said, and out the gate toward the Pacific. Every so often, the heaviest bits wash up on Ocean Beach. Cupping it now in my hands, I saw the polished grains of clear quartz and milky feldspar, bits of red chert, green serpentine, pink garnet, and black magnetite, the lodestone, right there where I sat, *Prospect Special Edition* folded on my lap.

I sipped from a mug of coffee and waited, like I did most evenings. Maybe I should have felt settled about things, having gotten so much of what I wanted already. I was a columnist, my name under a headline, *Between Two Bridges*, five days a week.

What I wrote onboard the *RMS Queen Mary* bought time for Tommie and Gorgeous George, the false story about their shipboard romance stopping rumors about Tommie and Coach, and about George and other male tennis players, at least for now.

Something as silly as my column wouldn't fix a world that would banish two first-class athletes from the sport they loved because of the people they loved. But it would protect them a little, for a while. In spite of my suspicions about Tommie, I was glad the tennis pooh-bahs didn't kick her out of her sport for loving Coach.

The column had shielded Helen from being dragged through the mud as Coach's killer. Helen had been the *literal* killer. But not the *real* killer. I didn't know for a fact whether that was Lowe or Frank. I wasn't done looking.

And I'd protected Coach from the trashy talk that would have ruined her legacy if her love story had gotten out. I never met her, but I knew she deserved better.

I'd used my column to protect people. Though I was going to keep trying to make it work that way, now I knew how hard it is to figure out who needs protection. Sometimes the people I protected would use me. Accepting that possibility was part of the job. And sometimes I'd have to lie to protect them. That would be a problem.

I lost my room at Rivka's, but I didn't lose her friendship. We met for dinner at our favorite place, Isadore Gomez's Café, every month or so to tell each other our stories, to check in. I still had her to lecture me when I made mistakes. I still needed that, even if I didn't enjoy it.

And I had this railcar to live in.

While I'd been on the ship, Momma and Jonesie moved out of their big, wind-stripped house on the Great Highway, to a fancy Edwardian in Sea Cliff, their digs becoming more re-spectable as their finances got more suspect.

The railcar passed to me through Jonesie. After the earthquake of 1906, his people recreated themselves as entrepreneurs, living cheap in Carville-by-the-Sea with others displaced by the quake and the fires. Now the rest of those railcar homes were gone, burned in developer-sponsored bonfires, replaced by shiny Doelger suburbs, where Frank lived, though Jonesie had hung onto his railcar out of family feeling.

When Momma made Jonesie trade up to Sea Cliff, he gave the railcar to me, in a fatherly gesture. He wasn't my daddy, but I tried to control my peevishness in the face of his generosity.

Inside, the railcar was narrow and bare, a metal clad monk's cell, clattering in the wind, cracked windowpanes admitting the ocean's roar, which I found purifying after the gossip work I did all day and most nights on the job. That was wearing on me.

A few evenings a week, Momma let me watch Elsie here at my railcar, which was just three minutes down the beach from the roadhouse, Jones-at-the-Beach, where Momma worked nights. Elsie lived with them fulltime now, but she had me part-time, and that was something. That helped both of us.

When I returned home from the *Queen Mary,* I expected to wrest Elsie from Momma. But then I went to their new house and saw her playing with toys in her room, saw how her tantrums had calmed, how she laughed more, how there was always either Momma or Jonesie or the housekeeper, Mrs. Shelton, there, as well as all kinds of other people coming and going. Their home was noisy and lively and somebody was always picking Elsie up, giving her something to eat or to play with, talking to her. I saw Momma holding her, singing some private song in her ear, like she used to do with me, heard her whisper, "You got a voice, baby girl. You got something to say." Elsie was doing all right with Momma, for now.

It made me nervous though. I didn't trust Momma entirely. And I'd promised myself to take care of Elsie. So I stayed close, dropping by their house unexpectedly, just to make sure she was okay. I was always ready if things tipped and she needed me.

Still, not being her sole person, her surrogate mother, freed me up to work in a way I hadn't done before. I'd never actually been alone in caring for Elsie because Rivka and the housekeepers had done it with me, but even together it was hard to raise her well and work well at the same time, very hard for me at nineteen years old. For the first time I knew what it felt like to focus. And that was good.

Now, in the evenings, I'd come out here on the beach before Momma dropped Elsie off, looking at the sand and sea and horizon, seeing the in-between state of things.

Today had been an all-hands day, everybody chipping in to put out the *Prospect Special Edition*. For the regular edition, I turned in a column about a dreamy Hollywood crooner boozing his way through a Nob Hill society dinner, spilling chicken à la king all over the stuffy hostess's satin gown, my usual sort of Friday story. Mac liked to send readers into the weekend thinking about embarrassments to the upper class. They liked that, the men as well as the women.

I was grateful that day's column went in the regular edition, not taking up an inch of space in the *Special Edition* about the Führer, whose mighty army was going to "meet force with force" because of Polish "violations of the German border." He said Germany had "suffered at the cruel hands of Poland," his followers thrilling to the aggressive message, ignoring the lie.

Great Britain and France would be in it any time now.

When would *we* jump in? When was the right time to step up and involve ourselves in trying to fix something that wasn't literally *about* us? Something that maybe wasn't our *business*? I worried a lot about this, studied a lot about it.

Adam Lowe was building liberty ships in Richmond and setting up shipyards all along the West Coast, profiting well from this limbo as the US expanded its fleet.

And, before and after my column work, I inched ahead in my research, trying to find out about the other women and men Lowe had controlled and hurt. I knew that included Momma, who wasn't telling me anything about her investors or other dealings with Lowe. "Don't dig for what you don't want to find," she said when I asked.

I was digging anyway.

I wanted to talk to Ben about this but I hadn't heard him clearly in my head in months. I thought he was still there, just whispering. Though his voice was weak, he still influenced me. Sometimes the faint voice is the one you need to listen to.

"Wake up, dreamer."

I tucked the paper into a pocket, stood, and brushed sand off my pants.

"Hey Momma, where's Elsie?"

"Let's go in," she said. "Colder'n a witch's teat out here."

I followed her around to the railcar steps, noting from behind her new dress and matching coat. She was barefoot, no hose, carrying her shoes in the sand.

"Why are you wearing that old thing? I thought you'd stopped that." She frowned at Daddy's field coat. "He wouldn't even wear it anymore."

"It's warm, fine for the beach. Where's Elsie?" I repeated, moving boxes of Helen's notebooks under the bed, pulling my research chart off the wall, folding it up, so we could sit at the tiny table without her investigating my investigating.

"Jonesie'll bring her over in a few minutes."

"What is it then?"

Momma didn't usually seek out time alone with me. We'd been relating fine with very little personal talk between us. She enjoyed my having the column, was glad I was making money, that people were starting to know who I was. And she liked when I used bits and pieces of gossip she gathered at Jones-at-the-Beach, making her a kind of shadow columnist, she said.

But the two of us usually talked in a storm—at the bar in the roadhouse, or at her home, with all the activity there, construction people and business partners coming and going. We weren't in the habit of sitting at the table alone in this railcar the size of our last tent on the American River.

"Heard your Daddy's in Paris." She laughed at this. "Lord almighty. Must like tobacco-voiced hobos over there. Imagine that."

"I heard. He needs to come back, get on a ship as soon as he can. Do you know how to reach him?"

She rolled her eyes. I would have to do the research to get him home before it became impossible.

Momma brushed some crumbs off my table.

"Anything changed?" she asked, almost lightly.

Everything in the world had changed. But that wasn't what she meant.

"No." I sipped my cold coffee.

She pulled a card out of her bag, set it on the table. "I made some phone calls."

The card was for Mrs. Inez Burns at a Fillmore Street address. I knew her name. She was number three on my *talk to* list. She rubbed elbows with the muckety-mucks. Well-to-do-men enjoyed her parties. In spite of her illegal profession, she was an insider with people like Lowe, though I doubted she'd talk to me about him. Too much turned on her reputation for keeping men's wives' and girlfriends' cases secret.

I turned the card over: "10:00 a.m., Saturday, September 9," written in my mother's deeply slanted cursive.

"You set up the appointment without asking me?"

"Somebody has to take care of it. It's better to do it early than late."

For a moment, I considered the possibility of letting Momma make my decision. I had so many to make, every day. But this was one your mother didn't make.

"You think something like this is safe? In Mrs. Burns' flat? No doctor?"

Momma leaned over the table toward me, the black of her eyes eclipsing the blue. "It's best. We both know that. Do things smart, not like I did."

That was the closest I'd ever gotten to an admission of guilt from her, and it came wrapped in the point that it would have been better for her if I'd never been born.

"I got to go to the roadhouse, meet an inspector," Momma said, rising. "So many of them coming by all the time now. Feels like they're after us."

I thought of Lowe saying Momma's name while I lay on the floor at his feet in the Observation Bar. They *were* after her.

"I'll take you to Fillmore Street Saturday, bring you to our place after. You can stay with us and recuperate for a few days. You'll be fine." She put on her hat. "Jonesie and Elsie'll be here soon." And she left, needing no further comment from me.

I moved back outside to the step and pulled an invitation out of Daddy's jacket pocket, admiring the embossed words.

Miss Sandra Abbott, Mr. Edward Zimmer,
St. Paul Catholic Church,
Three in the afternoon, Saturday, September 9, 1939.

Same day as the abortion appointment with Mrs. Inez Burns.

I rubbed my thumb along the invitation's deckled edge. This was the right kind of appointment for a nineteen-year-old girl.

"Helloooooooooo there! Look who I got!" Jonesie toted a squirming Elsie in his arms, big smile on his silly face.

She clamored down and ran to me, kicking sand behind her.

"Jujee! Look!" She held out a new stuffed bear in one hand, a lollipop in the other, hitting me hard in the legs with her chubby body.

I picked her up and she dropped the bear, wrapping both arms around me, sticking the wet lollipop into the back of my hair.

Rivka was right. Elsie was better off living with Momma and Jonesie than with me, for now. Though Kate Hopper Jones hadn't been the best mother to me, maybe she was a good-enough mother to Elsie. Still, I watched the two of them with vigilance, remaining ready. I would protect Momma from Lowe, but I'd protect Elsie from Momma. I knew this would take time. I was playing the long game.

I squeezed Elsie and walked toward the crashing waves.

She put both hands against her ears, "Loud! Too loud!"

The waves *were* too loud.

But I didn't retreat. I stayed there in the ocean's roar at the margin of sand and surf, holding Elsie tight, spinning around and around in the wind, Elsie's head thrown back, eyes closed, both of us shrieking with laughter, until we dropped, dizzy, to the gritty black sand together, the world whirling wild around us, sisters.

Author's Note

Not long after completing my first novel, *Copy Boy*, I knew I'd continue Jane's story in a second book, maybe more. I wanted to see how an ambitious young woman, who wants both a brilliant career and a fulfilling personal life, might try to gain these things in the period just before World War II.

In 1939, the entire world was asking Jane's own questions: how much am I willing to forgo in order to do what is right for others? And is it wrong to balance that drive to do good against my own best interest?

To explore these questions, I began with history and converted it to fiction. The character of Adam Lowe is a fictional creation, with entirely invented personal traits, but constructed of facts borrowed from the life of Bay Area industrialist Henry J. Kaiser, the father of modern American shipbuilding.

Before World War II, Kaiser succeeded in the construction industry, helping to build Hoover Dam and other Federal projects. In the buildup to war, he formed Kaiser Shipyards, to build Liberty ships. He formed Kaiser Aluminum, Kaiser Steel, and Kaiser Permanente Healthcare for his employees.

Kaiser was not guilty of the behaviors committed by the fictional Adam Lowe, but he did illustrate how enterprising individuals might amass wealth and power in a tumultuous political and economic time, when others without resources are suffering.

A pivotal scene in the novel takes place at the 1939 ladies' singles championship at Wimbledon. I knew of no better place than Centre Court to begin to explore the ways women in that era fulfilled their ambition or found it thwarted. Tennis was an early and persistent domain in which women have been allowed to exhibit their power and competitive spirit.

A friend and avid reader, Caroline Martin, recommended I read Robert Weintraub's biography of San Francisco tennis player and Wimbledon champion, Alice Marble, *The Divine Miss Marble: a Life of Tennis, Fame and Mystery.*

Alice was an amazing historical figure. She won the last Wimbledon Championship in 1939 before the tournament closed for the duration of World War II. She designed Wonder Woman's costume and (maybe) spied on an Austrian banker to steal information about Nazi methods, information purportedly used in the Nuremberg trials. For readers who like to explore the story behind the story, I highly recommend Weintraub's biography.

Though I did not choose to make Alice herself a character in my novel, I was inspired by the way she captured the popular imagination in that prewar era, by her renaissance woman talents, and by her long-term partnership with her brilliant tennis coach, Eleanor "Teach" Tennant.

The characters of Tommie and Coach are not intended to represent Alice and Eleanor, but rather the environment where they conducted their world class work.

Though I decided fairly early that half the novel would take place on *RMS Queen Mary*, I was never able to visit her in person. The ship, harbored in Long Beach, California, was closed during the Covid-19 pandemic of 2020–2021, when I was writing *Tomboy,* and on top of that, her owners entered bankruptcy proceedings in that period. A 2017 study conducted by naval architects and vessel experts, requested by Long Beach city officials, recommended $289 million worth of renovations and upgrades to keep the ship from flooding, and $23 million in immediate repairs to prevent it from potentially capsizing. As this book heads to its publisher, the city of Long Beach, California has taken over the *Queen Mary's* stewardship, aiming to refurbish her.

Because I could not board the ship, I relied on many books on the topic, as well as spending an inordinate amount of time on a website devoted to exploring the gaps between the ship's original and current state and design, https://www.sterling.rmplc.co.uk, published by Julian Hill. I also deeply appreciated the generous answering of questions by Chris Frame, host of the website https://www.chriscunard.com.

A good portion of *Tomboy's* first act takes place on trains. To learn about period train travel, I reached out to Chris Rockwell, Librarian at the California State Railroad Museum Library & Archives, who forwarded my questions to volunteer researchers Jeff Asay and John Privara. They sent a nineteen-page, single-spaced document outlining how to "get Jane to New York." They described every detail of that route, including ticket prices, upholstery quality, and sandwich options. I will always remember their thoughtful generosity.

I thank my dear friend, Dr. Elizabeth McClure, for answering my many questions about the physical and emotional consequences of concussions.

Any factual errors you find in the novel belong solely to me, not the people who generously answered my questions.

I also want to acknowledge the insightful support of my entire team at She Writes Press, especially Brooke Warner, Julie Metz, and Shannon Green, as well as deep-thinking, eagle-eyed indie editor Ellen Notbohm, and my critique group, authors Gretchen Cherington, Ashley Sweeney and Debra Thomas, aka the RBGs. It is a blessing to rely on such talented, trusted writer-readers. It's a gift also to have trusted proofreaders in the family—thanks for that to Claire Fox and Carol Strickland.

Finally, thank you infinitely to the many indie bookstores that inhabit a chunk of my heart, especially the tiny and mighty Capital Books, in Sacramento, California.

I hope you'll join me at shelleyblantonstroud.com for further historical details, events and discussion, as well as information about upcoming Jane Benjamin novels.

Discussion Questions

1. Why does Jane try to keep Elsie with her and away from their mother? Does she believe she's best equipped to mother Elsie, or does this effort represent some other motivation?

2. How do Jane's siblings affect her thinking and behavior? How does that relate to the way most of us are influenced by our siblings or other family members?

3. How does her gender fluidity affect the way Jane does her job? Why is there a difference between the way men and women did their work in 1939? How does that compare to contemporary times?

4. Jane and tennis player Tommie connect over their shared tomboy status, as well as their competitive instincts. What do you make of the way they each use or hide traditionally "male" traits to get ahead?

5. Jane has a history of lying. Often her lies help her to survive. What do you think about the writing she aims to do, given this tendency? What is the difference between fact and truth? Is it more important to tell the truth than to do good? How does this relate to accusations of "fake news" today?

6. Jane thinks part of her success relates to her willingness to cross boundaries she isn't supposed to cross. What is the relationship between such risk taking and achievement?

7. The *RMS Queen Mary's* cabin-class passengers are privileged in ways Jane is completely unfamiliar with. What do you think about her evolving attitude toward class?

8. On many occasions, Jane behaves selfishly. How do you react to this? Is it a survival mechanism? A character flaw? A function of her age?

9. When Jane and Frank spend the night together, Jane reacts to their budding romance in a surprising way. Will Jane be someone who will struggle in love?

10. Jane has relationships with many characters who might be considered friends: Rivka, Tommie, Sandy. What do you think about those relationships? What does Jane give and get through them? What does she need to learn about friendship?

11. What is the role of costume for the characters in this novel? Do clothes make the (wo)man?

12. The active story ends in September 1939, as England prepares to declare war on Germany. How is Jane's personal story related to those larger historical pressures?

About the Author

Photo credit: Anita Scharf

SHELLEY BLANTON-STROUD grew up in California's Central Valley, the daughter of Dust Bowl immigrants who made good on their ambition to get out of the field and into the city. She taught college writing for three decades and consults with writers in the energy industry. She codirects Stories on Stage Sacramento, where actors perform the stories of established and emerging authors, and she serves on the advisory board of 916 Ink, an arts-based creative writing nonprofit for children. She has also served on the Writers' Advisory Board for the Belize Writers Conference. *Tomboy* is the second book in her Jane Benjamin series. Her debut novel, *Copy Boy*, was the first. Shelley and her husband live in Sacramento with an aging beagle and many photos of their out-of-town sons and their partners.

SELECTED TITLES FROM SHE WRITES PRESS

She Writes Press is an independent publishing company founded to serve women writers everywhere. Visit us at www.shewritespress.com.

Copy Boy by Shelly Blanton-Stroud. $16.95, 978-1-63152-697-8. It's 1937. Jane has left her pregnant mother with a man she hates, left her father for dead in an irrigation ditch, remade herself as a man, and gotten a job as a copy boy. And everything's getting better—until her father turns up on her newspaper's front page in a picture that threatens to destroy the life she's making.

Just the Facts by Ellen Sherman. $16.95, 978-1-63152-993-1. The seventies come alive in this poignant and humorous story of a fearful rookie reporter at a small-town newspaper who uncovers a big-time scandal.

Expect Deception by JoAnn Ainsworth. $16.95, 978-1-63152-060-0. When the US government recruits Livvy Delacourt and a team of fellow psychics to find Nazi spies on the East Coast during WWII, she must sharpen her skills quickly—or risk dying.

The Great Bravura by Jill Dearman. $16.95, 978-1-63152-989-4. Who killed Susie—or did she actually disappear? The Great Bravura, a dashing lesbian magician living in a fantastical and noirish 1947 New York City, must solve this mystery—before she goes to the electric chair.

Water On the Moon by Jean P. Moore. $16.95, 978-1-938314-61-2. When her home is destroyed in a freak accident, Lidia Raven, a divorced mother of two, is plunged into a mystery that involves her entire family.

All the Light There Was by Nancy Kricorian. $16.95, 978-1-63152-905-4. A lyrical, finely wrought tale of loyalty, love, and the many faces of resistance, told from the perspective of an Armenian girl living in Paris during the Nazi occupation of the 1940s.